D0248358

INFINITE DESERT

INFINITE DESERT

A collection of short stories

by

MICHAEL WASHBURN

BOOKS

Adelaide Books
New York / Lisbon
2021

INFINITE DESERT
A collection of short stories
By Michael Washburn

Copyright © by Michael Washburn

Cover design © 2021 Adelaide Books

Published by Adelaide Books, New York / Lisbon
adelaidebooks.org

Editor-in-Chief
Stevan V. Nikolic

All rights reserved. No part of this book may be reproduced in any manner whatsoever without written permission from the author except in the case of brief quotations embodied in critical articles and reviews.

For any information, please address Adelaide Books
at info@adelaidebooks.org
or write to:
Adelaide Books
244 Fifth Ave. Suite D27
New York, NY, 10001

ISBN: 978-1-956635-01-0

Printed in the United States of America

Contents

Acknowledgements

A number of the short stories in this collection previously appeared in literary journals. "The Quest" first appeared in *Running Wild Novella Anthology*, Vol. 2, Part 1, "The Gift" in *Packer Current Items*, "Greed" in *34ᵗʰ Parallel*, "Speed Demons" in *Nomadic Sojourns*, and "The Enemies of Order" in *Meat for Tea: The Valley Review*. The author thanks the editors of these publications for permission to reprint the stories.

The Quest

Maybe the bar where I stood on a mild Saturday evening with a draft beer in hand was the most popular place to unwind in the eastern part of the Outback. All the leering faces made it appear so. I had not planned on staying at the hotel that this bar was part of, but there had been no time to plan my trip. One of the most controversial people in the world wanted me to run a national campaign for him, and though I shared many of his ideals, I barely knew the man. He dwelt in an embassy in a far-away capital, spending much of his time publishing documents that outraged people. I had accepted his offer of employment, foolishly maybe. Before fully embracing the role, I had to know who he was, and this meant reconstructing as much of his life as possible. In the meantime I had a spectacle to watch.

Everybody in the bar was listening to a shrink. He looked around the big room with oak panels set in long yellow walls, under evenly spaced chandeliers.

"So you may think you have an idea of the kind of people I was treating," said this man in a sweater and a pair of chinos. His dyed blond hair and spectacles made him look faintly affable, like an uncle you've been on good terms without welcoming him into your life. This quality coexisted uneasily with an air of institutional authority. The size of his audience, in an obscure

New South Wales hotel, clearly impressed him. He clutched a mixed drink in his left hand while making theatrical gestures with his right.

"Have I ever told you about Dennis? You wouldn't believe some of the characters who cross your threshold when you're a shrink."

People tittered, leaning in.

"Patients of mine have come from all sorts of backgrounds. This particular youngster, Dennis, was what you call a policy wonk—that is to say, a political analyst who prided himself on being knowledgeable about politics, whether or not people could appreciate his insights. A guy who stayed up into the wee hours to study every pause, every nuance in the debate speeches of also-ran candidates. A guy who could quote an article on free trade published twenty years ago in a defunct magazine. In plain terms, Dennis was a political junkie."

Already the psychiatrist had brought the listeners far into terrain that they never imagined. Here was a shrink with peculiar notions of transparency. The speaker went on:

"You may be wondering what brought Dennis to me. Well, for one thing, Dennis was grotesquely overweight. The guy would break any scale he lumbered onto. You could see his gut spilling out over the band of the plain gray slacks he invariably wore with a dress shirt and plain gray sports jacket. Being so fat, in my experience, is not necessarily a sign of psychological problems, but the shoe fits, if you know what I mean. And the condition perpetuates itself. *I'm bummed because I'm so fat and I deal with my depression by pigging out.* When Dennis didn't terrify women, when he actually succeeded in getting within ten feet of them, he told them something like, 'I am convinced that the current political configurations are indicative of long-standing fundamental economic, social, and cultural divisions that the election of a conventionally liberal candidate can only exacerbate.'"

A few people laughed out loud.

"I'm not kidding—that was how Dennis talked to women. And if that didn't finish them off, the odor from Dennis's armpits was the *coup de grace*."

More laughter now, a bit of applause.

"I'm a shrink, not a personal trainer or a liposuction specialist. Not that either could have done much for him, with his impulses and appetites. Speaking of impulses, folks, we're getting to the kicker, now. The right-wing, stuffed-shirt think tank that Dennis worked for as a policy wonk brought aboard a wide-eyed young female intern, earnest and idealistic in the extreme. Heather, I think her name was. She didn't take to Dennis, but she didn't actively spurn him, she couldn't do so if she valued her internship. Dennis, as you know, loved to talk about politics and political 'configurations,' and when people actually seemed to be listening to him, he misconstrued their reactions."

People around me in the bar recoiled a bit as if they sensed what was coming, even as they strained their ears further.

"On this one occasion, the innocent, idealistic, fresh-faced intern, Heather, I think her name was, stood in Dennis's office and politely listened to him expound on what he knew best. He was saying something like, 'I believe we are witnessing a realignment that unites the political right's traditional paleo-libertarian base with a conventionally leftist anti-state, though not, strictly speaking, anti-stat*ist*, polity.' Dennis noticed Heather was really pretty, even more so when she smiled, and he moved a bit closer to her as he continued to expound. The fresh-faced intern kept smiling and he kept talking and moved closer still to the supple flesh covering those delicate cheekbones, and it all seemed so natural and fluid to Dennis, as he later put it to me. Everything about Heather seemed to welcome and encourage him. He slid an arm around her. He kept talking animatedly as he moved in so close, his sagging belly was adjacent to her slender one. And closer still. She didn't seem to react negatively, so why not? Dennis kept prattling on, apparently thinking he'd cast a spell over her, taking her silence for assent. He later said through tears that he couldn't control it. Just as his hand reached its destination, Dennis fairly screamed, 'Yes, that's correct, a new configuration!'"

The listeners burst out laughing. I studied the eyes, the mouths of these merry spectators. Rarely had I seen people so caught up in such pure *Schadenfreude*.

I lay back in my chair, drummed my fingers on the table, looked around for a waitress to bring more beer. Before me on the table rested a lone glass with remnants of a Guinness I had sipped while processing the two days since setting out from Sydney in a rented blue Hyundai. How often I wondered about the nature of this place, about who really lived here. The open country was vast and new. Faces in gas stations, lonely vehicles on the shoulder of the road dared me to ponder their significance. While I felt a bit self-conscious about being here by myself, I was confident I'd never see these strangers again. I picked up the glass, eyed the amber liquid, and thought I must give it another chance. Maybe there were other hangouts to explore in this town. But where could one find such entertainment as we had here?

". . . and then there's Keith. Oh, Keith! He was a nearly seven-foot-guy with biceps and coarse black hair like a football player, and a rather, let us say, *complex* psychological profile."

I picked myself up, dropped some bills on the table, strode out of the lounge and into the lobby. An acne-riddled crew-cut teen clerk slumped behind the counter, watched the tiny screen on a plug-in device. Ignoring his curious look, I strode past the desk and mounted one of two curving staircases. On reaching the upper floor, I entered a corridor and ambled past bare wooden doors to the second to last door on the right. I was eager to turn on my laptop, connect with my back-office aide Devin, get up to speed on donations, and maybe have a laugh over the latest threats.

Once inside the dingy wooden walls of my room, the air coming through five inches of screen, and the whisper of the wind, made me think of the world's fluid motion that never thought of scum caught in crevices. Here was a lonely place, with a bed as plain as an inmate's bunk and a square unpainted desk on wooden pegs. I felt a heaviness in my chest as I took in labored gulps of air. I sat on the bed's edge staring at my laptop, debating whether to slam it into the plain stolid wall and bash it to a million bits. Then forget I had ever been part of a campaign, go back to the city, drop to my knees before my girlfriend Rachel, tell her that the thing that had given her such qualms about me was out of my life forever. But back in Sydney were plenty of people who did not wish me well, and one stood out for the sheer viciousness of his hate. His name was Gerald Foster, and he'd donated money to the campaign and then asked for it back when the hedge fund he ran imploded.

It *was* way too hot in here. That was how things were in these parts. Oh, the thought of stringing myself along from one hotel to another throughout the eastern Outback, in pursuit of the essence of a man, the substance missing from an aloof outline. Panting, I got off the bed, reached for the sides of the laptop. I enclosed my fingers around its edges.

Someone knocked on the door.

I moved in front of the little mirror on the wall near the desk, wiped my brow, doing those often futile breathe-and-count-to-ten exercises. Then I turned, extended a quivering hand to the knob, pulled the door inward. Before me stood a woman with creamy pale features, prominent cheeks, and fairly short black hair like an early-career Meg Tilly. She wore a plain purple shirt and jeans. My first thought was that her look conveyed a refreshing lack of pretension, but this gave way to a sense of the utter unlikeliness of her having a legitimate reason to be here. While detecting nothing sly or odd in her features, I thought no way could she be an innocent girl from around here. I had an impulse to slam the door and call the police. Then she spoke.

"Hello, sir. I saw you march out of that lounge like you were really angry. I thought I'd come and see if you're all right."

"Well, that's extremely kind of you, miss."

She looked at me curiously. I felt anxious as ever.

"Do you recognize me?" I asked.

"No, sir. Is there a reason I should?"

I began to laugh but checked myself.

"No. It's quite charming that you call me 'sir.' No, there's no reason you should recognize me, I'm nobody."

She appeared to sniff for a moment, absorbing a bit of the air in my room.

"Uh, so tell me, have you heard of this invention called the air conditioner?" she inquired.

"I beg your pardon?"

The stranger pushed past me into the room, flicked a switch beside the door that I hadn't noticed, and a unit opposite the door, mostly hidden by the curtains, came to life.

"I guess to young men from Sydney the whole Outback is Neolithic," she said in an exasperated tone.

Then she flicked the switch again and the unit fell silent.

"Why don't you come down the hall to my room. You can see your breath in there."

"Well, thank you again, kind lady."

"Natalie Roper."

"Thanks, Natalie. I'm Peter Logue."

Now I wouldn't be lonely or prone to the thoughts that made me want to harm myself.

We walked down the hall to the room nearest the stairwells on the same side of the hall as mine. Her room was the way I imagined a high school locker room in Maine on a February afternoon. Inside her deliciously cool space, ten times as many clothes, bags, papers, toiletries, coins, pens, books, and hand-held devices lay around than in my room. Natalie had propped a folding mirror on her desk, and a cord ran from a plastic blow dryer on her bed to an outlet by the door. With fast decisive moves she closed the door, sat down on the bed, locked eyes with me. I took the chair by the desk, which was as plain as the one in my room but looked so much nicer with all her things adorning it, saying *This is a place someone inhabits.*

"So, Peter, it's obvious you don't trust me. But it's exactly like I told you. I saw you storm out of there and I got really concerned. I wanted to make sure things are o.k. for you."

"Oh, I'll be fine. Who is that doctor in the lounge, Natalie?"

"That would be Doctor Myers. I'm sure you've met his kind. He's the sort of chap who walks into a bar and makes a couple dozen friends on the spot by buying everyone a drink."

"And just how do you know this? How do you know anything about him?"

"The company I work for moves me around a lot, Herr Inspector. I'm here a few nights a month," she answered.

"What sort of work do you do?"

"My employer is a hosting company for corporate events."

"Well, things are going to be fine with me, Natalie. Having said that, I find your concern highly unexpected and extremely touching."

"Why, thanks."

"I do have to wonder whether you'd have hung around down there all night if you hadn't happened to see me."

"Of course, Peter. It was quite a diversion. I especially liked the story about the guy with the huge trunk."

"You tell the truth, strange lass. I like that."

"Well, now, you don't know that anything I've said up to this point is true."

"True enough."

"Think, now. Is there anyone who hates you? I could be working for that person," said Natalie, if that was in fact her name.

Her hands rested at her sides on the unmade bed. They were such nice soft hands. At the moment, though I was aware that those hands could end my existence, she looked like the least threatening person in the world. Maybe she was acting on the logic that a possibility she was quite open about would seem more remote than one she made efforts to downplay or conceal.

"You could very well be in the employ of someone who hates me. Or you could be part of a ring that lures people out behind a shed a few dozen yards from here and deposits a bullet in the back of the head, in the manner of a Stalinist purge. That's a possibility I should consider, but it just doesn't seem useful right now. I *want* to be sitting here with you."

The woman chuckled.

"I am familiar with the phrase 'honey trap,'" I added.

"Look, I really do want to help you. I want to know what brings you, an urbane city man, out here, to understand why you'd ever give this place a thought."

"I'm not going to lie to you, Natalie. I just can't answer the question right now."

"Do you want to explain the repeated references, in the five minutes I've known you, to telling the truth?"

"I don't really care to explain. It all goes back to something quite traumatic in my past. Nothing I care to talk about now."

In Natalie's pale ingenuous face were signs of vast reaches of patience and curiosity, but I did not feel susceptible to those traits just now.

"My mental health, which you're so solicitous about, depends on being able to choose not to recall those things."

Natalie smiled faintly.

"Wow. How's that for an answer? I don't know, with all the repressed stuff in your head, maybe you need to go talk to Doctor Myers."

I laughed. Her smile broadened.

"Or you can just confide in me, and we'll get to the source of what's hurting you and we'll find a way to deal with it."

I studied this plain-spoken, seemingly quite ingenuous girl who had invited me into her personal space knowing no more of me than I did of her. Of course I did not know that, but sitting here in her enticing presence, pining for her, I couldn't believe the truth could be otherwise. If it was otherwise, then the truth didn't interest me at the moment.

She said: "I don't like to see someone as troubled as you appear to be. Perhaps it might help if I make myself a bit more available?"

With that, this stranger picked herself up, traversed the little space, and positioned herself within the demi-circle of my parted legs. Her straight knees brushed my folded ones. I was in thrall to a single, powerful thought: Rachel McGahan, my lover back in Sydney, had never given herself to me, nor I to her. We were *not* in a relationship! Even knowing Rachel platonically at this point was totally contingent. When Natalie's clothes began to fall away and I saw her breasts, round and pale and soft and flecked with dimples acknowledging this young woman's humanity, the impression of blooming health, of youthful bounty, of the potential to nurture, was so powerful that the reaction in my lower body was quick and inexorable. Within seconds, her fingers were working on my belt buckle. She unzipped me and pulled the band of my underpants to just below my scrotum. She had a lot to work with, and got right to it. Moments later our bodies rolled on the bed with such restless vigor I feared a guest would begin pounding the wall or cursing us out. This was a part of the country where people minded their business. But by the same token, it was a conservative place. Relentlessly, almost vengefully, I kissed her breasts and stroked her nipples, reveling in the readiness with which she received the moves from a stranger, from "this guy I met at the hotel." Partly to affirm the innocent decency of what we were doing, I kissed her in a way you'd never kiss anyone you didn't find lovely or had no reason to like. Natalie received the kisses as eagerly, as wholly, as anything else I did, giving more than her fair number in return. Somehow we got through the night without appearing to make anyone in the hotel mad.

In the morning, I gave Natalie my cell number and wrote hers on the back of one of my business cards before I turned in my key and set off in the rented Hyundai. Just before I climbed in, Natalie said, "You know, you could make an effort to exorcise your demons, Peter. Tell me about the trauma you went through years ago."

"I don't want to go there and neither do you."

As the car moved up the ramp away from the crummy hotel, I wished I had kissed the lone figure in the rear-view mirror for much longer, for the barren road must be my friend for many hours to come. I drove on in the wide landscape with grim ruthlessness. The Mulga trees dotting the lines plains on either side of the road were pretty, with their yellowing flower-heads, but they grew sparse as I cruised along. The sight of a Sydney Golden Wattle was a rare occurrence out here.

If I hewed to a straight line, it would be about five hours before I completed the new leg of my voyage. There'd be more hotels, perhaps even more lovers, out there on the broad plains, and more secrets as well. A driver out here was like an archaeologist exploring the mausoleums of centuries of ferocious love and congenial loathing on the frontier. That thought helped keep me going. Then there was the fact that every time I began to ponder the wisdom of this venture, I had an extraordinary bit of luck. Just as the thoughts I'd had in my room back there began to creep back, I came within sight of a gas station or a roadside shack. In one of the shacks I would meet a plain, decent person whose smile meant infinitely more to me than he or she could guess. On the road I flicked the radio on and off, scanning the great vistas, musing on the barrenness of the region where the candidate had spent so much of his early life, and, now and then, mulling what I might say to Rachel McGahan when I saw her lovely face again. I had violated the most basic forms and conventions of a relationship, yet I could hardly help thinking of Rachel. As I pondered these facts, my confusion was overwhelming. How much more productive it was to focus on the purpose of this trip.

For all the hype of the Outback as a scenic locale, the barrenness went on and on and on. If you got lost out here, and made the elementary mistake of leaving your car, you'd lurch and stagger and die in the brown hills or on a stretch of sage-dotted desert without a lot of grandeur. Yet in all but the darkest hours, the hills glowed with a sinister intelligence. I knew if I wandered among them I would feel the weight of unaddressed secrets pressing down hard. I was averse to stopping more than necessary out here.

On the morning after leaving the hotel, I pulled into the parking lot of a truck stop and diner. I drank oceans of black coffee without really touching my toast or exchanging words with the weathered faces at the other booths. Back on the road, alert and acutely curious about what lay ahead, I pushed up against the speed limit. Burg followed truck stop, hillock followed prairie under the cobalt blue until at last I began to see signs for Coburn, 50 miles, 25, 10, 3. The blue had almost a mocking quality, as if it wanted to impress on me how patient the world around me had been all the years I had been alive.

Every so often, I pulled over to the shoulder of the road and reviewed the twelve-page itinerary Devin had put together for me, which listed the candidate's known places of residence, schools, extracurricular activities, vocations, and public records of purchases made, debts incurred. God bless Devin, and all my employees, I thought. God bless Devin above all. If I brought even a bit of Devin's passion and commitment to this job, I'd accomplish something.

I took the Coburn exit, drove another three miles through lightly populated plains and hills, pulled into a dirt lot outside a plain one-story motel with white stucco walls and VACANCY in bright red letters on a big pole at the mouth of the ramp. Seconds later, I was in a tiny lobby talking to a middle-aged woman who wore overalls and sneakers and had a dyed cocoa perm. She seemed acutely curious at the appearance of a white-collar interloper as she handed me a key to a room down the hall. It seemed likely the typical inhabitant of these rooms was a semi-sentient blob in whose body the amphetamines had worn off just enough to allow him to crash for three hours before he climbed back into his rig. But that was the bias of a pampered city boy. Surely a fair number of poets, librettos, ballerinas, and cinematic *auteurs* had rested their heads here. Well, I would rest soon enough but first I must slake my curiosity. I passed through a narrow hall with framed pictures of the Ned Kelly gang, entered tiny room 14, dropped my bags, freshened up in the bathroom, and began to retrace my steps. The clerk smiled pleasantly enough as I passed through the lobby and out into the cool air of the valley in late afternoon.

No matter how carefully I reviewed the itinerary, I had no idea where I was going. I exited the parking lot and turned right on a black asphalt road running between stores and shacks. The afternoon was desolate and hostile. Here was a garage in whose dingy façade the windows were like two glazed eyes staring across the road at a boarded warehouse. Here were a gas station, a long-disused railway platform, a congeries of rusted barrels and dumpsters, a boarded-up shed. My feet tapped on the road as a breeze stirred my hair. Nobody was around. It did not take long to see how short the paved part of the road was. When I passed off it onto gravel, the echoes of my footsteps were deeper. They were like the monotonous claps of someone mocking a futile expedition. I turned north and made yet another transition onto a network of dirt roads, at the nexus of which I could see trails leading over hills in nearly every direction in the dimming day. Craving company, I kept going north, with my gaze trained on a vague rectangular form about half a mile away. Even now that clerk at the front desk was the last person I had glimpsed.

When I got to the low squat tavern, I hesitated before entering, maybe just as a reflex acknowledging how conspicuous I'd be. I told myself I must loathe that reflex, or loathe myself. After taking a deep breath, I pushed open the door and walked inside. In here it was dark and musty and not unlike a million other bars on the planet. Here were men playing cards at round tables beside and in front of a long counter running down the back wall, and at points in the interior there were posters, stickers, and banners bearing anti-Liberal Party slogans. A billionaire mining magnate in a certain western city had followers here. They chose to disbelieve all the reports about the mines being unsafe, and one report in particular that was under a suppression order, or the question of the mines' trustworthiness never occurred to them. The expansion of mines and their administrative infrastructure throughout the country introduced a power structure that could only detract from the authority of the first and most obvious one.

Behind the bar, a young man with short red hair leaned on the counter, talking to a burly guy on a stool who might have been a miner or a trucker. I eased myself onto the fourth stool over from that guest. Across from me, behind the bar, still more slogans exalted mining as a way of life while calling for doing away with regulations. Here was nothing surprising. On the west coast of our country, iron ore, the provision of it to China's steel industry, had made the people of Pilbara, a few of them at least, among the world's richest, so the arguments for prospecting to go full blast elsewhere were obvious. Now as smoke got into my nostrils I realized I had not noticed a young lady sitting a few feet to my left along the short part of the L formed by the counter, and she was making eye contact with me. She wore her golden hair short and a pouty fullness marked her cheeks. I thought she was passably pretty in a conventional way. I realized she had probably been watching me since I entered.

"You waiting for someone?" this stranger said.

"Ah, no. Just stopped by for a pint."

"You're not from around here, are you?"

"No, ma'am."

"Obviously. Why are you here?"

"For research that I can't do anywhere else."

"Oh, so are you, like, an intellectual type? Are you *special?*"

"You might say so."

"Well, tell me something I'm ignorant of, then."

"We've arrived at a new configuration."

"Huh?"

"It's a lie only if I say it to mislead you."

The bewildered woman picked herself up off the stool and retreated to a far corner of the darkened place. I wasn't too sad about not having to talk to her anymore. Now, at last, the redheaded guy behind the bar lavished his attention on me. I ordered a Guinness draft and sat there appreciating my solitude, relishing the thought that I could re-engage with the world, as I knew it, on my own terms, or not at all. I kept drinking, patrons came and left, one song on the juke segued into another. If I accomplished nothing else, at least I'd have helped a struggling, underdog establishment. I did not want to give in to my romantic urges, especially after talking to that dingbat, but I began to imagine what it would have been like to grow up in these parts. I imagined you must grow into habits of thought. Mind you, I wasn't thinking only of the rusting ornaments that you must take down from a wall and carry into the lonely fields. Beyond the dingy money-grubbing establishments, out there in the hills, were poor households where tired aging men could not help thinking about the rules that kept industries in the area from flowering. But the rectangle of empty space in the hall where a door stood propped open did not invite the inhabitants to go out and engage with the world. Outside, voices do not resound, they do not echo, they falter and die in the dimming lonely spaces.

More patrons came and left as I lingered there. A thirty-something fellow with straight dark hair, a thin mustache, and a pair of glasses sat down a couple of stools to my right. He looked like a nice enough chap. I found the courage to talk to him. He ran a local delivery business, had been in the area for only two years, had barely heard of my candidate. I had so little interest in him that I could not have said at exactly what point he got up and left. The ebb and flow of patrons continued. I felt a growing urge to talk to Natalie. I fished out the card with her number on it, pulled out my phone, mulled what I might say. An argument began in my head. I told myself there was no point in calling, that Natalie was the cheapest and most expendable kind of surrogate. She was already joking to her friends about this neurotic she had met at the hotel. I told myself I did not believe that for a moment. The vividness of the experience with Natalie came back to me when I saw a pair of women enter, walk toward the other end, stop to talk to a vague blond form. Now I was so bent on getting drunk that I hardly cared when one of them pointed in my direction. More people deposited themselves on stools or got up and left, a young couple in jeans and tank tops, a woman with bags of flesh wobbling under her arms. She shifted on her stool and yammered while lighting cigarette after cigarette. An old farmer in overalls and a mother on the cusp of thirty who looked as if she could never decide whether she wanted to be here.

When next I lowered my gaze, a forty-something man with scuds of frayed auburn hair and a ruddy weathered face, dressed in jeans and a gray windbreaker, made eye contact and ventured a joke about the game that I was too ignorant of rugby to get. I thought of all the times when I'd struggled to make conversation. But I had no reason to pretend to be interested in the frenzied actions on the screen.

"Look here, man. I'm interested in one thing. If you want to talk about the game, that's fine, but you'll need to find another bloke."

He turned his creased, rugged face away from the TV, toward the white-collar intruder. I knew what kind of awesome force was latent in the muscles poking out of his short-sleeved windbreaker. An impulse to deck me flashed through his eyes. I introduced myself, then laid the candidate's name on this stranger. Perhaps you knew him, I suggested. He wanted to know why I should have the faintest interest in the fellow. I kept myself on the margins of this conversation.

"I'm his former roommate. Now certain people are questioning who he is and what he's about, stating all kinds of malicious nonsense, or at least I hope it's nonsense, and it's up to me to act as a kind of character witness. I'm trying to piece together a bit of the chap's life *before* his uni days."

"I get it now, mate," the stranger said.

The place had grown crowded, bodies squeezed past us, and not all the looks were friendly. But the kid behind the counter attended to me promptly enough. Like Dr. Myers's audience the other night, I had eased into a mood where nothing goes down better than a good yarn. I saw that my appeal had caused stirrings in this stranger's memory.

"Well, first of all, it's been twenty-five years since I was friendly with that bloke," he began.

"You had a falling out?"

"No, sir, we didn't have a 'falling out.' I just mean that I haven't seen him or made any effort to keep up, nor has he."

"But you won't say who wrote the last letter."

"Come on, now, don't get smart with me."

"I didn't mean to, mate. Can I get you another drink?"

He consented to have one on me.

"Can I ask you your name?"

"Arthur Dawson."

As soon as his next draft beer came, he spoke more freely. It turned out that Arthur's interactions with the candidate were a bit less extensive than I had hoped. Sure, they had hung out at the same dance hall, had drunk and partied together, but it would be a mistake to call them chums. Arthur said that if I mentioned his name to the candidate today, the latter would not recall the two of them having been mates, but would not have too many negative memories, either. Ah, there was the rub. Would not have *too many* negative memories. My curiosity piqued, I thought about what might be the right way to proceed here.

"So tell me, please, Arthur . . . uh . . . help me understand what were some of the things that bugged the candidate about living around here."

"Is there any particular reason you're wondering?" Arthur asked, his expression of bland indulgence hardening a bit.

I began to respond, began to find the voice of an apologetic amateur publicist, when Arthur cut me off.

"No, never mind. I know what you're about, mate. A bloke don't become fully real to you until his trials and traumas are out in the noontime sun. No need to convince me of that. And I reckon you ain't speaking from a general prejudice against this place, you probably don't give a damn about this backwater or any of the folks you might meet in these parts, no, you've got a natural curiosity about your onetime roommate who's now somebody important. That's fine. I'd be lyin' if I said I wouldn't have the same impulse."

I wasn't sure all of that was true, but I nodded to indicate he should keep talking.

"I need to tell you, by way of background, that at the time I knew your man, I was working for a fellow named Ray Balfour. My employer was a farmer, slightly better off than many of the farmers in the vicinity of Coburn. That Ray Balfour was a man ahead of his time, oh yeah. I'll explain what I mean by that in a minute. When I wasn't working for Ray, I liked to shack up with my girl, Sally Richert, or sit on the front porch of the house of my mate Marty Palmer. Marty, too, was a farmer, of a different generation. I guess he had twelve years on me. He said he admired my youth and strength. Blue was his favorite color. Marty had been lonely since his wife walked out. I told him, buck up, now, Marty, I may be stronger and faster but you've lived longer and you've got maturity. I'd be grateful for a bit of your wisdom, mate. He was happy to dispense some of that, during the long afternoons we spent on his porch staring out at the yellow plains, but he was even more willing to dispense with a bit of his Scotch, in return for my company. And he loved to stare and stare, not just at the plains, but at the blue above the miles of tilled land."

Arthur laughed.

"Ray Balfour, the bloke I worked for, was ahead of his time. Though this was long before the age of e-mail and the internet, what folks nowadays call the information age, Balfour had added a few things to the routines of a farmer. He had a printing press in a room of his farmhouse, and he put it to good use. He used it to make himself a pioneer of the business side, the information side of agriculture. He put together reports on the crops he raised. These highly professional-looking, bound and stapled price lists, under the heading *Balfour's Bumper Crop Report*, began turning up in every store, pub, diner, filling station, bowling alley, library, and theater in a hundred-mile radius. You'd find neatly printed columns with all the goin' prices for the barley, wheat, maize, or oats that yours truly and the other hands bundled and loaded onto the beds of four red pickups. In content and design, those reports were so many cuts above anything anyone else could produce, and they went into such wide use, that before long they *set* the going prices for crops in most people's eyes, rather than merely advertising one farmer's prices."

Arthur took a long draught of his beer and looked warily around the crowded bar.

"He was driving folks out of business left and right, mate. Marty Palmer was hurting, Basil Jones was hurting, Gus Davison was hurting, Mick Ryan was hurting, Joe Vartle was hurting, Colin Lynch was hurting. Paul Newcomb was hurting something awful and fairly begged Ray Balfour to come up a bit on the wheat and barley prices. That was bad enough. There was an outcry but it went only so far. Most people didn't work for Ray, and now here's what hardly anyone got."

His eyes flitted about the place uneasily again before he went on.

"In a community full of second and third cousins, where young people on one farm dated people on another, it wasn't hard for Ray's employees, his *operatives* you might say, to filch sensitive information or get a relative or girlfriend to do so. Ray made his hands go and find out, in a sneaky way, what the competitors' prices were going to be, and then he undercut them. He did it ruthlessly, mate, he did it methodically. When I used to walk into the middle room of Ray's farmhouse, my eyes popped out of my head. These big boards with detailed maps of the area greeted my eyes, showing all the farms and the prices those farmers charged or planned to charge. I knew if I didn't keep my knowledge to myself, it would be the end for me financially. But I couldn't *bear* what was happening to Marty and Ed and Gus and everybody. I—ah—forgive me, mate," he said, swallowing hard.

I responded with a patient indulgent look.

"So what did I do? I went to your man. Your man! The founder of the most controversial website in history. Even all those years ago, he was bright and well-spoken and he knew a couple of newspaper editors. Once he had the low-down on Ray's methods, of course he wanted to go public with it.

He wanted it on the front page. This was so long before social media, as you know. There wasn't much the young upstart could do if he didn't have editors on his side or the ability to get them on his side. But he told me could do it. He could get the awful truth into print, get it out there in the world for all to see. And there'd be an outcry from here to the moon."

Embarrassed at having briefly choked up, Arthur was speaking briskly, as if to carry me from the awkward moment and discourage me from looking back.

"Of course I had no idea what the outcome would be. I spent a lot of time with Sally in the loft of a barn not three miles from where we're sitting. I went to see 'ol Marty Palmer, a man you could confidently expect to be sitting on his porch at a certain time of the afternoon on a Sunday, sipping Scotch from a chipped glass, gazing out at the thin yellow stalks and the endless blue. I join him there on the bench on his porch, I drink some of his Scotch, and he tells me he doesn't think he's going to have such bad news for his two sons and two daughters. I say, 'I really don't know what you mean, Marty.' He says, 'No, Arthur, I reckon you don't.' I ask whether he's had a bad year, and he says damn straight he has, it was all he could think about for a long time, but he ain't too concerned about it no more. Again I tell him I ain't got a clue what he's goin' on about. He says, 'Don't fret, Arthur,' extends his hairy right arm, and pours some more Scotch into my glass."

The words were coming so fluently I thought I'd awakened a latent gift for storytelling. Arthur Dawson wasn't done.

"I have to say, I may've given you the impression that my mind was on weighty stuff all the time. 'Course what my mind was really on, no small part of the time, was Sally Richert. I fairly wanted to impale her, mate. I know I'm talking like a pervert now, but honestly that's what I thought about."

"Well it's wonderful that you're so honest," I said.

"And so, after a few highly satisfying nights with Sally, who should I run into but your man. Now a candidate of no small renown. It turns out that the editors he approached wouldn't take a chance with a story that some would consider, what's the word, libelous. The decision was horrifying for the young upstart, let me tell you. It killed him that he couldn't get the truth out there, he couldn't make the world, or at least our little corner of it, more transparent. I told him I was sorry, and went back to my routines. Shagging Sally and busting my ass on Ray Balfour's farm. A man needs work, needs to lose himself in it, all that crap. Then I went to pay a visit to 'ol Marty Palmer. He wasn't out on the porch, so I walked right through the door, and nearly slipped on the wet chunky matter on the wooden floor. Minestrone with chunks of beef and stringy noodles. Those noodles had once been conduits for ideas, impulses, memories, passions. Marty's brains were all over the floor and on the glass frame of the clock on the mantel across the room from you when you walked in. Marty lay on the floor with one hairy arm at his side and the other at about a forty-five-degree angle, and the gun resting on his crotch. There'd be a bit of a surprise for his kin, particularly because they didn't know about the reverse mortgage he'd taken out. Under its terms, the property was subject to foreclosure when the borrower died or moved out. It was fair to say Marty Palmer had fulfilled one of those conditions. I do miss Marty."

I thanked Arthur by buying him yet another beer, but this weary stranger hadn't exhausted his usefulness. Far from it. In an offhand voice, I asked Arthur who else around here might have known the candidate back in those days. The answer was that there weren't really many people left at all. They'd died or moved on.

"All of them?"

"Well, no, of course not all of them."

Arthur told me at length of a fellow who had hung out and gotten drunk with him back in the days. That place was still standing, and the man in question, one Dave Morehouse, was the manager. Arthur couldn't think of anybody else I might try, but perhaps Dave was good for a lead or two. He told me how to get to the dance hall from here.

"Much obliged, Arthur." I dropped bills on the counter to cover his next two drinks.

Outside it was much cooler than when I'd strolled up the gravel path to the bar's entrance. I quickened my pace, passed onto the paved road, and made a left into the driveway of the little motel. In an angry reflex I scanned the motel's windows, but no one was watching or the darkness behind the dingy rectangles kept me from knowing if anyone was. Back behind the wheel of the Hyundai, I fought once again with the urge to call Natalie. There could be no hope of seeing her again and I wasn't out here to goof off. The road leading out of Coburn's downtown was all but deserted. I passed a couple of cars without getting a glimpse of the driver. The Hyundai's windows were up because of the wailing that assails the ears when they are open. I gazed out the windows on either side. It was too desolate and dark to see where the sky met the earth. To think that the candidate, the invisible presence in an embassy so many leagues away, had once driven, ridden, walked on these pitch-dark roads.

After half an hour of cautious driving through the dark, I felt immense relief as a neon sign for the Greater Coburn Dance Hall came into view. The building itself was one story, long and flat, reminding me of the site of an indoor skating rink I had visited as a boy. I swung into the driveway and maneuvered the car into a space between two of maybe eighteen vehicles. My feet crunched on gravel as I climbed out. I could see my breath. I walked twenty feet back toward the ramp, turned, strode through the swivel door at the juncture of the long wall facing the road and one of the shorter walls. Inside, '80s rock blared as a few kids danced. On the far side were a bar, pool tables, and a juke. Just a handful of people sat at the bar. Two men stood with cues at one of the pool tables, while a young couple used the other.

No one appeared to give me a thought as I traversed the length of the building and sat down. When the petite, conventionally pretty brunette finally noticed me, I asked her where to find Dave Morehouse. She nodded toward the first pool table, where a guy in his late forties stood. He hadn't looked this way nor did I think he'd seen me come in. For a minute I remained at the bar, unable to decide how or whether to approach him. The Men at Work song from '82 or '83 playing on the speakers ended and an Air Supply number came on.

I brooded. I fidgeted. Then I thought of the wisdom that an older colleague once impressed on me, when I was a financial reporter. *If you wait for every little circumstance to be just right, you will never get anything done.* I walked straight up to Dave Morehouse, waited for him to turn around and extended a hand. The middle-aged proprietor looked mildly astonished and a trifle annoyed. Perhaps he thought I was a yuppie tourist who prided himself on having "roughed it." But he must know about the campaign, I thought. Well, to judge from his weary nonplussed look, maybe not. I said I was gathering material about the candidate. Maybe he could tell me about the times when the younger version of the candidate, and Arthur Dawson, and their mates used to hang out here. He looked at me crossly but there was something mechanical about the anger. Dave Morehouse let out a sigh.

"Yeah, I've heard about the campaign that's going on. I can't say I'm a supporter. Tell me what you need to know, chum."

I asked him to recall that time of life, to recall what the future candidate liked or didn't like about life in these parts. The man I researched did not stay here too long, I noted. He could have, but he did not. He moved on to another town.

Dave narrowed his eyes the way you do when someone artlessly dancing around a topic.

"Yes, I recall well the days when Arthur and your man and I used to hang out here. We caroused like a bunch of teenage idiots. I don't really have much to tell you except that your man made a complete and total ass of himself whenever he ventured on the floor. But I never faulted him for that. I don't think the girls around here had a very high opinion of me as a dancer or potential boyfriend. Young people from all over come to this hall to dispel notions, it went on all the time here. Oh, I did more than my share. When I recall the one event from that time that you might say had some significance, your man falls by the wayside. He wasn't a player."

I listened.

"No, he wasn't a player at all, Peter. Maybe it wasn't fair to put him in the position he ended up in, but I can't say he acted well. I don't really care to talk about it, to be quite honest. Part of me wants to crack this pool cue over your head and send you whining and wailing back to Sydney without your coveted story, fuckhead. But I guess I'd bring trouble on myself. The simplest thing may just be to give you what you want and send you on your way."

I had to interject.

"Dave, look here. I had no say over where I was born. Should I beg forgiveness that I'm from Sydney? I've tried to be a good guest in the Outback and I do have my reasons for wanting to know a little more about the man who's running for high office."

This seemed only to compound Dave's annoyance. He hadn't been expecting an argument. But he continued.

"Listen, mate. If you think you're the only urban twat who's ventured out here with a noble purpose in mind, you're barmy. Every so often, a reporter from the city, a young bloke who looks and sounds quite like you, ventures out here to do a bit of research on 'social currents' or some such nonsense. Teen pregnancy, alcoholism, heroin use, juvenile incarceration, Abo rights and living conditions, or what have you. And the bloke decides that because I manage this place, I must have some kind of insight into these things. I don't like it much, as you may have inferred. But since you have a bit of a personal connection to a former mate of mine, I'll humor you. How's that?"

I nodded. He went on.

"I used to be friendly with a few guys here, not just Arthur and your man. The owner of the place took to me, he began to groom me for a leadership role here. Part of that role, of course, would involve keeping up with all the petty stuff going. The cliques, the intrigues, the drugs, the fights, all of that. Sadly you can't be aloof from all that if you expect to manage the place someday. You can't be an elite pretty boy.

"This kid I knew, Tim Reynolds, was a really decent guy, but some people regarded him as a mama's boy and an elitist. I always thought he was as nice a bloke as they come. He was a guy who'd bent down and tie your laces when you were too plastered to do it. I got on with him. Tim worked as a bank teller during the day, but he was one of these people I saw only at night. I had hardly any sense of his daytime self. Whenever you might run into him, it struck you that he was handsome, a lot of girls noticed him. A guy with his abs and cheekbones, with his bright demeanor, couldn't walk around here without turning a few female heads. One girl in particular, Kirsten Ware, was always asking about Tim, did I know his whereabouts, did I know when he might show up. I didn't want to tell her anything. I honestly didn't want to have to answer for the truth or falsity of what I told her. They met here, I won't say regularly, but there were maybe three consecutive weekends when I saw them out there—" he said with a gesture at the floor on which a handful of youngsters were shuffling.

"If Kirsten wasn't the only girl interested in Tim, Tim sure wasn't the only guy who took a liking to her. Vince Zarou, the son of a trucker, pined for the young lady and, according to rumor, jerked off over pictures of her. They say you should never trust rumors, Peter. But based on how I saw Vince act around Kirsten, I say you can."

I began to try to imagine what it must have been like to be around Kirsten Ware. What were the nature of her charm, her captivating qualities? Then I thought, *No, I don't really want to go there, things are complicated enough at the moment.*

Dave Morehouse continued: "This Vince was a vain little bastard. There wasn't much money in his family at all but he walked around in a Brooks Brothers suit sometimes, like he was worth something, just for show. I saw much more of him that I ever wanted. I had a part-time gig at a factory but I spent a good part of my time at the bar you just left, two stools up from where you were sitting. My customary seat. Three nights a week, you'd find me on the other side of the bar, and on weekends I worked the security detail. The gossip came after me like a swarm of bees. I had a fair idea of what Vince was going to do. Well, he wasn't actually going to do it himself, he was going to assert his claim to Kirsten by proxy. And he had a most intimidating proxy in the form of Anthony Carr. The brutish son of an abattoir worker, a huge guy with a twirly mustache like Rocky Sullivan, and a tattoo of a bull with steam coming from its nostrils on his right biceps. I lifted weights four days a week and I would have gone to *extreme* lengths not to mess with Anthony Carr, let me tell you."

Dave briefly looked around the place, as if vestiges of the people lingered out there.

"The plan was *numbing* in its stupid simplicity, Peter. When Tim and Kirsten were out there shuffling on the floor, Anthony would come up and bump into Tim really hard, send him sprawling, and claim that Tim had caused it. Tim would vocally object. Anthony would challenge Tim to take it outside, and Tim, not wishing to appear craven in front of his girl, would accept the challenge. When the night came, that's precisely how it unfolded. They went out back. It wasn't a fight by any definition. Tim ended up with spinal damage. In a wheelchair. I will not even begin to describe to you what Tim's life was like, in the few years he remained alive."

I asked about the fate of Anthony Carr.

"Two years in the hole, which was probably at the high end since striking Tim was partly defensive in nature."

"Two years? *Two years?*"

"You heard me correctly. As I said, that's at the high end. People have dropped a chunk of concrete from an overpass and taken a stranger's head off, and the sentence was two years."

"I'm sure I *didn't* hear you correctly!"

He gave me a cold contemptuous look.

"So I'm a liar, then."

"You said you'd heard things. You must have testified."

"Look, Peter, there was no way to prove what I'd heard or hadn't heard."

"That's not true. You could have gone to the police, set forth the facts, and they could have fixed you up with a recording device and got you to talk to Vince, to pretend to congratulate him and get him to say something about, you know, his brilliant plot coming off."

Dave looked at me with the cold, clinical sternness reserved for cancer patients in denial.

"You come across as a smart guy. But I see now you spend an inordinate amount of time watching cop shows."

"No—that's what they do in such cases."

He chuckled faintly.

"What they have done, on occasion, perhaps."

"I can't believe what you're telling me."

"Post-hoc analysis of a situation is the easiest exercise known to man."

"You sound like you're talking about the goddamn Vietnam War. This is a personal situation. People you knew. Friends. A young guy with a family and a girlfriend who couldn't stop thinking about him!" I said.

"Well, to tell you the truth, I could stop thinking about him, and before long I did. But, it might interest you to know, one individual did think about the matter. Rather obsessively, I would say. On the night of the incident, the man who'd go on to found a notorious website and run for prime minister from the confines of a foreign embassy observed the movements on the floor from a vantage point right there."

Dave pointed to a spot on the walkway between the dance floor and the back wall of the place, exactly halfway down the floor. In the middling light and the low babble from the speakers, I imagined a lone figure, leaning against the wall with his hands in his pockets, watching the unfolding scene with growing distaste. Feeling queasy, a parched chalky sensation in his throat, as the reality of the plot grew ever more blatant.

"If there is any upside to this matter, it is that the world will not see Tim Reynolds as a middle-aged man. Believe me, from the way he spoke after this business, that is the most merciful outcome. And Kirsten? Don't even ask. You don't want to know." Dave finished.

"Thanks, Dave."

On the road back to Coburn's business district, I passed just one car going the other way. Its headlights were like the eyes of someone whom you'd spurned at a dance, hours ago before you got really wasted, and whom you were unlucky to pass by now. The lights grew in fury until they passed. Then the road was dark and barren again. All around me sheds, rusting barrels, empty dumpsters and other rusting things dotted the plains. A short time later, I lay on my back in my bed in the grubby hotel, thinking about people I'd failed, wondering where my own shabby youth had gone. No noises came from outside, not even from the tavern on the other side of the road.

In the morning, I turned in my keys and walked outside but didn't climb back into the Hyundai right away. Across the road, fifty yards to the east, the tavern beckoned. Surely they would be open. To operate just as a bar, eschewing the full-service route, was no option in this economy. I walked through the door and sat down on the same stool as the night before. Instead of the young guy with red hair, a brusque woman in her forties, a brunette with an elaborate perm, moved behind the counter. I ordered coffee and the spike it gave me was enough to trigger my repressed brooding about calling the women who'd let me into her life. I pulled the card with Natalie's number from my wallet, put it on the counter, stared at it. The coffee made my tongue feel like debts were coming due for all the stupidities it had uttered. I drank the searing liquid hurriedly as if my body craved assurances. I couldn't leave just yet. The woman behind the counter took an awfully long time to attend to me when the coffee in my cup ran low. I began to think about the unasked question. *"You're not from Coburn, are you?"* I tried to think of a comeback.

No. I couldn't engage. With abrupt moves I dropped bills on the counter, went back outside, walked up the road, turned into the lot, and climbed into the Hyundai. Later, in other settings, I would barely recall the drive out of Coburn and onto the freeway ascending like the artery of a burn victim through the arid interior of the continent.

Now there came a stretch where the arable land began to give way, the dirt and sagebrush yielded to sand. All around, everywhere, was the mocking blue. Settlements visible in the distance on either side grew fewer and tinier, the distances between branches more intimidating, the corridors of shadow punier. The counsel of researchers and travelers without number about not leaving your vehicle no matter what reverberated in my mind. Turning up the radio, I kept my eyes on the point ahead where the clear cobalt blue met the pavement. Even now the details of the plan were vague. Oh, to imagine myself languishing at a bar on the open terrace of an establishment at Bondi Beach, raising a bottle to my lips, talking with other patrons: "Yeah, I'm pretty busy during the week." Nothing in my life, nothing at all, could have coherence and integrity until I got certain questions about the candidate sorted out. I gazed at the horizon, eased my foot down on the gas. The past could not fetter me. I may not have had much of a plan but there were things that must become real to me.

I drove on in a dogged, workmanlike fashion, repressing thought, refusing to entertain the notion that so simple a route through the desert could pose challenges. Referring to Devin's map, I thought I knew exactly where the settlements lay. Even so, it was not long before my muscles began to loosen, the glare of the arid plain pulled at my eyes. I had a dazed feeling like when you're up late and fighting to keep your eyes open. Grudgingly, I pulled over to the edge of the road. Alone on the highway, gazing into the glare, I had a vision of ambling over the plains in the heat for hours, passing beyond hours to fluid time that rolled and expanded in all directions. I saw myself kneeling, panting, cursing, weeping, falling on my belly as the sun swelled.

My cell phone rang. With immediate trepidation, I raised the device to my left ear, looking around.

I listened as the voice of a woman I vaguely recalled meeting, I couldn't say when, sometime in the last ten years, flooded my mind with a thousand hopeless longings.

"Peter."

"Oh, hello, Natalie. Where are you?"

"Excuse me?"

"Where are you?"

"I'm at home."

"You can't see me from there, can you?"

For a moment there came no answer. I thought the call had ended.

"Is everything okay, Peter?"

"Uh . . . I've never liked that question much, Natalie."

"Do you want me to hang up?"

"No! Please don't."

"You seem awfully confused. That was the reason for my question, mister. Now maybe you can help me because I'm a little puzzled."

"Please explain."

"I got a call from a stranger just now, Peter. I'd just come out of the shower and I was toweling off and my phone rang. I dared to hope that it might be you."

I wondered why I hadn't called her. Rachel was one reason, surely, but there was another, flitting at the edges of my consciousness.

"So who was it?"

"It was a woman calling from a bar in Coburn."

"Ah, yes. I think I know whom you mean."

"She said she found my number on the back of a card you left on the counter."

Of course. I was a scatterbrained idiot. Having lost that card, I hadn't pursued the argument about calling Natalie far enough even to recall that fact. The card had my office's number on it but not my cell number. The woman who had served me coffee had picked up the card and called Natalie. Since leaving the hotel where I'd met her, my thoughts had generally been about other women. Now, Natalie's lovely voice, the coy supple voice of a poor but intelligent girl, was doing things to my mind. Again I wished I'd invested more time in kissing her before heading off from that semirural setting into the Outback.

"This woman wouldn't identify herself, Peter. She said that when she found the card on the counter, she went to the window, just in time to see you heading for the exit ramp out of town. And she said—"

Natalie seemed to fight briefly to get the next part out, as if she didn't quite believe it.

"She said it looked like another car was following you."

I heard her breathing through the little device, anxious and labored, on the precipice of awful suspicions. Instinctively I turned around on the driver's seat, scanned the expanse of highway up which I had driven.

"Uh . . . did she describe the car?"

"A black something-or-other . . . a Mercury, I think."

"You think?"

"Cars to me are like sports teams to you, Peter. I've never been able to give a damn about them."

"But you said you *just had* this conversation."

"Short-term memory isn't my strength."

I recalled the response I had once made to a girl, Becky, back in my suburban neighborhood many years ago. *Your mind is a toilet,* was my immortal witticism. I couldn't fathom why this should occur to me now as I idled on this deserted highway talking to a woman who was even now a stranger, yet who had vital sensitive information to impart.

"That's not all, Peter. This woman . . . how should I say this? I kind of got the sense she didn't like you much."

"Really."

The breathing came through, labored, pained.

"She said that all morning, before and after you came in, people repeated things you'd said the night before."

"Oh, come on. You're crazy. She can't have said that. What kind of town is Coburn?" I said with disgust.

"I am not crazy, thank you very much, and she did say it."

I listened to her breathing, still on the precipice of something else.

"Oh, Natalie, I didn't mean to lash out at you. I'm sorry."

"It's okay. Maybe you'd like to tell me where you are."

"I'd tell you if I knew. I'm on a highway somewhere."

"Then tell me where you're going."

"Roxbury."

"I can't fathom why anyone who had a choice in the matter would go there."

I let this pass.

"Maybe I'll catch up with you, Peter. We've got each other's numbers. Promise me we'll talk again soon," she added.

"I can make no such promise."

"Please, Peter!"

"I promise not to rule out the possibility of seeing you again. That will have to do for now."

I could hardly believe what had passed from my lips. It flew right in the face of all my longing for her. Having made my share of mistakes back in university days, I knew that when you are desperate to love someone, a virtual stranger can appropriate the role of a central person in your life.

"I'll call, Peter."

"Please do. I'll try to be a little more coherent."

We hung up. I exhaled, rubbed my eyes, and put the Hyundai back in drive. After forty minutes of hurtling through the nothingness, I came to a rest stop with a filling station and convenience store. I refueled and got a sixteen-ounce cup of coffee. Newly invigorated, I drove for eight long hours until at last the road began to decline as I approached a valley where a spate of blue, white, and gray wooden rectangles appeared far off on the horizon. Here and there the red of a barn flecked the sand-flecked dinginess of the houses and public buildings. It was about three miles from the mouth of the exit ramp to the town proper. The town was not an impossible object after all. I was going to be there in minutes, and even now the brightness of the blue above had not dwindled.

Coming off the ramp, I swung left onto Roxbury's main street. Here were a feed store, a post office, a notary public, a saloon, and some plain drab houses, all of them rickety two-story edifices of unimaginative design. We all know what winds and sandstorms in the Outback can do. The rickety appearance must have just been on the outside. The buildings must have had really sturdy infrastructure. Finding the hotel was almost too easy. It was another two-story affair with a narrow balcony running along the pale blue façade of the upper floor. An alley divided it from an oblong hardware shop with faded brick walls that looked as if rendered by ragged crayons. Though the hotel had just two floors, they were spacious. A sign out front mentioned a tavern with happy hour and live music. Maybe, just maybe, a stay here would not be an ordeal. On the side of the hotel opposite the alley was a lot with only a red Audi and a white Datsun taking up space. I swung in between them, got out, and went around to the lobby. Inside, an old man with a thick white beard stretched the bands of his suspenders far enough to pluck a key from a hook high up on the wall to his left.

I mounted the stairs to the upper floor and walked along a hall, toward the front of the hotel, until I reached 212. Beyond the thin wooden door was a plain bed whose ends just barely fit between the wall on the side through which I had entered and the western wall of the hotel, abutting the lot. A desk, surmounted with a cheap white plastic phone and a little lime green rotating fan, sat below an oval mirror in a tin frame. An unpainted oak dresser stood by one of the two windows at the front of the room. A rug with a plain blue and white floral design lay on the wooden boards. I moved to one of the windows, looked out on the lazy scene below. Not even a cat or a tumbleweed disturbed the placidity of the road. Exhausted, I peeled off all my clothes, flicked on the fan, and flopped onto the bed. I dozed off, woke up, dozed off again.

Upon waking up around 2:00 a.m., I reached over to pull the chain on the little lamp, illuminating the plain room. I lay there brooding. After so long on the road the idea of travel had grown repellent. The highway was a tunnel, yes, a dark reeking tunnel through which I had crawled for three days for the tiniest gulp of air, the briefest flicker of light. On the side from which I had set out was a pocket of stale air in which I had stumbled after strangers with next to no reward or fulfillment. That was what I had to look forward to, when this folly in the desert was over, unless I could pinpoint a shadow moving among the sands, the buttes, the valleys, the dried riverbeds.

In the morning, I had pancakes, orange juice, and black coffee in the tavern on the hotel's ground floor before climbing into the Hyundai, cranking up the air conditioner, and carefully reviewing the pages with Devin's map and itinerary printed on them. I was eager to track down Gladys Whitcomb, a former teacher of the man I worked for. As far as I knew, she was the only living person who might have memories of the candidate as a pupil. I put the car in drive. The roads on the outskirts of the town were barren, the sands painfully bright, the rocks fairly glowed even at this early hour. To a frightened lonely mind they whispered, *We may only be rocks but just you dare touch us.* But it was cool inside the Hyundai. In spite of myself, I felt a faint but unmistakable surge of confidence about the prospects of finding the retiree, whom I doubted was going anywhere in a hurry.

I drove on in the brightening day, turned onto a new road once, twice, and yet again. At length there came the disused well that marked yet another turning point. Then I was on a narrow road through an expanse so barren you had to wonder how anyone with declining strength and mobility could even think of living alone here. Ahead a cluster of buildings grew slowly more distinct. I drove for another minute then eased my foot on the brake and pulled into a dirt lot beside one of the two-story houses. Its sides were long boards painted a dull gray and the inverted V of the roof had tar-black shingles. In the spaces behind the dull clouded windows I could detect no life. I climbed the flight of unpainted wooden steps and knocked three times on the door. I waited and waited but there came no sign that anyone had heard, so I knocked again. Then I heard footsteps on the road and a stranger's voice.

"Can I help you, sir?"

The stranger packed a lot into those five words. His question wasn't friendly. It was along the lines of, *Do your actions have some legitimate purpose that I'm missing?* I turned around and saw a man in his mid twenties, with symmetrical features and short dark hair, wearing a cotton t-shirt inside a pair of overalls, and dull sneakers that had once been the color of milk.

"G'day, mate," I said, and the affectation was so sublimely awkward I immediately wished I could withdraw it.

I hastily added: "I'm looking for Gladys Whitcomb, a retired schoolteacher. I believe she lives here."

The young man shook his head, eying me as if I'd invented a nonsense pretext for scoping a potential burglary site.

"That lady hasn't lived here in two years, and the current owners of that house don't appreciate having their privacy disturbed."

"Hey, I'm truly sorry. Honest mistake." I descended the stairs and turned to walk back toward the car.

Before I got there, the stranger spoke again.

"Hey, fellow."

He stood in exactly the middle of the street, at a point where anyone at a window of one of the four houses could have had a good view of him. But as yet there were no signs of anything or anyone moving or breathing within those crudely joined walls.

"I suppose you think it's due to some kind of freak accident that people live all the way out here."

From his tone I knew there was no point in trying to justify myself. With a quick shake of the head, I walked back to the lot and climbed into the Hyundai. In my rear view mirror, that figure in the middle of the road receded every so gradually, his unforgiving eyes locked onto my course.

Back at the hotel, I passed the elderly clerk without a word and mounted the stairs to the upper floor. In my room, I stripped naked again and lay down on the bed under the fan's breeze. I was hardly pleased with myself. I'd made an honest mistake but without doubt, I needed better information before inserting myself into strangers' lives.

The phone on the wooden desk rang.

I swung my legs over the side of the bed, assumed a sitting position, drew a deep breath, and reached for the receiver.

"Hello?"

The voice at the other end sounded prim and slightly whiny, like that of a parent whose child is in your kid's playgroup, and who has a report to lodge about your kid's misdeeds.

"Do you want to see Natalie's head explode?" the voice asked.

"Who's calling?"

"This is Peter Logue, is it not? The perfectly vile man who can't leave others in peace."

"Who are you? Arthur? A friend of his, maybe? Did Arthur put you up to this? Or maybe some other chump in the bar in Coburn. Listen, now. You *can't* frighten me," I nearly hissed.

"That's interesting. Not many people in the world are unable to feel fear on some level," said the prim voice.

"That's not what I said! I said you can't frighten me."

"Really?"

"Really," I said.

"We'll see about that."

"Do you want to tell me who you are, anonymous coward?"

"I am all the aggrieved people of the Outback, telling you to turn around and go home."

"Are you, now? I'd say that's quite an insult to the good respectable discerning people of the Outback."

The voice chucked.

"You know how hot it gets out here during the day. Really. It will do things to you that there aren't scientific words for. Don't hang around here."

"I don't plan on wasting a minute."

"You know how hot it gets elsewhere. Do you want to see *Rachel's* head explode?"

"Excuse me?"

The caller hung up. I stood there amid the faint hum from the little plastic fan on the table, watching a flap of the curtains stir languidly. I replaced the receiver, dressed, splashed water on my face, walked out of my room and down the stairs, and entered the tavern. Behind the bar, a woman named Molly with blonde curls dangling on and just below the shoulders of her white button-down blouse was doling out beers while bantering with a few of the locals. She moved from one end of the bar to the other with seemingly inexhaustible energy. Noticing me, Molly moved up with alacrity and served a Guinness. Outwardly she was as gracious a hostess as I could have hoped to find. I needed to meet someone who knew about retired teachers, who could help out with directions, who knew where I could buy a tube of sunblock. The glare outside was a malicious force eager for any chance to take advantage of a dumb traveler. It was so discouraging and there were so many things I needed help with right now. There was the matter of that call. Maybe if someone had access to a few of the articles on the campaign and was privy to my experience in the bar in Coburn, it was not so hard to connect Natalie and Rachel. Still, I had to consider the possibility that someone might mention Natalie *to* Rachel. Maybe I needed to go home at once. I drank a second draft beer, a third, a fourth.

"Hello, sir, are you having a good time?"

The stranger who had wedged herself between my stool and the next one was a woman of about 5'5", with coils of thick dark hair falling a few inches past her shoulders. She wore a purple tank top and a pair of cutoff jeans. She was cute, if a little on the stout side. With zero interest in talking to her, I nodded and looked back across the counter at Molly who was pulling bottles out of a freezer.

"Cheryl," said the young woman who'd approached me, extending a hand.

"Peter."

"A few of my friends and I think you're cute, Peter."

"Oh, please. 'Cute' is a teenybopper expression. Could I at least be handsome?"

"Do you always go out to bars by yourself, Peter?" Cheryl asked.

"Of course not."

"You don't know anyone here? Just breezin' through town?"

"You might say that, Cheryl."

"Do you want some people to socialize with?"

"Now, Cheryl—please hear me out. I'll take a chance on the possibility that you're worth a word of explanation. I may be here alone but that doesn't mean my circumstances are lower than yours. Some people here in the Outback cherish their privacy, and I've found I'm quite like them. But more importantly, I strongly believe that people who lose themselves in drink and social circles tend to do so because there are things in their past that are just too awful to face or accept."

At the last few words, Molly's head and a few others turned in our direction.

"Well, mister high and mighty. I'll leave you alone. If you *do* decide you want to hang around with some cool people, even if we're not on your level, we'll be over there." She gestured toward a table in the corner.

"There's Luke, and there's Matt, and there's Emma," Cheryl said, gesturing at a trio of young people seated at the plain wooden table. Then she rejoined her friends.

I settled up at the bar and went back upstairs. I wrestled with calling Natalie. What could I say to her? At this point, I was slightly incoherent and I'd just humiliate myself again. I lay down, dozed off, woke, got up, tried to freshen up a bit. The whirr of the plastic fan was faintly reassuring. I thought of hiding my cell phone someplace where I couldn't see it, where it could exert less temptation. I went to the bathroom down the hall and downed water to dilute the booze. Back in my room, I thought once again of calling Natalie. Why had I blown her off? Right now anyone, save maybe the caller this afternoon, might have been preferable to my loneliness. I considered going out, but this wasn't a place with a lot of options and I thought I'd be lowering myself if I retreated into the arms of that stout woman who'd come on to me downstairs.

There really were more important things to be thinking about now, what with a sinister black car having followed me through the desert. I wondered who could be the leering, seething occupant of that vehicle. Maybe it was Gerald Foster, who had donated money to the campaign and then asked for it back. We were in no position to give any of the money back. In truth, I had no idea whether the financial data he relayed to me concerning his fund really had any basis in reality. Maybe one or several of the fund's limited partners had grown alarmed at the rise of a candidate and a party devoted to transparency, and had told Foster he'd better withdraw his support or their thousand-dollar-an-hour lawyers would be on him.

Could the caller have been Foster? I thought again of the voice I'd heard on the phone in that barren hotel room. I sat in my car trying to wring every nuance and inflection from the memory of that voice, as if it were a sponge. Slowly my mind began to associate the voice with the man I'd met in a bar in Sydney one evening, a place in King's Cross that reminded me of a mine where the workers threw a bash. On that occasion I had believed that Gerald Foster could come to play a critical role in the campaign. I had not known how right I was.

Now from somewhere outside came a new flow of noises. Yes, there was some kind of ruckus going on behind the hotel. At this moment it seemed critical not to descend into windy musings. Someone out there in the blue and yellow afternoon wanted me dead. I went back to the bathroom and downed water, avoiding looking at the mirror. Knowing full well how precious water was, I consumed it in heaving gulps until I felt I knew what waterboarding feels like. At last my nerves felt more or less at ease. Back in my room again, I took my cell phone, dialed Natalie's number, and waited. After six rings I went through to voice mail. Presumably she had her cell phone on but had chosen not to answer. I hung up. I wondered what was going on outside. The elderly clerk at the front desk did not acknowledge me as I passed through the corridor.

I walked around the front of the hotel, moved through the lot, and entered a big plot of dirt and grass dividing the back of the hotel from a cluster of dumpsters and, further south, the outskirts of a grimy gray complex housing a water tower. Way down the field, thirty yards from the hotel, nine youngsters were whooping, laughing, singing, scurrying, and mock-tackling each other. At this hour the heat had relented faintly. The air had a lucid but not altogether pleasant quality. Out here it was easy to note people's physical flaws and crude words echoed dully. The sinking pink semicircle in the west cast an odd sheen over the youngsters' raucous faces. Scanning the playful throng, I spotted Matt, Luke, and Emma, to whom Cheryl had introduced me earlier, but not Cheryl herself. The boys were shirtless, a tableau of trim figures and toned muscles. One of the girls jumped onto and rode piggyback with one of the guys, who ran into another boy carrying a girl on his back. Laughing, the second boy narrowly avoided falling on his side, staggered a few paces, nearly fell again, braced himself with his bare right leg, gently deposited his charge onto the grass, and allowed another rider to mount him. Nobody appeared to notice me. They were having fun and would not welcome an adult's stiffening bones and gathering weight.

Terrified of going back to my room at this point, I mulled my limited options. Where to go? Where? The sky over this barren town was bereft of clouds. On the other side of the hotel, on the desolate street, dry drainpipes on the side of crude buildings gathered rust, the barely perceptible click and whirr of a fenced-off generator did not challenge the quiet. With reluctance, I retraced my steps to the front of the hotel and passed through the lobby into the tavern. Like robbers who crave phenobarbitol in advance of a bank heist, I was ready to do just about anything to soothe my nerves further in the event of phone calls. Forget going home for now. I still had to find the teacher, had to force the possibilities in this remote place to their realization.

To my disbelief, Molly was still behind the bar, moving with the same energy as before. I found a seat in the middle, began a tab, and the Guinness flowed. I chatted with Molly about little things. She was awfully nice. Her life in this town moved in cosy grooves, with no surprises. In a one-story hovel not too far from here someone might be waiting patiently for her. At length, a few of the revelers began to trickle in from outside. Luke and Matt had found shirts. To my relief, they did not appear to notice me as they passed through the room to one of the tables, grinning and leering at a few youngsters. Molly asked politely what had brought me to the town. She seemed genuinely curious. Her manner contrasted with that of the aggressively stupid people I had run into. I told her that my boss was running for high office and he was still a cypher to many. Then I asked Molly about a retired schoolteacher, one Gladys Whitcomb. Not only did Molly know of the woman, she was able to tell me in detail how to get to where Gladys lived. The route from here to there was simpler than I could have imagined. I kept drinking, enjoying Molly's company. Then, as I might have expected, Cheryl appeared once again in the gap between my stool and the next.

"Nice to see you finally relaxing a bit, Peter. Are you enjoying yourself just a bit now?"

For the first time, I really studied the face before me. The smile conveyed a warmth fighting to break through thick crusts of sarcasm. The face surrounding it might have been quite lovely without the beginnings of pouches at the edges. It was the face of a woman who perpetually wanted and expected to be happy.

"I'm doing fine, Cheryl. But, you know, I just got done talking about myself to Molly here. Why don't we talk about *you?*" I replied in an even voice.

"Tell me what you'd like to know, Peter."

"Tell me what you wouldn't like me to know."

"Huh?"

"I said tell me—"

"I'm not the one who's got problems here, Peter. Everyone in here can tell there's something you're terrified might happen."

"Don't be silly. I suppose you can read my mind."

"What are you afraid might happen?"

"We all have fears but I dispute your use of the word *terrified.*"

"You *are* terrified. There's some possibility you won't face."

"No there isn't. I happen to have heard that women don't shit."

"Jesus, how drunk are you?" Cheryl demanded with a cross look before moving back to the table where Luke, Matt, Emma, and a couple of others waited.

Molly kept serving and I continued drinking long after I should have quit. In my peripheral vision, I could see Cheryl pointing and whispering. Poor girl, I'd never meant to offend her, but maybe it was for the better. Having bungled relations with enough women in the last few weeks, I saw no need for more disaster. Even in this state I knew that if I opened my mouth it would be the giddiness talking. I drank so much I was a little afraid about the morning. My recollections of leaving the tavern and dragging myself back through the lobby, up the stairs, and into my room were never clear or linear. At some point I ended up back in my plain bed, face up, fully dressed, without even the presence of mind to turn on the little plastic fan. More voices came from outside. People were as raucous as ever.

In this state, I fell asleep.

An image came of a room in an upscale restaurant. Fine silk cloths cover the tables, and scarlet curtains form the backdrop to the graceful moves of waiters in sleeveless black blazers, white shirts, and black ties. At a table here are two individuals. The first party has gone to no small trouble to make himself presentable. His jet-black suit and tie dare you to guess their price, and his cologne evokes a lineage of refined maleness from Alexander of Macedon to Laurence Olivier. He has been wise to take care with his appearance. Seated across from him is a woman with platinum hair and such supple pale features that she could not banish her emotions from her face. Though she clearly relishes an elegant setting, she wears no earrings. By all appearances the woman is comfortable, but somewhat unsure of how to construe or respond to the fellow's manner. He is affecting relaxation. There's a fact he badly wishes to impart to her, yet he grapples with the fact.

Man: It a violent country. Oases like this one are rare indeed.

Woman: So why did you ask me out? I can't say I understand you at all. I really have no idea what you're about. I don't know who you are. There are lots of single women here in the city and more than one place where you could safely meet them.

Oh, I know, I've met my fair share but I can't say that many of them "got" me, for want of a more precise term. In any event, thank you for your candor.

Is that what you wanted to hear?

Of course not. But thank you.

Now I'm even more bewildered.

It isn't really all that complicated. I believe nothing is too precious or grandiloquent to offer as a sacrifice to truth. That's not a bad creed to live by at all, you know, you just need to look at how much misery it averts in the end. I have young people working for me and not one of them is in it for some prospect of growing gray and bloated on a beach with a glass of rum in hand. Death hovers over each of them.

At this moment, even though unconscious, I was vulnerable to the expectation, the near certainty that the cheap plastic phone on the table was about to ring. My impulse was to dash the phone against the wall. I swung my legs, got up, deposited my fully clothed body in the chair. I could not recall where I was. Here was a hotel room, where I was alone and miserable but perhaps downstairs they would welcome me in the lounge where a shrink held forth about lunatic patients. Or maybe the diversion I needed was in a tavern across the road, where I'd hear tales of men with pitchforks mounting hunts for liars across the vastness of plains and deserts. Or, perhaps again, children in a large sandbox wished to invite me to play with them. I scraped my temples with the tips of my fingers.

Feet clomped on the floor in the hall.

Come on, where was I?

Possibilities afoot terrified me, and, if so, then I had told an untruth.

Where was I?

I tried to deny the approaching sounds. I thought of Bondi Beach.

Indeed, footsteps. Even as the moment of crisis drew near, I focused on the receiver in the white plastic tray on the bare little desk. The world could emerge through the tunnel's mouth before me. Instead, a succession of events occurred. I shifted the chair so that I was facing the door. I tried to keep my attention on that cheap plastic phone, but later I'd recall the door swinging open and the light bulb in the ceiling coming on. Four strangers in the room, or it might have been nine. No, they were not strangers. The weight pressing down on my legs was the body of a well-fed young woman with dark hair falling to her shoulders and a ruddy face swelling just a bit at the periphery. A face I knew. Yes, the face belonged to Cheryl.

No, of course it didn't. Cheryl was a woman I had met against my wishes in a bar in a part of the city I did not know. But in truth the buttocks working methodically over my groin as the others danced and laughed belonged to none other than Cheryl, who maybe had never despised me after all. Or maybe she had and this was her way of saying it. On the face above me was an indulgent look faintly tempered with pity, as if she knew the degree of my fear. Her buttocks kept working. She wanted me to relish the sensations now. With a swift move of her right arm, the mouth of a bottle met my lips. I did not need what came now, but it came on hard. At least one horrifying possibility did not materialize. At least *I* didn't come. Not now, not with these yahoos prancing around in my private space. I stood up and the face before me, pretty though descending to flab at its extremities, began to whirl. I was unable to avert my gaze from the face, though it wasn't what exerted force over my body, sucked me right into this devil's hop. I grew aware of large soft fingers on each of my bare forearms, guiding me gently the way you might move a scarecrow when its belt is undone and you don't want it to fall to pieces in your hands. Then the fingers began to clench, the agent behind them started to pull me more aggressively.

The face before me was neither distinct nor indistinct. It was artless, smooth, and easy, part of the unquestionable texture of the world. I whirled and in my confusion nearly tripped a couple of times, catching on both occasions a glimpse of one of the male revelers spinning, laughing, raising a bottle. It is hard to say at exactly what point the lower edge of the shirt covering the form before me began to rise. Soon I was looking at a pair of nipples that kept their bright alertness even as the pale nearly amorphous flesh around them bounced and roiled. The hands that had been on my forearms pushed me, hard, harder still, into the warm receiving flesh and I kissed and sucked as if I hadn't aged mentally since the age of three months.

Upon waking, my relief at finding my body fully clothed and devoid of caked vomit was immense. I got up, looked around again at the plain unassuming room. Though I had thought of it as my private space not long ago, I didn't care to spend another minute here.

The road leading out of town was not quite so barren. After a few minutes of driving, a filling station came up on my right, the glare from its green plastic sign assailing my eyes. The road before me shimmered as I briefly debated whether to pull in here. After consulting the readout on the dash, I swung into the lot, parked, got out, and chatted with a twenty-five-year-old in a blue outfit and cap while one of his mates filled the tank. The young man wanted to know what I was doing out here. I told him I was here for professional reasons. He asked who my employer was. "No one you know, mate." I gestured to the northwest. He looked unsure where I was pointing, whether at the mountains many miles off or the barren sands.

His directions proved useful. I drove on the same road for another twenty minutes, turned right onto a side road, drove for fifteen minutes, then took a left onto yet another side road. Now there came houses at intervals of forty to fifty yards on either flank of the road. None of them had more than one story but most had a garden, a driveway, and a mailbox accessible from the road. These structures were about as interesting as kids' sandcastles at Bondi Beach. Up ahead, the eighth house on the right gradually came into view. Here was a squat but oblong blue building with a fairly well-kept garden, its hydrangeas scoring the monotony of its petunias inside a white picket fence. The house was spacious of its kind, but it was as plain as they come, its façade disclosed absolutely nothing.

I swung into the driveway, parked, and walked around to the path leading through the garden to the front door. I knocked. Within seconds, the door opened to reveal an aboriginal woman, her black hair in thick knots, a polite guarded look on her face. I asked to speak to Ms. Gladys Whitcomb, mentioning that I knew a former student of hers. The aide seemed to infer that I was the agent of that former student's sympathy and consolation. I did not feel too bad, not having lied. The door closed. I waited there, and waited some more, already a minor casualty of the heat.

At last the door opened again and the aide beckoned me to follow her. I moved inside. This was not heat's domain. The house's owner had tried to foster a climate in which the aging

of flesh is like the progress of a turtle over a continent. Punctu-
ating the hall were the entrance to a modest dining room and
kitchen divided by an island with a sleek glittering surface, and
the closed door of the room where I guessed the aide watched
TV and slept. It was a straight path through the hall to the large
room at back where Ms. Whitcomb passed her days. I thanked
the aide and moved over the varnished boards to the entrance
to that big room. Here it felt even cooler than in the hall. Filling
the chilly air was the pungent aroma of gum trees occupying
pots at either end of the wall on the house's north side. There
were all the habiliments of a retiree's house, a TV on a tray with
yellowing magazines on the shelf below, a stack of dog-eared
digest-sized crossword books between the TV and a squat mini-
fridge housing the retiree's myriad medications. Languishing in
a mechanized swivel chair was the retiree, a tiny wizened figure
with a face like an ancient loaf that someone had forgotten to
throw out, and wispy white hair that was increasingly hard to
notice. Her rich blue eyes, which would follow you wherever
you went in the room, their moves in sync with your own, were
her most noticeable feature. Though the cool air and the scent
from the trees might have fostered an illusion of longevity, there
could be no doubt as to the rate of that little fridge's opening
and closing.

I took a seat on a plastic chair the aide had moved beside
Ms. Whitcomb specifically for this meeting. Those eyes moved
when I moved, stopped when I stopped.

"Hello, Ms. Whitcomb. Peter Logue. I'm an associate and
former roommate of a man who was once your pupil."

I had not been looking forward to this part at all, but when
I told her the name, I saw that my concerns about upsetting her
were quite moot. Gladys just nodded, regarding me the way
she might look at a sneaky estate lawyer. I tried not to speak

too quickly, not to allow any suspicion that I was skipping over anything that might make me appear in a different light. When at last she spoke, her voice was strong and clear.

"Peter Logue, is that your name?"

"Yes, ma'am."

"Hmmph. Nice white-collar name. I've met plenty of poufters like you. The type who work at a desk all week and, when they've really got some energy, go down the hall with a colleague and play badminton in a neat square room, and then return to the desk. A nice life all right. Do you know what things may come upon you at noon out here, sir?"

"Ms. Whitcomb, could we please talk about the man I work for?"

She studied my face for a bit, then nodded.

"I remember him quite well as a boy."

"Do you, Ms.—may I call you Gladys?"

"Indeed. He was one of the brightest pupils I had."

Someday, I thought, I would have what they call good interviewing skills and I would ask thoughtful but probing questions with craftily hidden agendas. For now, though it was beginning to sound formulaic to my ears, I posed my question about what the candidate-to-be had liked or gotten frustrated over when living out here.

Gladys reclined in the lift chair, her body at roughly a forty-five-degree angle, still regarding me a bit suspiciously. At the same time, another quality made itself apparent in her features, something peculiarly akin to gratitude.

"In spite of what I said before, I'm glad you're here, young man."

"Are you? I mean, thank you, Gladys, I'm thrilled to be here."

"I may as well tell you. I'm much too old and frail for them to operate. They've given me another six months, at the very most, before the illness encroaches to the other kidney and this crumpled-up sack gives up."

"Gladys, I'm so sorry—"

"No, you're not. You'd be sorry if you had timed this differently. But you're not truly sorry, Peter. Anyone who empathizes with a cancer patient from a safe distance is just observing the expected niceties, blowing wind."

I decided not to argue, though resenting the implication that I had lied.

"Your associate was, as I have said, exceptionally bright as a boy. Perhaps too bright in a community where some people, frankly, consider it their inalienable right to be stupid."

Enthralled, I wondered where this could be going.

"He read with the comprehension of an older boy, and even in his first essays he showed a good grasp of the way words go together. He could study a period of history, analyze concepts and trends, apply them to the present. Of course his comparisons didn't always hold up, but I'd say he was remarkably precocious."

"I'm getting the impression that teaching him was one of the brighter spots of your career."

"You speak too hastily. Was he different from a lot of the boys I taught? Most certainly. Did that mean it was good for me to have him in my class? That's another question altogether."

I looked at her, patient and encouraging, but she picked up on something uncomprehending in my expression.

"You have no idea what I mean."

I shook my head.

The wizened lady let out a sigh and allowed her body to go even limper. If not for the mechanized swivel in the platform supporting her, she would have been gazing at the ceiling. I did not envy the aide who looked after this widow day after day.

"Perhaps you fancy yourself an expert on life. I, for one, don't think you've been out in the world much at all. There are things out here that'd cause such terror you'd want to play badminton in your cute little office until you die."

I let this pass.

"In a small community, giving a particular kid higher grades than others, and recognizing the kid's 'brightness,' on a consistent basis, is tantamount to favoritism. A teacher does not make friends that way. These people, they had a right to know things. They'd want to know, if I commended someone's child for a paper, why I hadn't also given kudos to the Bennetts' child, and the Muirs' child, and the Burkes' child, and the Simpsons' child, and the O'Neals' child, and the Whites' child, and the Randalls' child, and so on."

Despite the growing queasiness in my gut, I kept up my polite comprehending expression.

"Oh, no, it simply doesn't do. But there are ways around the problem. For example, one of the other boys, little Tommy Burke, sat next to the bright pupil and grew quite adept at aping his classmate's handwriting. When we had exam booklets filled out in pencil, it wasn't so hard to Tommy to make a few alterations in one of them, changing the meaning of the text so it suggested that the Nazis, not 'the Germans' but 'the Nazis,' had started World War One."

"You can't be serious."

"That error, and a number of other artfully inserted howlers, helped keep me in the good graces of the people paying my wages and considering me for a more senior position and salary bracket, Peter. Favoritism is an evil thing."

"Favoritism!" I said, feeling a medieval anger rise within me.

"Let me ask you, young man from the city who says pretty things, what are the parameters of your existence? What is the highest that you can aspire to?"

"I don't see what this has to do with sabotaging a boy's grades."

"You're a guest in my house. I asked you a question."

"Well, if a certain person got elected I suppose I'd get a cabinet position."

"You suppose. You have the safety of making suppositions from a rather comfortable place, Peter. There was little point to working in my stifling little world if I couldn't at least get a promotion and a raise. I was working and trying to keep myself youthful and attractive for a nice fellow. At twenty-nine, I did meet a guy who liked the fact that I was in a traditionally feminine occupation, but that man, my first husband, badly wanted a family. He left me. Since I'm really leveling with you, Peter, I might as well remind you of how envy sprouts wings when you are a childless spinster looking at a family's young success story. I met another man, and we stayed married for thirty-seven years until his passing, but those were thirty-seven years of staring at walls from opposite sides of bed, never broaching a certain subject."

So that was it. The candidate-to-be's grasp of modern European history, and possibly other subjects, had undergone gross distortions to assuage the status anxiety of a sad insecure woman. I stood up with a sad resigned air.

"I am so delighted to have received you here this morning, Peter. I will go to my Maker without a single festering, un-confessed secret. Right now I feel lighter, fresher, than I can ever remember having felt."

Fifty minutes later, I pulled over to the edge of the road again and pored over the map and itinerary. At this point in my sojourn in the Outback, my goal was to track down a mysterious guy who had briefly been a co-worker of the candidate-to-be. Even in this information-sodden age, the whereabouts of one Terence Wright weren't easy to pin down. Wright had been a colleague of my boss during a dreary and depressing phase of the latter's life, when he was sending his resume to auto dealerships in need of back-office clerks, banks looking to hire greeters, bars willing to take on marginally competent bartenders.

The vastness of the desert was as scary as ever. If I got lucky enough to locate Wright, to engage with him face-to-face, I'd be conversing with a fellow with firsthand knowledge of the tensions that led to the candidate-to-be's dismissal from a firm. It could be quite a story, rich with implications about the man I knew in the present, but the conditional part of the above sentence coiled and swung frighteningly like a minotaur's tail. If only I could locate Wright. I buried my face in my hands, unwilling to face the lonely roads again.

But this quest had yielded truths before and surely it could once more. Surely it could. Mighty winds would displace concealing sands and I would wander and drop to my knees and sift with both hands until I found a fact, now about a boy, now about a guy in the full bloom of early manhood, now about a stand-offish adult with silvering strands at his temples, and the intelligence disclosed to me would vault my sense of this elusive human being into an exhilarating or terrifying galaxy. Steeling myself, I put the Hyundai back in drive and slid once again into the eastbound lane. Having driven hundreds of miles to the west and north of Sydney, I had changed direction decisively and had moved in an arc, southwest shading to southeast, now pretty much east, on a course that would bring me back to the densely populated areas after many more hours of driving.

On the way to the retired schoolteacher's home, there had been buildings and people here and there. On this side of Ms. Whitcomb's tiny settlement, the loneliness of desolate roads enveloped the driver once again. Rotating my head nervously from side to side, I tried in vain to spy a town, a village, a shack, the barest rudiments of infrastructure, a utility box or telephone pole. Here was sand, sand, sand. I drove on through this barrenness with my right hand resting limply at the lowest point of the steering wheel, only occasionally rousing the hand to nudge the wheel as the road titled in barely perceptible gradations. The desert went on for so many miles all around that communities, governments, social systems could have arisen out here and flourished and died off the grid over centuries. The desert glowed in the glare, the sands were so vivid it hurt to look at them.

Many miles ahead, if Devin's map didn't lie, was a town called Evanston. With a few more hours of determined driving it would become as vivid in its way as these hostile sands. At length there came a fork in the road that did not show up on Devin's map. The map described a fairly clean arc through the desert. Here was a bit of a puzzle, but there didn't seem much point in trying to raise Devin on the cell phone. Surely he had done the best he could with what he had. Of the two roads stretching into the distance, the more southerly one looked just a bit cleaner and better paved, the gray of the pavement contrasting more with the sand and sky. As the moment of decision neared I swung the vehicle to the right, pursued a strip of road briefly indistinguishable from what came before the fork.

Then the road began to grow choppy. After half an hour of uneasy driving the land began to break up. At first the hills and buttes came as a relief for the sheer fact of their unpredictability. For a while the road's altitude did not change markedly, but then beyond the left shoulder a great hill arose, a majestic fold in the monotony. But hill is not really the right description because there appeared to be no other side on which the land fell dramatically away. Anyone who got lost out here was done for. The vehicle plodded on at the base of this hill, curving as the hill curved, left, right, left, and right again.

The rhythms of the engine were reassuring. They eased me into a sense of the powerlessness, the irrelevance of any particles of sand that might have found a home inside the chassis, on the gray rods and black flaps of CV boots in constant motion. For so many hours the whirring had seemed to invite some agent to disrupt it, but now the car had proven itself, had exposed an urban naif's lack of automotive expertise, or so I needed to believe. I repeated to myself that the car was fine. I looked out at the horizon to the east. The blue met the gold in a line so even that I relished an illusion of exactitude, of a line more even than artificial means could achieve. I tried to deny the truth, I tried to comfort myself with a notion of geometric precision, or people living in isolation in communities of twenty or thirty or a hundred, never fearing quakes or movements of catastrophic fires or masses of sand across the continent or evenings where they would look up at clouds, against a backdrop of surging violence, and tremble, huddle together in fear, and taste acid rain.

I thought, soon a town must appear, soon the ugly green of plastic signs, the pennants of used car merchants must fleck the monotony of sand and sky. But between my position on the road and these welcome prosaic destinations, there must be pits, craters, sites of meteors' impact decades ago, and I could only guess what lived in those barren disused spaces. In vain I told myself that fear had no place here, that someone must come bringing truth, welcome or not, to the continent. It was impossible not to wonder what entities dwelt in the depths of this country, what agents they might send to sabotage the intricate machinery on which my life depended.

The borders of the road grew unmistakably less distinct, sand gnawed the edges of the metal shell enclosing my body. Though the air conditioner was going full blast, the glare outside stung. At any moment the car might fail, all directions might bleed into sand and sky. For now the vehicle's hum was just faintly reassuring. The road was less distinct, but it was there. That would have to do. Here it was hard not to think of what a sandstorm could do in a blink to the integrity of the hill. I kept thinking, ahead was Evanston, it was going to become real.

Now the road, such as it was, began to veer wildly from the base of the hill. From a certain point of view, this was yet another relief, lessening the tedium and the driver's vulnerability, but the arc of the road, portions of which shimmered even now in the glare, was utterly confusing. To the west was the hill, to the east were distances with barely distinct ranges of cliffs and buttes hundreds of yards off.

There could be no point in consulting Devin's map, but I had to orient myself. I pulled over, parked, reached into my breast pocket for the phone. At this point an odd swell appeared in the shadow of the hill falling on the car's hood. I gazed out the driver's side window, rotated my eyes skyward. On the crest was a black car, looking quite picturesque between the ochre-white sands and the limitless blue. I clutched the wheel with both hands, tried to peer through the other car's windows, anticipating movement. I felt myself the object of a regard still fiercer, still more probing, than my own. I put the Hyundai back in drive, floored it, and watched the dark rectangle in the rear-view mirror recede and recede.

Unable to stick to this course, I spun the wheel to the right and struck out into the desert. I drove about three hundred yards before I thought, no, this only fulfilled the desires of the black car's occupant, this would ensure my end more reliably than any bullet or explosive. So I reversed course, made it back to the road, plowed ahead on a more or less easterly course, looking out at the top of the hill whenever I was not frantically gauging the shifts and curves ahead. At last the road intersected with another, more or less perpendicular, route, running north to south. I swung onto that road and drove well above the limit until that long row of connected hills was far behind.

But there were many more hills out here, amid the unfamiliar roads, and the light was beginning to change. The valley was a barren unforgiving place and I had no idea where I was in relation to anything else. To that extent, at least, the driver of the other car had won. I pulled over, sat there beholding the landscape once again. Surely the vast reaches couldn't be so intimidating when you knew exactly what and whom you were looking for. It was not the remoteness of this place that got to me just now, but, on the contrary, the possibility of meeting strangers. But there was so much they were desperate to conceal about themselves, and I was unsure that desperation was greater than the terror that drove them from what others had failed to conceal.

I know what you're thinking. A bloke don't become fully real to you until his trials and traumas are out in the noontime sun.

I suppose you think it's by some kind of freak accident that people live all the way out here.

I am all the aggrieved people of the Outback, telling you to turn around and go home.

Do you know what things may come upon you at noon out here, sir?

Let me ask you, young man from the city who says pretty things, what are the parameters of your existence. Perhaps you fancy yourself an expert on life? I, for one, don't think you've been out in the

*world much at all. There are things out here that'd cause such terror
you'd want to go and play badminton in your cute little office until
you die.*

The voices coming to me now were malevolent spiteful
sirens, daring me to unveil truths even as they warned me off in
the plainest terms. I drove stubbornly on in the gathering dusk.
Far ahead, about seventy yards off the road to my right, I made
out a building of some kind, a fairly big one, I could tell even
from far off. As I closed the distance, I discerned that it was a
disused factory. Yes, they had left and gone home long ago. All
along the brick façade facing the road ran two indistinguishable rows of boarded windows. The wide yellow smokestacks at
either end were thick with soot and dust, but you would look
in vain for a puff of smoke, for a shadow flitting past a window
or within the penumbra of the balcony at the upper floor on
the narrower end facing north. I stared at it in passing. Soon
the factory was receding from view. I scanned the road ahead
in vain. The factory might not have been active in years and
there was no point in calling Devin without a reference point
he could use to plot a route to Evanston. At least my route had
grown random enough that it seemed unlikely that the other
car could follow.

Far off, once again on the right, something rather more
modest than a factory gradually came into view. Here was a
little shack, tin on all sides, flimsy and pitiful in every detail.
It might have been a makeshift thing put up years ago in the
midst of a road project. Out in front of the shack, a woman in
her forties sat on a trunk. She had skin the color of strawberry
milk and clumps of stringy hair that perhaps quite a few years
ago had been a luscious amber. The woman wore tattered dark
blue shorts and a frayed white undershirt. She did not move. I
eased my foot on the brake, parked at the shoulder, got out and

approached her. The crunch of my feet on the shoulder's gravel was a fitting announcement of my obnoxious presence. To my dismay, the stranger seemed bent on not noticing me even as I got within ten yards. In as polite a voice as I could summon, I told her I was looking for the road to Evanston.

Without turning her head or making eye contact, she said, "Get lost. Or more lost."

I allowed hurt to creep into my voice, I wanted it to register.

"Why are you being rude? I've been driving for many hours. I'm asking for your help."

"Hell of a long time. You from Cans?"

"Sydney."

"Of course. You didn't know people out here exist."

Now I couldn't hide my annoyance.

"Oh, please. Urban snob gets what's coming to him? Disturbing you was never my design. I would like to know the route and then I swear I'll leave you alone forever."

"I reckon you got lost on your way home from a gathering somewhere."

"Yes, ma'am. You've nailed it exactly. I was attending the annual spoiled-and-pampered convention. Between sips of Rosé and bites of chocolate-dipped lamb, we talked about how to get a corner on the export markets and drive local grain producers deeper into destitution. Turnout was great. We invited aborigines because we could charge them a whopping fee, just enough to make them default on their mortgage payments, and then we'd have another Stolen Generation, and we were also mindful to invite lots of Chinese businessmen so they'd get an idea of what plots to think about buying up, once we've herded people who say 'reckon' onto reservations. That's the grand design. Because I am from the city, I am utterly incapable of feeling empathy or love for a redneck."

She did not lower herself to reply.

"If you must know, I'm not a smug young man at all. Almost everything I've ever touched in my life has turned to shit, and I'm truly pathetic. Nearly every day I think about an occasion when a woman I was interested in saw me naked on a bed in the full glare of an overhead light. That light was much crueler than the sun here in the Outback could ever be. It was humiliating. My life's an indescribable mess and I can't make anything of myself and I've come out here in the hope that I might curry favor with certain people by arming myself with a certain understanding. The only thing that separates me from people who take a swan dive from the top of the Sydney Opera House is the possibility, however remote, that I might achieve such an understanding."

I fairly panted by the time I finished. She did not smile or say a word, but kept looking ahead.

"Look, I'm here for the sake of knowledge and understanding. I—"

"Make a left 17 miles from here and you'll get to Goulburn Township," she said in a voice so cutting I wanted to check that my nose was still where it should be.

"Thank you for your help, ma'am."

She didn't say a word. Of course I could not take her directions at face value, she might well have been trying to get me killed. Maybe Goulburn was in the wrong direction. But if that was the name of a real place, and it was around here, then it was all I needed to know.

I followed the stranger's directions. Little did I suspect that they were accurate as far as they went but that Goulburn was a gaggle of singed teetering crusts of walls and doors, of stone and brick remnants of one-story buildings not inhabited in years. Not only had a fire come to the township, but the winds had given the remnants of each structure a thick coat of sand. It was impossible not to wonder about the odds of this place being on any extant map in the universe.

I paused to think about whether it was really necessary to hunt down the next person on the list, to fulfill a quota of strangers who had direct experience with the man running for prime minister. I had already met a number of people who had left me with little doubt as to the sources of the candidate's hunger for truth, his disdain for the niceties that paper over the dregs of our experience on this planet. But I couldn't say how many testimonials made for a full accurate portrait. If there was a guy out there who had intimate experience with the man to whom I had prostrated myself, I would find him in the hope of validating my trust.

But how would I ever find anyone amid the vastness of sand and sky? Out there was the desert. Out there were feral things and feral people, their eyes reddened, their minds deranged by the rising of sands amid gathering winds on evenings when people in the staid quarters of our cities relaxed with a glass of gin before screens where the faces of commentators looked out blandly, mouthing words that located the source of crisis no closer than Bali. Australia's a modern nation whose people live on the coasts, but I had to make my way out there. Though it was obvious the land didn't want me, my need for knowledge, certainty, affirmation wouldn't go away.

Fixing my gaze on the space out in front of the car where a road should have been, I pressed down hard on the gas. I moved across a barren land with rows of dusty buttes far off to the right, cutting into each other without rational design. I forged ahead, smashing through the barren yellow and orange and ochre, the pitiful stalks with their bits of shadow, for nearly an hour before reality asserted itself once again. On the road about forty yards behind me was a black car, moving at a speed expressing neither hurry nor lassitude. It was fine with where it was. The distance was close enough to monitor every move I took but not quite near enough to make me panic just yet.

I was not going to give panic a window of opportunity. There seemed little he could do at that distance, so maybe I should forge ahead in a straight line to minimize the chance of getting lost. But I slammed my foot on the gas and cut to the right, over a patch of desert that had no greater or lesser claim than anywhere else. I drew near the buttes. My car gained speed and within a couple of minutes the driver of the other car had lost me. In the spaces amid the buttes were plains and corridors through which a driver could cruise in the knowledge that his emergence on the far side of the row of buttes was too immediate to allow for any panic, any concern about getting lost.

I reached Devin by phone two hours later. He had done research on the Goulburn Township fire and was able to place the settlement in relation to others in the region. With his help, I found a road on the far side of Goulburn Township that wended on a northeasterly course until it joined with a road going east and then dipped to the southeast. With growing confidence I drove on in the dimming air and at length began to see signs on the road for Evanston. The signs were extravagant in their promises. "Food," "Gas," "Lodging." Lots of establishments filled with simple people who'd be easy to talk to were coming up. Here was that point in a journey where a driver must not get careless.

At last I turned onto the winding exit ramp, drove seventy feet, made a left onto a two-lane street, and pursued it until the generic shapes of a Best Western motel came into view on my left. Here were two floors of plain small rooms with an office in the lower right corner of the building. I parked, went inside, and paid the tired middle-aged clerk for a single. I went back outside and mounted a wooden staircase with unpainted boards and a plain square landing halfway up. The room on the second floor was nothing much, a modest bed, a dresser surmounted with an aging TV, a fridge, a sink, a plug-in coffee brewer on a formica counter. I dropped off my bags, and in the throes of a gratitude I had rarely felt as an adult, tried to ring Devin. No luck. Well, he deserved some time with his girl.

No. I was not going to humiliate myself again. I thought I had a pretty sound understanding of the need to be cautious precisely when you feel you are close to attaining a goal. At this time of the evening it was possible that many miles from this desolate outpost, in a fashionable corner of the city, a woman sat at a chic wine bar, a new place serving $15 glasses of rosé, quite by herself I hoped, reflecting, meditating, remembering me as I was at the moment I walked out of her life. There was no need to disturb or complicate whatever serenity she found at this moment.

I showered, put on fresh clothes, and set out on foot from the Best Western. There wasn't much of a path, just a narrow untended dirt causeway with squalid clumps of grass at the edge of the street I had taken to the motel. It was the kind of area where drivers during the day notice kids with green or purple hair, claiming tiny zones of defiant aloofness where they can smoke joints and listen to Joy Division. Soon I passed the point where the exit ramp joined the street. I left the causeway and entered a field on the far side of which stood a one-story structure with beige stucco walls, a flat roof, and a neon Budweiser sign in one of the front windows. When I passed through the front door, a mostly blue-collar crowd greeted my eyes.

Later, I mounted the steps leading the motel's second level, moved past six plain doors lining the walkway on the east side of the place, entered my room, and flicked the overhead on.

Natalie sat on the bed looking at me.

I stood there in the doorway, feeling as if my passage through the desert had drained every particle of water, every mite of strength from me. My throat felt as if I had been dry-heaving for three hours. At the same time, a rush of memories came, I recalled the flash of joy at the moment the seed had taken flight from by body at Natalie's instigation as she stood before me with a calm gentle smile.

She read the question in my eyes.

"The woman in the tavern in Coburn had your card. I already had your cell number. I got her to give me another number on the card, an office number. I called it and I got through to a young guy who sounded really smart and nice. I pled with him for, like, half an hour, I said I needed to meet up with you about something urgent. He got it. He told me where you were going."

I thought: *Oh, Devin! You're a better judge of the forces at work in my life than I am.* But if Devin knew about my connection to Natalie, perhaps Rachel might find out. Then again, perhaps not. Devin had never been more than a friend of a friend to Rachel, and in my absence there was absolutely no basis for them to speak or interact at all.

"How did you get in here?"

"I told the clerk I'm from your company and I was supposed to meet up with you here. It was a simple matter to have him call Devin call the front desk and verify everything. It might not work in Sydney, but here's another matter."

I went to her. Right now she was everything I had denied myself in the past week, yet she was, quite unmistakably,

Natalie. My body felt devoid of tension as we lay on the bed, there was only a leisured swelling in my loins at the expectation of the touch, the caress of her soft hands. I exulted deeply in the absence of raucous voices outside. Beyond these walls was a vast zone of clear quiet space punctuated by the rumble of eighteen-wheelers on the road intersecting with the highway.

Later, in the dark, as Natalie's hand roamed over my chest and abdomen, pausing at odd points to caress me, she asked whether I had truly managed to relax. Not for the first time, I wondered whether things about me were as obvious to everyone as they were to her. She told me how deeply she cared for me. She urged me to open up about unexorcised traumas. There must be some reason, beyond pure adolescent idealism, why I would devote myself to the campaign of a candidate I never saw in person. I wondered what I could disclose to her now.

"No," I said to Natalie.

"Peter. You've come an awfully long way on behalf of the truth."

Lying there in the claustrophobic dark, I considered her words.

Then, slowly, I felt myself at last begin to yield.

The Gift

South Australia, 1935

The strong desert wind swept across the desolate land and carried dust through the dry air. Sand flew this way and that in brief, spastic flurries, and spun in dense clouds up towards the grey sky. Herb Johnson's gas station stood tiny and humble, a black and white beacon looking lost in the vastness of the arid landscape. Behind the station lay Herb's farm, wide strips of green crops and plowed earth sectioned off by long brown fences, with an adjoining barn and decrepit farmhouse.

Herb was out in his folding chair, lying languidly between the battered old station and the two fuel pumps that stood together before the highway. Once in a while, perhaps twice a day, Herb would spot a glint of sunlight reflected off of a faraway windshield, and a dust cloud coming up behind it. The distant shape moving along the highway would grow and grow until the features of the car grew distinct. The money Herb made in the ensuing transaction wasn't much, but Herb was doing all right selling crops and produce to men in several nearby towns.

The screen door opened, and Jack O'Loughlin, one of Herb's hired hands, came outside holding a bottle of beer. Herb took off his Stetson and put it on the ground beside him. Jack offered no casual greeting, no polite "Mornin'" as the other hands did. The young man's haggard, bleary-eyed countenance was a clear sign of a hangover. Jack didn't say much and often took on an air of sharp recalcitrance, but he was an expert mechanic and hence was of use.

Herb glanced at Jack, then turned to the stretch of grey road. Davey, Herb's son, came out next, followed by Louis, another hired worker. Davey clapped Louis on the back and addressed his father.

"Louis and I are goin' out tonight, okay, Dad?"

Herb spoke without taking his eyes from the highway.

"No. You've both got work to do."

"We'll get it done."

Herb didn't reply. Davey grinned at Louis. Jack sipped his beer. Herb picked up a gun catalog and began flipping through it distractedly.

Jack gazed westward, out over the vast expanse of yellow sand and toward the great black mountains that thrust upwards like jagged coals in a furnace. His squinting eyes roamed over the great plains of dust and rock and turned down slowly, suspiciously, onto the strip of dust rising behind a moving object. Jack pointed this out to Davey, who showed his father. Herb got out of his chair and stood with the three teens and they waited expectantly.

In a minute or so, the young men and Herb realized that the cloud was not coming up from behind one object but three. Three men were walking towards the small station. "Abos," Herb said in a nasty tone.

As the three walkers drew near, Herb and the teens noticed that a pack of dogs trotted along at their heels. Soon it was possible to make out the characteristics of the approaching figures.

The walker near the left side of the road was a young man, roughly Davey's age, clad in a simple loincloth. His hair fell to his shoulders and was only a few shades darker than his skin. The middle walker looked at least four times as old. On the right approached a large aborigine, even more muscular than Louis, with a headband strapped across his wide brow.

Herb watched uneasily as the aborigines walked up to the front of the station. Louis stood with his arms folded, and Davey looked at the three men nervously. The old man came forth with the long-haired youth and raised a gnarled hand in greeting. Herb stepped forward and nodded hesitantly. Then the old man spoke words Herb could not begin to understand. Herb looked to Jack, whom he knew to understand some of the language, for help. Jack walked over, expectant. An exchange began between the aborigine and Jack, and Herb waited as they conversed in that bewildering dialect. The muscle-bound aborigine stood by the dogs, looking on silently. Davey jerked his hand up to swat a fly buzzing around his face.

Jack turned to face Herb.

"We'll call this man here Thomas. He's the leader of a group about thirty miles west of here. He asked me to greet you—"

Herb cut in. "Ask 'im what the hell he wants from me."

"He wants to trade with you."

"Now that's strange. Usually if blacks want somethin', they go and steal it. At least that's been my experience."

Jack continued. "Listen to his offer. Just listen. Thomas wants to trade with you. You've got something that would be useful to his people."

"What might that be?"

Jack turned to the old stranger and there was another brief exchange. Thomas made motions and gestures with his hands. Jack faced Herb again.

"I think what Thomas is interested in is the hunting rifles, Herb."

Herb sneered.

"The huntin' rifles? What for?"

"These people hunt for food, Herb. The rifles would be invaluable to them. He's offering you your pick of two of those dogs. Why don't you make the trade? You'd both come out ahead."

"No way in hell would I do business with an abo. Where'd he ever hear of a rifle, anyhow?"

Jack spoke to the stranger again briefly.

"Apparently, a traveler came by their camp a few days ago. He spent a night there. In the morning he went out with some tribesmen and killed a kangaroo with this 'magical object' Thomas just described to me."

"I see."

"Why don't you make the trade? There's no reason for these people not to have what we have. Two rifles and some ammo for two of those dogs. Make the trade, Herb."

"No. No way'n hell am I tradin' with a black abo. They wouldn't know how to use a rifle anyhow."

"Come on, Herb—"

"I jus' gave you the final word, Jack. Now tell them t'clear out 'fore I get mad. Tell them, Jack."

Jack let out a long sigh and looked down. He relayed Herb's stubborn refusal to Thomas, who nodded. The old stranger and his long-haired companion turned and walked back to the muscular guy and the dogs. The three started off down the long road.

A few moments after the aborigines had begun their journey westward, the long-haired youth turned to glance back at Herb. The glance was quick, momentary, but its coldness would live on in Herb's mind for some time.

The three walkers sent up a thick cloud of dust as they moved along. The whites watched them plod on and on until the grey horizon dwarfed them. Herb lumbered into the station. A moment later, Davey and Louis followed him. Jack went to the green folding chair, sat down, and put on Herb's Stetson.

II.

It was around three in the morning. Davey and Louis, both drunk, came rolling toward the station in Herb's pickup. Both boys were lightheaded but not too far gone to have discussed their plans for sneaking into the farmhouse without waking Herb. Davey swerved to avoid crashing into the fuel pumps and stopped the vehicle just in front of the quiet station. Louis laughed and he and Davey stumbled out of the pickup and slammed the doors. Davey looked for the station's front window, trying to catch his reflection in the glass, and felt a stab of surprise when he could not. A sense that something was terribly wrong penetrated his shroud of intoxicated serenity. His fear grew when he noticed jagged shards of glass littering the ground in front of the building.

"Louis," he mumbled. "Louis, look at this!"

Louis, who was one degree closer to sobriety than Davey, said, "Damn. It's been bashed out. What coulda done this?"

Davey shook his head.

"Let's go inside," Louis said.

The euphoria that ten beers had brought to Davey was gone. He was worried now. He began to rummage for his keys.

"Don't bother. It's not locked."

"What?"

Louis opened the door and they entered. Then Louis found the light switch.

"Oh, Jesus," was Davey's reaction to the scene that greeted their eyes. Louis was only able to stare.

The room had been ransacked. The drawers from the oak desk at the east wall lay scattered on the floor, their contents emptied out all over the bare boards. The couch at the opposite wall was on its side, one of the legs broken off. The bookshelf that had stored all Herb's old gun catalogs lay flat on the ground like a felled tyrannosaur. The lamp from the overturned night-stand lay in halves, its glass dome shattered. All over the walls were deep, jagged scratches, made perhaps with a hatchet.

The far wall, which had born Herb's two hunting rifles on small metal hooks, was bare.

Davey stumbled over to the west wall, kneeled, and began retching violently, and the beer that left his body made a final touch to the devastation. Louis, the faster and more rational of the pair, darted through the wrecked room and the adjoining hall, burst out the back exit, and ran towards the farmhouse. Seconds later there was frantic knocking on Herb's bedroom door.

III.

"I can't believe it," Herb said, and took another swig of booze. Herb sat at his kitchen table. Gathered around him were Davey, Louis, and all Herb's other employees, with the exception of Jack.

"I just can't believe it. One of those goddamn blacks must've broke in, tore the place up, and grabbed the rifles," Herb muttered.

Whatever doubts the others may have had, they dared not contradict Herb in his present state. Clearly Herb couldn't believe that a mortal could be disobedient as the one they were thinking of right now.

"Looks that way, Herb," said Louis. "Looks like they broke in and tore the place up and stole the rifles."

"Why the hell'd they have to wreck the station besides?"

"I dunno. I guess they was really angry. I guess they take what they won't be given. And that's aborigines for you, Herb."

Herb drank some more booze. "I guess I shoulda expected somethin' like this."

Louis narrowed his eyes for a moment. He'd found a way to allude to the elephant in the room.

"Where's Jack?"

Herb spoke again. "He musta run out on me. That bastard. But you know what? I don't care. The strange thing is that those blacks took only the rifles and a coupla boxes of shells. Not the compass. Not the radio. Not even the damn cash register! All the money's there, right? Of all the things they coulda stole, they took the stupid rifles and some ammo. I don't get it."

He put the bottle to his lips for a full minute before he spoke again.

"Fact of the matter is, we can't let 'em get away with doin' what they did. We gotta hit back."

"What're we gonna do?" said Louis.

"Give me that phone."

IV.

Constable Ryan picked up his telephone and listened patiently to the gruff, bellowing voice at the other end.

"All right, Herb," he interrupted. "Now, give me an estimate as to the value of the stolen merchandise."

"Oh, I dunno. Maybe five hundred dollars. There's at least twice that in property damage."

"And around when do you think the incident occurred?"

"I can't say. It was after eleven, I know that."

"All right, now, listen. This is serious, but it's not that serious. We'll get your rifles back. Keep in mind that the aborigines are highly primitive, uncivilized people. They have no organization beyond tribal identity. It's all they can do to hunt to stay alive. I don't even know that they have the same ideas about private ownership as we do. Personally, I don't know or care much about their culture. They aren't too sociable but they sure as hell don't bother anybody most of the time."

"What're you gettin' at, constable?"

"I was going to say that you can't really blame them for this business."

"Far as I'm concerned, they're guilty as hell. They broke in, wrecked, my station, took my rifles. That's askin' for it."

"I agree that we have to get back the rifles and punish the vandals. Now, I'll come by your place first thing in the morning. I know where to find that group, I've been there before. We'll go and get your rifles back and I'll see what I'm going to do. Now get some sleep."

Constable Ryan hung up his phone.

V.

The sun beat down mercilessly on the hood of the constable's car. The vehicle crawled on and on along the narrow strip of grey, looking insignificant and lost before the majestic blue horizon. Its occupants were Herb Johnson, Louis, Constable Ryan, and one of the constable's deputies. Anger seemed to roll off Herb in waves. The constable was nervous because Herb had chosen to bring a large shovel along in the car and clearly wished to use it to realize some violent fantasy.

The road stretched out before them like an endless streak of grey paint. The constable had visited the camp once before, and he thought he could easily find it. Still, he wondered whether their car would ever arrive or whether it would just plow on down the road forever, lost in this desolate world of sand and sky, baking in the almost unbearable heat.

Finally the road curved sharply to the right, and the constable knew the direction in which to turn. He brought the car off the road and out into the wide plain of sand. They drove on for another ten minutes before approaching a steep incline. The car's engines grumbled in sincere protest as the constable edged the tired machine up, up, over the peak of the hill. As the men passed the peak and started down the other side, they were granted a full, unobstructed view of their destination, the aborigine camp.

Huts lay scattered about the grounds like brown rocks strewn on a barren shore. Children ran in and out of the huts, some of them followed by dogs. More dogs roamed the outskirts of the camp or lay sleeping at various points within. Adults stood here and there or sat motionless outside the huts. Some of them held spears and boomerangs. In the middle of the camp, the flayed carcass of some large animal roasted over an open fire.

The constable's car accelerated in its descent. The men in the car noticed, lying on the slope of the hill, a disemboweled dog. Flies buzzed frantically over their sumptuous feast. As the car reached the foot of the hill, several of the tribesmen began shouting, and half a dozen dogs started barking fiercely. The car rolled into the camp. The aborigines who had gathered in the center scattered, picking up kids and spiriting them away from the fearsome invading machine. Constable Ryan pressed the horn to warn the aborigines running to and fro of the danger of the moving car. The shrill blast elicited screams of terror from some of the fleeing tribesmen. The constable cursed. He hadn't meant to scare them. Now they'd never cooperate.

He slammed on the brakes and the car skidded to a halt near the center of the camp. The doors opened and the men clambered out. Louis kicked at the wild pup growling at his feet. Herb ran back and forth through the camp, swinging his shovel in a mad frenzy. The constable hoped that Thomas would not present himself, at least not until Herb had calmed down.

Five feet to the right of the car sat an abandoned child, naked and wailing querulously. Upon the constable's command, Louis and the deputy began moving from hut to hut and peering inside, searching for Thomas. The constable looked around for anyone who hadn't run off in terror at their dramatic entrance.

From one of the huts to the east of the constable's car emerged Thomas. A moment later, Jack O'Loughlin, the mechanic, stepped out behind him. Herb and the constable saw them, and Herb suddenly had to admit to himself what must have happened. It was Jack, not the aborigines, who had wrecked the station and taken the rifles. He had met the tribesmen somewhere near the station and given them the stolen items, and come back with them to the camp. It all made sense, although Herb didn't fully grasp Jack's motives.

The constable drew his revolver, ready to arrest the young fugitive. But Herb acted faster. He bore down on Jack in the heat of his fury, and, before Jack knew what was happening, was upon him. A powerful sweep of the heavy shovel set Jack out on the ground. The mechanic cried out in surprise and pain, clutching his stricken head. The furious attacker raised the shovel into the air, obviously intent on doing something similar to the old tribesman. But Louis was too quick. He leapt head-first into Herb, knocking his employer down. The shovel rolled out of Herb's reddened hand. Herb kicked and clawed and struggled to break free from Louis's hold with amazing determination and vigor. The constable came over to help subdue Herb and the deputy put cuffs on the wounded mechanic and dragged him to his feet.

Herb quit struggling and Louis and the constable allowed him to get up. Constable Ryan picked up the shovel. All he wanted now was to get everyone into the car and clear out of this sad place. He waved his revolver in the direction of the old man. Thomas moved back a few paces. The deputy opened the back door of the car and shoved Herb inside. Then he entered the car himself and pulled Jack in by the handcuffs. Constable Ryan and Louis climbed into the front and the constable turned the ignition. The automobile came to life.

Louis watched nervously through the window as the scattered tribesmen started to return to their camp. Dogs ran down from the hill and adults approached the center of the grounds. The car's tires kicked up sand but could gain no traction. Constable Ryan cursed and slammed his foot down on the gas. The car lurched forward reluctantly as he spun the wheel. The vehicle came around in a semicircle and began to rumble with excruciating slowness toward the hill.

The constricting belt of tribesmen parted as the constable drove through. The deputy said in amazement, "Lookit the old guy!" Thomas ran behind them in a comic, fitful limp. Suddenly he stopped running, drew his emaciated arm back in an arc, and flung a small white object at the departing car. The object flew through the air and struck the grimy rear window, producing a thick spider-web crack, and then clattered off the trunk and onto the ground. The car swerved and rumbled further and began its precarious ascent of the steep dune. It went up, up, over the peak once more, and plummeted downward. The aborigine camp was lost from sight.

VI.

"Damn it, Ryan. What're we gonna do with 'im?" Herb said.

The constable wished he had an answer. Jack appeared to have lost consciousness, and the blood from his head wound leaked down into his collar. Louis's undershirt, tied around Jack's skull as a makeshift bandage, was doing little to arrest the flow.

The heat came down in searing, almost visible waves, washing over the constable and the others in the car. It seemed to have doubled in intensity since the drive to the camp. The constable knew that out here, in the Australian desert, there was no escape, no shelter from the sun. It pounded down unrelentingly, like a blacksmith's hammer.

Every twenty seconds or so, Herb mopped his dripping brow with a dirty hanky. "Ryan, we gotta somethin'. This boy's lookin' bad," he kept saying.

It was no lie. Now Jack seemed to waver in and out of consciousness, and every now and then a weak moan escaped his parched lips. The blood trickled down incessantly, caking on his neck and shoulder. The constable wished that Herb would shut up. But Herb went on.

"I don't think you're gettin' me, Ryan. I think this boy here's a goner. If he ain't now, he will be soon."

"What the hell are you suggesting I do, Mr. Johnson?" the constable replied, his voice tinged with hysteria. The journey seemed as if it would never end. He had yet to find the road that led back to Herb's farm.

"What I'm suggestin' is that this here boy's had it. He ain't gonna make it."

Herb wiped his forehead with the hanky and continued.

"I'm thinkin' maybe it wouldn't be the best thing for you if he dies comin' back in your car. Which he looks about to do."

The constable responded with the nervousness and unease that Herb's voice was peculiarly lacking.

"So? What the hell can I do? You hit him. We're gonna keep going until we get to your farm. We'll fix him up—"

"Come on, Ryan. He ain't gonna last ten minutes."

"So what the hell do we do?"

Herb spoke calmly, assuredly.

"I'm sayin' if he's gonna die, it don't hafta be in this car."

Constable Ryan slammed on the brakes and the car came to an abrupt halt. He gazed through the windshield and out over the wide desert. For a minute the men sat silently. Then the constable spoke.

"All right. Bring him out of the car. Everybody out."

The men got out. Louis and the deputy each held Jack up by a limp arm. Another feeble groan escaped Jack's throat as they dragged him twenty yards from the car and dropped him in the dust. The constable gave the cuffs back to the deputy.

"Do his ankles."

The deputy knelt down and fastened the cuffs to Jack's ankles. He met little resistance from the dying mechanic.

"Good," said the constable. "That's good."

The deputy rose and the four men stood in a circle around Jack.

"So, are we just going to leave him here?" asked Louis, gesturing at the ragged body.

"Damn right," Herb replied. He mopped his brow. The deputy was fanning himself with his hat. The constable spoke to Herb.

"Nobody's going to find him here, right?"

Herb chuckled. "Look 'round you, Ryan. The only thing's gonna find this boy is buzzards and dogs. They'll eat well tonight, I reckon."

Louis spoke. "I still wonder. I wonder why he took only the rifles and ammo. And why he cared so much about those aborigines."

Herb looked at Louis and grinned.

"Ask him if you're curious."

Louis looked at Jack, then looked away.

"And about those blacks. Seems you care for them too," Herb said.

"Not much. But I ain't no psychopath."

Herb addressed the constable. "It's much easier this way, Ryan. Ain't nobody gonna know. You ain't got a thing to worry about. Now," he said, addressing the group, "'less anybody has any more comments to make, I'd rather not stand here in the sun any longer."

The constable nodded and the four men walked back to the car and got in. A minute later the car was gone, the dust still settling to the ground.

VII.

Herb and Louis stood together outside the gas station, waving at the constable as he drove away. Gazing at the crack in the rear window that the little box of ammunition had made, Herb wondered how the constable was going to explain it.

Davey had come out to meet them.

"You didn't get the rifles back, Dad?"

Herb studied his son for a moment.

"No. The camp was empty. They all split. I'm afraid we won't get 'em back, ever."

"Damn. There's nothing anyone can do?"

"Nope."

"Damn. Hey, Louis. Feel like a drink?"

"Sure do."

The two boys walked around the station and towards the old farmhouse.

Herb sighed. He applied the hanky to his brow. He felt weary, and even a little upset.

When the constable's car began to drive off from where they'd left Jack, the mechanic had started screaming, a shrill, penetrating wail. It had sounded horrible. The noise echoed across the bright desert, pursuing the men as they sped away. It hadn't seemed to stop until the constable finally found the grey road and brought the car onto it. The noise did not cease in Herb's mind until another unnerving sound replaced it—the constable crying.

Herb knew his unease was ephemeral. He'd finally made it back home. Jack lay abandoned out in the empty desert and was probably dead by this time. Constable Ryan was safe. Herb was safe. He had run into trouble, and perhaps he had acted in anger, without thinking. But he'd met the ultimate requirement. He'd lived to go on ruling his domain.

Herb walked over to the green folding chair and sat down. He reclined comfortably, scooped up his Stetson, and dropped it on his head. He gazed down the long highway. The heat would not diminish intensity for at least another three hours, Herb thought. He'd wait.

Visionary

Harold Ross doubted he could make the car go much further, and his throat felt as if he'd been arguing for hours. All around in the hot white afternoon were sand, dust, dirt, and barren cement, and he was a good two hours from the city on the coast. Looking out into the blaze, surveying the gold and copper sands and cliffs, he began to wonder whether the car or he himself would give out first without water.

Those who can really dignify themselves as journalists go off to cover elections in Moldova or high-profile L.A. trials for *Time* or CNN, he thought. They do not track down clusters of people and write profiles of them. Harold's alma mater had moved high up in the rankings and gotten huge gifts, and a newspaper with a modest circulation had expressed interest in a story on where the school's alumni had ended up in life. Harold needed the work but felt this was a new low in his crummy career. He thought of what others had done by the time they hit thirty. His research for the profiles would surely make him feel even worse.

The car rumbled on. All around were dirt, cacti, slivers of shadow. He imagined wandering out there in the dust and heat until he fell down. It was a setting, he felt, that would magnify the significance of any lizards or birds that came to behold you in your fear and despair. When you saw their eyes, you would know they knew quite well they were not the last things you had expected ever to see.

The groans coming from deep inside the car intensified. His exhaustion grew. His clammy hands gripped the wheel like a life preserver. Thank God he was no idiot about one thing, he had not underestimated the amount of gas he'd need to get to the coast. But taking an obscure side road to avoid paying tolls was a poor idea.

At last he made out a cluster of buildings far off on the horizon. There were maybe five or six of them, on the right side of the highway, their surfaces glinting in the harsh light. With his luck, they were probably a bunch of disused factory buildings.

As the car drew nearer, the industrial character he'd perceived from far off proved to be an illusion. Here were white rectangular two-floor buildings with long shuttered windows. The place looked like a studio lot without cameras and crews or a farm barren of animals and crops or a town with no commercial buildings at all. No one was around.

As he pressed on the gas, the car did the opposite of what he wanted. It slowed and faltered as an ominous hiss rose from its depths. Harold just barely managed to edge it onto the road's shoulder before it gave up. He cursed and punched the wheel in fury before getting out and heading off down the road toward the cluster of buildings.

Now he saw what maybe he should have guessed. Buildings this nice wouldn't lie exposed. A chain-link fence with a fringe of barbed wire at the top ran all the way around the cluster. As if anyone could fail to get the message, signs warned passersby not to trespass.

Harold felt hot and weary almost to the point of falling down. He held out hope of getting the attention of someone, anyone. Some of the shutters on the long windows were open, but he could not see a soul.

Now he spotted a woman, about fifty yards further down the road, walking in the same direction, her back to him. Her shirt and dress were so light it had been easy to miss her in the glare.

"Hey! Hello!" he called out, and realized his voice was too feeble.

He began to run, thinking he might terrify her before he ever got to explain himself and make his plea for help, but her pace did not change. When at last he caught up, she heard his clumping feet and turned around, not with alarm, but, it seemed, suspicion at meeting a stranger out here.

Now that he was close enough to take in her features, he had to wonder what she was doing out here all alone. She was on the frailer side of sixty and had the weak, drained look of an outpatient in slow, wobbly recovery. Her steps were so halting she must be in great pain. He realized now that she was moving toward a gate, barely detectable in the vastness of linked metal. He found his voice.

"Hello, miss. Can you please help me? I need water and jumper cables for my car back there. I'll die if someone doesn't help."

The eyes in the wizened face gazed at him.

"What have you made, sonny?" she said.

"Excuse me?"

"What have you brought into the world?"

"Are you all right, miss?"

"I asked you—"

"Yes, I heard you both times, but your question's nonsensical. My car broke down and I'm about to drop dead of thirst. I can barely talk. Can you please help me?"

Those eyes took him in, seemingly with a mix of derision and pity.

"Come with me, sonny."

He followed the stranger another twenty yards and then she tapped out a code on a panel to the right of the gate. It slid open. They entered the compound. The stranger knew exactly where she was going, but Harold looked around in wonder as they moved amid the long freshly painted buildings. Even the dirt had an austere refined quality and the light seemed milder, more forgiving. Their feet clumped softly but even now it seemed there was no one they should worry about disturbing.

"Follow me, sonny," the woman said as she turned right, opened a door, and entered the long building running parallel to the fence and the road.

He thought there might be soldiers waiting in there to kill him. It was as logical a thought as any he had had lately. But here to his surprise was a long space full of what looked like the denizens of an overpriced shrink's waiting room. That was Harold's first impression.

The people here, who ranged in age from twenty to seventy, sat in chairs or reclined on couches or lay on their backs on cots with their limbs splayed. All the men had a lost, troubled look in their eyes. Their features looked drained, their skin pale. Why they lay about here during a busy time of the day for most people was a mystery. Not one appeared to take notice as the woman led him through the room and up a flight of stairs.

On the upper floor were more men and a few women, as lost and weak as the others. One stood at a window gazing out at the desert. Another sat on a plush red chair with his right elbow resting on a knee and his hand paused in the air as if he wanted to explain a thing but had just forgotten what it was.

Two young men in dark blazers stood talking at a point near the end of the room. Upon seeing the woman enter this space with Harold close behind her, they showed not concern or alarm but the annoyance of teachers dealing with a disobedient kid.

She gestured for Harold to stand by the stairs and then walked up to the two men. Harold could not hear the whispered exchange that followed. Then one of the two men took the woman into another chamber and the other walked up to Harold. He was in his early twenties and had the brisk, assured manner of a successful day trader.

"You know this is private property, sir. You can't just walk in here off the road."

The young man looked more concerned than Harold thought his innocent incursion should warrant.

"What do you want me to say? That I won't do it again? I never planned to stop here. The quicker you can help me, the sooner I'll be a memory."

It must have been his exhaustion that made his thoughts tumble out in such unmediated form, Harold guessed.

From the small room where the other young guy had taken the woman came the sounds of gentle chiding. None of the other people on this floor spoke. It was as if depression had robbed them of the will even to do that. Harold's interlocutor looked intensely at him.

"We'll get you back on the road. That woman who led you up here has a nervous condition and she doesn't need attention of any kind from strangers. So I'm just going to lead you back outside. No need to say goodbye to her."

"What is this, some kind of clinic?"

The man in the blazer thought for a moment, then nodded.

"Yes. For a highly specific type of patient."

The youth in the blazer led him outside, disappeared, and reappeared seconds later with a bottle of water. Harold took it with gratitude and stood in the glare, looking around at the buildings, imagining that they were all full of people like the ones he had seen. A man in overalls came around the corner of one of the other buildings carrying a metal case. Harold led him to the car. Not quite half an hour later, Harold was back on the road heading for the coast.

When he got near the city, he was in a different climate. The air was cooler and the sky overcast. A drizzle began. The rain came pretty hard by the time Harold navigated the dark downtown streets in search of his hotel. The edges of the dark buildings barely stood out from the deepening blue, yet it was impossible not to notice how many sleek towers had sprung up since Harold last visited the city. Here was a popular place for the educated, affluent, hip young set.

At last he found the hotel, one of the impressive new buildings. Minutes later he stood in a suite on the thirtieth floor, gazing out through the windows at a great city in the night. Out there, in the vast dark, lurked millions of minds of varying degrees of sentience. Lights were still on in the office towers. Behind those lights, he thought, were a few of the more sentient souls who knew all too well that they existed in time and who felt acutely the relationship of every second to the one before and the one after and were aware, as only the deeply, relentlessly ambitious can be, of what a losing proposition life is. Some people will deny with bravado the value of success as conventionally defined and will go on doing so, with variable eloquence, until it is painfully clear who has won it and who has not. At that point, the defensiveness of those who have failed is hideous. "I could publish a book tomorrow if I wanted to." "I'm swear I'm gonna make those bastards suffer." "Watch how you talk to me. Do you know who I am? *Do you know who I am?*" On and on.

The ambitious had chosen a path that would not avoid all the agony, far from it, but might at least afford moments of smirking satisfaction near the journey's end.

Harold sat down in one of the plush scarlet chairs facing the dark forms of the towers and the dwindling number of illuminated windows. He sipped whiskey, brooding, thinking that if he had taken one wrong turn in the desert he would not be here now. He would have liked to call people he planned to write profiles of for the newspaper, but the hour was late.

Sipping the liquor, feeling it inflame the spaces in him that had so desperately needed cool refreshment hours before, he had an odd sense that the strangers out there behind the lights in the towers could see him, even with all the lights in the suite off.

In the morning, he drank some coffee, took out his laptop, and began making calls. He prided himself on his ability to type as fast as people talk.

The first alum he reached was Josh Blanton. The life of a rising hedge funder wasn't so busy as to preclude talking to a journalist for a few minutes, but Josh clearly didn't relish Harold's aggressive manner.

"Come on, Harry. You know I can't talk about LPs or investment strategies," Josh said.

"What's your AUM?"

"Now, that's public and it's frankly something I'd have expected you to look up before you made this call. Being a professional journalist and all."

"Just tell me, please."

Josh gave a pretty awesome figure.

"Obviously the fund's having one of its best years ever," Harold said.

"I hope your profile offers more insight than that. But, yeah, we're beating expectations yet again and branching out into some new areas of R&D."

This led to an off-the-record discussion, conducted in the most general terms imaginable, at the end of which Harold felt as small as he ever had in his life. As if sensing how Harold felt, Josh adopted almost a friendly tone.

"This sounds like a decent gig you've got here, Harry. How many profiles are you going to file?"

"However many alumni speak with me."

Josh laughed.

"Well you're one for one, right? I'm sure your luck will hold. Will I see you at Heather Neill's opening at the Hurst Gallery? There should be a bunch of us there."

Heather Neill. Back in undergrad days when people said all kinds of things they did not mean or quickly forgot they had said, this classmate had blathered on about becoming an artist. You can't take what a kid says too seriously. Heather's ambitions might have lasted an even shorter time than her boyfriends. But now Heather had realized those dreams and an opening was to take place at one of chicest galleries in the city.

"I'll be there, Josh. Think she'll deign to speak to me?"

Now Josh's tone sounded cruel.

"Maybe if you pretend to be a sad loser who desperately needs this writing gig, she'll take pity on you and cooperate."

Josh laughed again. Harold wasn't sure why.

"Ah, well, we'll see."

"I'm going to jump on another call, Harry. See you soon."

They both hung up.

He could have lied and told Josh that hundreds of alumni were eager to talk to him. But to Harold's mind, at least, that would raise questions about the merits of what he planned to write. Harold's brother had lived in New York for a time, and, like many people, had vivid memories of 9/11 and the weeks that followed. Some readers of the *New York Times* had written letters faulting a series that ran in the paper, entitled "Portraits of the Fallen." It consisted of profiles of victims of the attacks, about one to two hundred words, and the readers slammed it for lacking depth, for failing to convey any real sense of the people these profiles were about. The reaction was predictable, Harold thought, imagining a wretched reporter in a cubicle with ten of these portraits to file by five o'clock. The reporter would try desperately to learn about and give readers a sense of a complex human being, with decades of life behind him or her, based on a couple of quick calls and a minute or two of online research. That wasn't Harold's *modus operandi*. He felt he could be an accomplished journalist someday because he sought and yearned to get at *why* people were where they were in life.

He made a few more calls without reaching anyone. Then he got through to Stuart Thorne, a successful playwright, at a venerable theater on the edge of downtown.

"Harry Ross. Oh yes, I remember you quite clearly. Some of my memories crept back over just the last few days," Thorne said.

"We haven't seen in each other since graduation. What are the odds that you'd be thinking of me?"

"Math is a false god, Harry. You know, I'm helping with the rehearsals for a new play of mine. You may have heard the canard that there are no original stories. Even the boldest and cleverest tale hearkens back to some biblical or Homeric proto-type. I'm not sure I really buy that, but perhaps, from a certain point of view, there are no original *characters*."

"I'm kind of lost, Stu."

"Which is better than being literally lost, I'm sure you'll agree. The point is simple. Everyone on stage is a dreamer, a visionary, an ingenue, a proto-fascist, or a fool, and hence a derivation of someone you've known at one or another time of life."

Harold took time to process all this.

At the end of their exchange, Thorne mentioned the opening at the gallery.

"Ah yes, I heard about it from another alum. I do plan to be there."

On the night of the opening, the weather again was markedly different from what Harold had gone through in the desert. The skies dimmed earlier than he expected this time of year and a drizzle flecked the windows of the cab taking him from the dank downtown to a trendier part of the city. The figures moving on the sidewalks seemed distant, hurried. But when the cab pulled up in front of the gallery, a glimpse of the bright lights and smiling guests behind the windows made him feel briefly like the star journalist he had dreamed of becoming.

He walked through the door and made his appearance, or rather, the art presented itself to him. It was as if all the high-end galleries in the city had pooled their resources. On the east wall, huge canvases transported him right back to the desert, so vivid were the cliffs standing in silent majesty over the arid valleys, so stunning the contrast of their jagged yellow and ochre forms, like the ruins of an apocalyptic Dreamtime, with the cobalt blue above. Scars ran through the desolate valley floors, twisting and curving and bisecting the barren riverbeds. Here were images of a locale so blistering and hostile they evoked terror.

On the same wall, closer to the back, were images of an environment no more inviting. The viewer felt transported to deep space. The gallery was a starship and through its windows the viewer gazed out at constellations whose lambent purple and silver-blue nebulae and regions of unfathomable black were the backdrop to the streaking of blinding comets. At this distance the amber and silver and red planets lacked the overt fierceness of the deserts in the other paintings, but in the midst of this panorama they did not look at all like sanctuaries. The viewer's mind conjured all manner of beasts and monsters.

A server passed by with glasses of white wine. Harold took a glass and whirled toward the opposite wall, where the images wrought by a modern-day Hopper might lull the viewer into a trance. Mysterious figures sat and lolled in dimly lit, lushly rendered bars, cafés, and clubs. Lovers strolled through a park in a business district where nature had made a tentative peace with the towers poking above the dense foliage. A blonde sat at a desk in an office, facing the viewer. Through the window behind her a crowded avenue, a dull purple mountain, and a cobalt sky beckoned the viewer to step out into the bright day, but the woman's look was somber.

Harold turned to the rear wall, which the owners had lined with a fantastic array of Pollock-like abstractions. The streaks and splotches on the vast canvases were manifestations of what would be, for lesser artists, mental and emotional states of ineffable strangeness. The deep blue, fiery scarlet, lush green, and abundant ochre were stunning in their individual darts and weaves and bursts. Together they conveyed an intertwine of lives so deeply lived in every moment that Harold began to wonder whether he himself had lived, as opposed to just existing. On yet another canvas was nothing but blue. It was the gateway to a gorgeous, forbidding universe.

As Harold sipped his wine, he realized that the art had so mesmerized him that he'd shut out the talk all around. Now a silver-haired man in a black blazer came up to Harold.

"Is this your first visit to the galley, sir?" the stranger asked in an urbane voice.

"The first of many, I should think."

"What are your impressions?"

"I've never seen anything like it."

How often Harold yearned to be clever but came out with banalities. As if sensing Harold's unease, the man grinned and repeated the trite phrase.

"You've never seen anything like it."

"Who's your favorite of the artists here?" Harold asked nervously.

"There's only one artist here, tonight, my good man. Please meet my daughter."

A woman with an alert, intelligent look, dressed in a black turtleneck and pants, had glided up to the spot directly to the man's left. She had coils of silky golden hair, pale unwrinkled skin, and lips the color of raspberry jam. She was stunning but Harold didn't feel taken with her for the tired old reasons. He wasn't some horny guy. He felt awe in the presence of the creator of this art.

"Hi there, Heather, I'm Harold Ross. I'm working on a feature, I can't say for whom, about where alumni of our school have ended up in life. I was hoping we could chat about how you become so accomplished."

He gave a wide grin, intended for both her and her father, but now the latter nodded and walked off toward a cluster of guests, leaving him alone with this visionary.

"The introduction wasn't necessary. I remember you, Harold."

"You do? I wasn't the most popular kid."

"I can't fathom why you think I mostly paid attention to the big men on campus. Imagine trying to talk about Duchamp with one of them."

"The range here, Heather. It's . . . this is going to sound banal, but it's astounding."

"You have as many or more universes within yourself, Harold."

"Do I? You sound like David Foster Wallace. Remember that passage in 'Good Old Neon' about how we're always trying to see each other's inner lives though these tiny keyholes?"

He quickly regretted his literary allusion, knowing he was showing off. But her response surprised him.

"I've read that passage hundreds of times, Harold. It's hypnotically eloquent and beautiful even if the ideas aren't new. He's talking about personae and how few of them we ever present to one another."

"Yes. Exactly. *Personae*. Funny, I was just talking to a theater guy about this. Imagine the odds. But math's a false god. I know I'm not particularly eloquent right now, but I feel, I don't know, I feel incredible, like I'm riding a comet's tail."

He wasn't playing the sycophant. This amazing woman had pulled him right through a window of the starship into a galaxy he'd never envisioned. To stand here and talk to her was exhilarating.

"You're not the first guest who's expressed himself in these kinds of terms."

That hurt a little.

"So, as I said, I'm working on this article, and I really hope you can find a bit of time."

Her eyes didn't flit or swerve.

"I'd be happy to offer some comments for your article, Harold."

"That's wonderful. Now, how late—"

"Oh, I don't mean tonight. I've got not one but two parties after this."

Harold was lucky to get one or two invitations per year.

"Believe me when I say I've got a piece of performance art planned that'll blow your mind, Harold," she added before giving him a card, smiling enticingly, and walking off.

He drank three more glasses of wine while taking in the art. Only now did he realize that he had not seen Josh or Stuart or any alumni other than Heather. They might be out there in the crowds or might have come and gone while the art had him in a daze.

Now he noticed a girl in bright red overalls standing to his right. Once again he yearned to be clever, but he came out with, "There's nothing even remotely like this work in the whole city, is there?"

She didn't turn her head and for a moment he thought maybe she hadn't heard this inanity. Then she replied.

"I guess you don't know too much about this artist."

He groped in vain for a savvy answer.

"Well, I am a classmate, you know."

"Then I wonder how much you've kept up with her. I happen to know that her work is also at the Jameson Gallery and the Müller Gallery, and she has more openings later this year."

He looked around the gallery, trying in vain to spot the brilliant, astonishing artist. She was in the midst of a crowd somewhere. Surely, he thought, the feature he planned to write wasn't so trivial, so inconsequential for her reputation, that she should put carousing and partying first.

With the darkest anger rising inside him, he walked through the crowds toward the front entrance. Then he spotted that most stereotypical piece of an artist's attire, the black turtleneck, under coils of golden hair. Heather stood on the edge of a cluster of guests, her back to him. At this moment he felt a bit like the creep who'd shot John Lennon, a lonely outsider with a fast and easy route to fame.

"Heather!" he called out.

She didn't reply. He cried her name again. Either she didn't hear or, having given him enough of her time, chose to ignore him.

"HEATHER!"

Still she didn't turn. He grabbed her right shoulder, harder than he meant to, or at least with more force than he wished to give the appearance of using, and now she turned around with a look of annoyance.

"Ah, Heather. Sorry. Look, it's just that I'm on a deadline and I was kind of hoping we could talk tonight."

She didn't say anything, but shook her head decisively. He still stood there, expecting at least a more legitimate reason for her refusal, but she just looked at him. Many others in the gallery were also gazing at the rude interloper.

Without another word, he walked out of the gallery and headed to a bar, where he sat drinking for three hours. All the while he thought of the desert.

In the morning, he sat in the hotel room looking out at the city, sipping pungent black coffee, and fingering her card, whose edges felt really sharp.

He dialed her number on his cell, put it to his ear, and listened. The call went through to voice mail.

"Hi, Heather, it's Harold Ross here. Sorry if I was a bit rude last night. I'm eager to learn more about your creative process and the challenges you may have encountered. Please give me a call. Have a beautiful day."

Even as the words came out, he winced at the message's banality. Then he sat there, looking out at the towers where the people who mattered were hard at work, but his phone did not ring. In his growing anxiety over a call that never came, he thought back to the sands, the far hills, the bright red buttes, the barren road, the cluster of buildings, the strange unsmiling woman, and all those lethargic people. They looked as if they had been working so hard, in some secret parts of the compound, that they were borderline catatonic. Harold thought he had everything figured out here. How remarkable that he should pass through that place and then meet an artist of such astonishing range, but then probability was a false god. He did not know what to make of anything anymore. He raided the minibar for whiskey before noon.

The next call was to a journalist, a real one, who'd graduated two years ahead of Harold. The phone rang twice before he got an answer.

"Bryce Nelson."

"Bryce! It's Harold Ross. How are you?"

As soon as the pleasantries were out of the way, he got right to his theory.

"So you know that artist, Heather Neill? The one with the fantastically rich dad. There's this place a couple hundred miles out from here where I suspect he takes care of artists who're in financial straits, and encourages them to make as much art as they can, but in return they have to give up certain rights."

"Harry. I've heard of ghostwriting but this is preposterous. It's insane."

"That doesn't mean it's not true. You could do something with this. I write for the *Bulletin*, which is nothing. You write for the *Herald*."

Harold gave the best directions from memory that he could.

"I'll check it out."

"Thanks, buddy."

The next day was mild in the way that lulls people into complacency about the passage of time. No manner how many corners he turned in the downtown grid, the sun never met him full on as it did in his visions of the desert. Realizing he had not eaten in a while, he looked in vain for a deli. He had a terrible feeling about the course of his life. He nearly challenged a few strangers for looking at him a second too long.

As he turned a corner four blocks from the hotel, moving east then north, he caught a glimpse of bouncing golden coils as a stranger turned west onto the parallel street at the end of the block.

"Heather. Heather!" he cried, running north, giving a light push to one of a trio of old men shuffling up the street.

The three men gasped and cursed as he ran past them. Within seconds he was at the intersection where he was sure he'd seen her. Thirty feet down the street to the west, a man in a dark suit helped the blonde into the rear of a limo.

"Heather!" he cried, running fast.

The woman got into the limo and the man closed the door and went around to the front passenger seat and climbed inside. He noted that Heather's window, if indeed it was Heather, was halfway down. He screamed.

"Heather! You spoiled bitch! You phony! You've got the world thinking you're a great artist but I know your dirty fucking secret!"

The limo pulled away from the curb. He screamed even lounder.

"Come back here or you'll be sorry! Yes, that's a threat!"

As night fell he was too drunk to do much besides sit in his hotel room looking out at the blinking lights and the illuminated windows. Then his cell phone rang.

"Hey, Harry. Bryce Nelson here."

"Who? Oh, Bryce! What've you got, man? Gonna do a feature on that compound?"

"That's what I wanted to talk to you about, mate. It's not where you said it would be."

"What on earth do you mean?"

"Exactly what I said."

"You followed my directions precisely?"

"No, I didn't go out there myself on such short notice, Harry. We've got stringers in the area. I asked them to go and take a look, and they found desert."

"Are you banging Heather Neill, Bryce?"

"*What?*"

"You're asking me to believe that she's got such range and versatility and talent that she made all the art I saw last night, and much more besides. That's literally impossible."

"I don't think you know much about art and artists. Besides, you were hot and tired and thirsty and delusional. You probably did imagine all or part of the experience in the desert."

"I'd know if I'd imagined something. You're calling me a liar."

"If you like. But the larger point, Harry—"

The pause was ominous.

"Yes, Bryce?"

"I'm not going to say it."

"Now you have to."

"Look, Harry, it's one thing to resent the successful, but this is the weirdest case of cognitive dissonance I've ever seen."

"How dare you—"

"I'm hanging up now. Good luck with your feature."

"Bryce, wait. I'm sorry. Who are these stringers you sent? Tell me whom they work for. Can I talk to them?"

"I said I'm hanging up."

"Bryce, I'm so deeply sorry for yelling at you. I swear on my grandma's grave that place is there. Far west of Coburn and south of the interstate. I'll show you myself. No one's ever meant to get past the gate. If you can get inside, as I happened to do by sheer luck, you'll find the source of Heather's genius. This could be the investigative piece of the century."

A long pause followed. Finally Bryce spoke.

"All right, then. Those stringers don't work for me and I honestly don't know how seriously they took this thing. Text me the directions and I'll check it out myself. Even if I don't finagle my way inside, I can get lots of people asking questions."

"Thanks, man."

Bryce had one more question.

"Tell me, Harry. Was it ever your dream to be an artist?"

"Yeah, either that or a novelist. A real creator. A visionary. Look at me now."

"Well, I hope that mini fridge isn't empty. Good night."

The contents of the mini fridge couldn't sustain him over the next twelve hours so he made forays to a bottle shop and brought vast quantities of booze to the room.

On the street the next day, he began looking around aggressively for galleries to check out. Then he realized that there were none downtown, that his mind had grown hazy. Strangers hurried by, pushing past him, not making eye contact. It was almost as if they were channeling the indifference and rudeness he had shown so often. He swore at them.

There were no galleries down here but he pretty distinctly remembered a bottle shop. He thought he even recalled how to get there. As soon as he set off, he spotted those familiar bouncing golden coils at a point down the street. He began to run and pitched forward hard onto his belly. He got up, cursing and screaming at the distant figure.

"Heather! I'm Harold Ross, your classmate! Come back here, witch! *The world's going to know you're a fraud!*"

People on the street gasped and pointed and a few of them reached for their phones. He ran off, taking a roundabout route back to the hotel.

At dusk he sat in the chair, sipping whiskey, thinking of a line he'd once read in *Modern Times* by the popular historian

Paul Johnson. "Facts have a way of asserting themselves." The book was largely about the failure of utopian schemes. His dream of a glamorous journalistic career had been a kind of fantasy, an ill thought-out one, but now Bryce Nelson had agreed to help him and soon they'd both be famous.

To Harold the lights of the towers out there were emblems of order, safety. Outside was a world with rules you didn't have to like or respect, you just had to adopt a mode of being that didn't contravene those rules too blatantly. No one out there suspected Heather Neill of being a fraud, but certain facts would assert themselves, in the most public and unerasable manner, soon enough.

A knock came. He picked himself up clumsily, spilling whiskey on his pants, shuffled to the door, and opened it. In the hall stood a pair of men in sports jackets. They held up badges. Their names were Blake and Carpenter. They invited themselves in. Blake did most of the talking.

"We've gotten a number of reports of disorderly conduct and menacing by a man who gave his name as Harold Ross. We canvassed hotels in the area and had reason to believe you are staying here."

"I'd say the empirical evidence is on your side."

"People in the other rooms have complained about a lot of yelling in here."

"The TV was up too loud. Sorry."

"Did a character on TV do that?" Blake asked, pointing to shards of glass lying in a puddle in a corner.

"An accident."

"What are you doing in town?"

"I'm collaborating with Bryce Nelson, a journalist for the *Herald*, on a major investigative story. I can give you his number."

Blake and Carpenter exchanged looks. Harold sighed.

"Let me guess. Something's happened to Bryce."

The lawmen nodded.

"Once again, banality thwarts our knowing the sublime."

"It was a fire," Blake said.

"Of course."

"You're going to have to check out now, sir."

The lawmen left and Harold began to gather his things.

Two days later, no hotel would admit the haggard man on the street. The hostels were full. He hobbled around on the busy streets, cursing at strangers, unable even to remember where he had left his car. They must have towed it by now.

On the morning of the third day of his displacement, he spotted those bobbing golden coils again and ran after them. Heather was in the company of what looked like a troupe of art students, six girls and two boys with a bright happy demeanor, and he guessed they were on the way to a café where they would talk at length about her genius. But he got to her first.

"Heather! Your time's up! Certain of us know your little secret!" he cried.

The foaming beast that leapt on her was so ferocious that members of the troupe screamed in terror, bringing half a dozen strangers quickly to her aid.

"*No! Let me have her!*" Harold screamed.

They pulled him off the artist and punched and kicked him and one man thrashed him so hard with a belt buckle that his forehead needed five stitches.

Not having suffered any serious injuries, Heather didn't wish to seek the toughest penalties available. She had something else in mind. Heather's lawyers worked out a slightly unusual plea bargain with the defense counsel.

Pedestrians on the streets of the great city got to take in the sight of a feral, balding, deluded man prancing about in his underpants inside a steel cage mounted on four columns between a pair of towers in the center of downtown. Nothing he did was private. His ravings conveyed over and over the abjectness of his envy for those who truly deserved their status in the world.

The caption for this bold work of performance art gave the busy men, women, and kids hurrying by a chuckle.

"Most Likely to Succeed."

Greed

"It's not the best you could get for the money," said Claire. No one would call her a rude and tactless woman, but she had her moments of candor.

Claire was not looking at Jeff's suite any more. She stood at the window and gazed out over the skyline where random lights flashed far above the streams of traffic and the odd siren. It was a calm night that helped to crystallize and refine whatever thoughts might be forming. The winds whispered as they had done for ages, as they had done before all of this. Jeff had a lot on his mind tonight. He fumbled for something to say to the guest peering out into the night with a glass of Scotch in her fingers, on one of which a ruby with a gold frame glittered like an adornment in a Renaissance painting of Artemis. Her brown hair reached almost to her shoulders, its richness offset by the glimmer of an earring that must have set her, or some obsequious man, back a few thousand dollars. She could attract a mate from a mile off. *A professional woman.* So much of one thing, and so much of something else entirely.

Jeff poured himself another glass of Scotch before walking over to her side at the window. A siren flashed below as a highway patrolman's orders echoed through the night. Without success, Jeff tried to convince himself that it had not been awkward to invite his colleague up here for drinks. Well, okay, he did feel screwy, but all the real conversations among his colleagues took place in the context of lunch or drinks. Jeff had met Claire at a bar where forty employees had gathered, after Jeff's third day on the job, to say farewell to the president of media relations. Now, leaning against the windowsill and sipping his liquor, Jeff groped for a way to jump-start the dialogue.

Without preamble, Claire asked, "Do you know anything about astrology?"

Jeff mumbled, bringing an impish smile to her face.

"Just a random question," she went on, "you don't need to answer it off the cuff. I get so caught up in cash flows and stock gyrations all over the world, and then it strikes me that there's some explanation for things that I've just never deigned to consider."

"I'm a Libra."

"Never mind, it's a loopy question," was how Claire came to his rescue.

"Do you like your colleagues, Claire?"

"Oh, they're all right. If you work in the research division, I guess you should expect to meet some socially challenged types."

Claire, if you haven't noticed, I'm the one who's challenged here.

"There's a guy, Steve Pomper, who's a pencil-whipper," she added, "but otherwise you can rest on your geek credentials among these folks."

Jeff envisioned a department full of geeks hard at work on their spreadsheets and reports. *Claire, you're no geek!*

"Tell me more about what they hired you to do," she prodded. "You seem to straddle the worlds of management and financial services, which I find awfully impressive for someone this side of forty."

Only by three months, but we'll let it go. Jeff smiled nervously in the gaze of her clear blue eyes.

"Is this like a trial, where you'll screw your case by discussing it?" she asked.

"No, but look, they hired me two weeks ago. *I'm* not up on the whole picture yet. You understand."

"Of course I do, hotshot." Claire flashed her rows of perfect ivory at her host.

"We have a vision for this company, just don't ask me to explain it right now. Welcome aboard, Jeff."

The smile that Ed Masters flashed was a keenly honed reflex. Ed walked with Jeff through the fifth floor of Echelon's offices in the heart of downtown. They turned a corner and continued toward the quarters of the company's chief operating officer, Paul Jarratt. In the space outside this suite, Paul's receptionist managed to look cheesy and urbane. After a few minutes, she ushered them into the office where one of the world's most powerful men sat behind a desk on which a few papers lay beside a briefcase and a cell phone that the executive might have just used to talk to a divorce lawyer, or an embalmer.

"Gentlemen," said Paul, getting up.

Ed flashed that smile again.

"Paul, I don't think you've had a chance to meet Jeff Grimes yet. He's our new director of financial services for North America and the Pacific. Jeff, I think you know who Paul is," he finished with another chuckle.

"How was orientation?" asked Paul.

"I must have met three hundred people in the last two weeks," replied Jeff, "and I'm not sure all of them were thrilled about meeting me." He grinned. Get it, guys? *Levity.*

"To be honest, Jeff, I wish things were in much better shape," said Paul. "I have only the vaguest idea of where all the money's going and who owes what to whom and what we can or should do to restructure the whole damn mess. We're depending on you to do a man's job. Welcome aboard."

"Well, thank you."

"I suppose you want a corner office?"

"Er. . . ."

"Don't worry, you've got one. Nice view of the skyline, or so they tell me. I've been so busy that I haven't made it down to that part of the hall."

"Once I'm settled in, I'll have to invite you down there to soak your gills," Jeff put in, and wished he hadn't. Was that a wince on Ed's face? Maybe the COO's compulsive drinking was a *verboten* topic. But Paul plowed right ahead.

"Operations in Houston, Phoenix, Portland, operations in Fiji, the Solomons, and a dozen other places I couldn't point out on a map. That's a hell of a purview for one man, Jeff. You come with outstanding recommendations from three Fortune 500 employers. But now comes the test. I'm sure you care about your family, your professional reputation, and your future."

Jeff blinked. No one had spoken to him this way before. No one. Ever.

Then Paul grinned. "You're the man on the spot, Jeff. Are you guys doing anything for lunch?"

"We're neighbors. We should have lunch one of these days. There's a new Vietnamese place up the street," said Mark Healy, leaning his head into Jeff's office on a dreary Wednesday morning.

"I'd love that." In reality, the idea of going anywhere with this officious busybody made Jeff want to retch. After reporting to Paul Jarratt in a few minutes, it would be time to take the elevator to the ninth floor and step into the chamber to which Ed Masters had referred obliquely the other day.

Throughout the meeting, Paul was in a mild state, his mind not really on the figures that Jeff earnestly rattled off to him. When the time came, the way to the chamber did not suggest horrors worthy of Poe or the young Ian McEwan. Amid the familiar institutional gray, Jeff passed two smiling secretaries who walked in and out of offices whose occupants Jeff did not see, but there was hardly anyone on this floor, it seemed. Then Jeff came to the door of the chamber, entered his PIN on a console, and stepped inside. As the lights dimmed, Jeff sat down in a gray chair with scarlet armrests and thought that all that was missing now was popcorn. Then, on the screen before him, there appeared a shot of a hotel that Jeff placed, from the dust and the light, in a town in the Southwest. Prescott, Arizona, maybe. Lightly clad men and women strode through a pavilion, outside a hotel with tiny balconies on its façade, dingy rectangles demarcated by black rails. It looked like a hot day, but not unpleasantly so. The camera followed couples walking arm in arm through the dustbowl of the courtyard, many of them in their twenties, newlyweds maybe. Then a bit of text flashing on the screen revealed that Jeff had not been too wide of the mark, for he was looking at the Regal Embassy Hotel in Scottsdale, Arizona. The camera cut to a room where one of the couples sat at a conference table across from a manager in a dark blue double-breasted suit. It was then that Jeff realized he had to flick a switch to "Audio On" to hear the couple, who had not had the time of their lives. Apart from the pricey reheated food, the husband had strode past another couple having intercourse in a hallway near the rec room. Now the wife was complaining about a man who had groped her from behind as she passed through the lounge on her way from the indoor pool back to their suite. The swine in this place thought that any women who entered their vision with her navel exposed invited this sort of attention. She was sick with anger. While scrambling to reply point by point, the manager stressed that any fellow who did not act like a gentleman would find himself barred from the hotel. He asked why the wife had not acted sooner, but nothing he said could change the couple's impression of the Regal Embassy.

By now, six hotels in six cities had shut their doors, while the chain's management had let 3,000 workers go without notice. Jeff had already come to a decision about Echelon's investments in the franchise. He watched two more clips, dealing with a supplier of lawnmower parts and a seller of package tours, respectively, before shifting to footage of the operations of Echelon Financial Services in the Central and South Pacific. This film's cast included a certain Raymond Carr, the regional director of development, wearing dark shades, looking like MacArthur on the general's return to the Philippines in 1944, and just as certain of victory.

If you don't know how to act, you shouldn't be here, Jeff mused as he poured himself a glass of merlot and tried to strike a casual pose in front of the throng of guests waiting to get a drink. *But you'll never get the finesse without venturing to a few functions like this one.* Jeff's hand trembled, spilling a bit of the wine on his pristine cuff, before he passed the bottle to a man in a blue serge suit and drifted around the room at the Mercury Club. Then Jeff spotted Claire and approached her, grinned nervously. With effortless poise, Claire glanced around the room before speaking.

"Thank you so much for the drinks the other night. I just wished you'd talked a bit more about yourself."

Jeff stammered until she broke him off with the lightest of laughs.

"I'm hoping you can save me from having to talk to Steve Pomper," she said with a sideways look at the mid-level executive who was chatting up two other women from Claire's division.

"You really don't care for ol' Steve."

"Oh, sure I like Steve. He's got the administrative skills of Adolf Eichmann and the personal demeanor of Rush Limbaugh."

Jeff glanced over at the executive for two seconds before realizing that Steve was returning the gaze, and then he looked away in embarrassment.

"You know what Ed Masters told me?" asked Claire with another gesture.

"'I have a vision for this company, just don't ask me to explain it right now.'"

"How astute, Jeff." Even as she sipped what must have been her sixth glass of claret, Jeff sensed that Claire was not a mean drunk, unlike some of the women he'd had the ill luck to date, just a lass who got tipsy and spun her everyday world into a carousel of buffoons.

"Have you been following cash flows to any interesting places?"

"Oh, don't repeat this to the Financial Action Task Force," she replied, "but I do know where a lot of hard currency ends up. It gets wired to offshore banks that don't have brick-and-mortar branches but are registered in tiny countries you've never heard of."

"Try me," Jeff challenged her, but then a hand fell on his shoulder.

"Jeff Grimes, I'm pleased to meet you," came a voice from behind. Jeff turned.

"How are you, Jeff? Ray Carr."

Jeff faced the regional director, who was older but was technically his subordinate.

"Mr. Carr—er, Ray. I've heard so much about you lately."

"You know something, Jeff? No one even mentioned you to me until after you came aboard."

When Claire drifted away, it did not register on Ray, who charged ahead.

"Jeff, we can wield so much power in the Central and South Pacific. We can flex our muscle in front of those dinky tribes, and they'll hand over *any* resource."

Regretting Claire's departure, Jeff grinned nervously.

"Yeah, just dangle some dollars and those native babes spread their legs," Carr said. His mouth was like the opening of a mine with the odor of decomposing miners wafting up to the surface.

"Is that the wisdom you picked up on your travels out there?" Jeff asked.

"Yeah. Though it's hard to think about geopolitical lessons when you've got a fat native girl sitting on your face," Carr snorted. "Yeah, you can have a whole nation eating out of your hand, taking care of *all* your needs, if you want to."

"And that's a good thing, even if they are pretty broke?"

"We can extend our sovereignty by giving them an extension or two on their loan. They'll grovel and beg, it's a lot of fun to watch."

"But they still won't make good."

"Oh, one of them did pretty good by me," said Ray Carr with a wink.

Jeff stammered again. *Okay, consult the etiquette manual. How do you call someone an evil stupid gluttonous fuck in a diplomatic way?*

"You look like you need another, Jeff."

"That was my fourth."

"Then you definitely need another. Come on, guy!"

Jeff sat in his office listening to the patter of rain on the air con-ditioner. For the past hour, he had gone over all the plans for his upcoming trip, the first leg of which was a flight to a tiny Pacific island, and the second, a flight to Brisbane and thence to Melbourne. He reached into a drawer in his desk, and fingered a small box containing something he would give Claire if he ever convinced himself that it would not be careless to invite her to dinner some time. When Jeff answered the knock on his door, he found himself facing Mark Healy across his desk.

"Sure, Mark, I'd love to go to the Saigon Garden this evening."

A few hours later, the two men sat at a table to which a smiling waiter with slick dark hair came promptly. Mark broke the silence that followed their orders.

"I heard you had a chat with Ray Carr at the party the other night," he said.

"Yes, as a matter of fact, I did."

"He just might have thought you were going to become fast friends with him."

"So?" Jeff tried not to sound impatient.

"Jeff, that guy . . . he, ah, gets a little drink in him, and it loosens his tongue a bit too much."

"I think his tongue was already pretty active."

"He thought you'd both be reporting to Paul, not that you'd have executive authority over all financial services here and in the Pacific."

"Oh, he said *all kinds* of things."

"Even so," replied Mark, sticking his fork into another dumpling, "Ed Masters knows Ray, and I know him, and we both think he's done a man's job at Echelon. You know what Adam Smith said, about how countries can get seriously fucked up through public malfeasance, but not private. Some of us feel that caution is the best approach to any task."

Jeff considered this *non sequitur* before he spoke again.

"In an incestuous corporate culture, people get very careless. I'm always asking myself if I've been careless. Maybe I have recently. I'm glad to be getting away from all this for a while."

"Well, bring something back for me, will you?"

"Of course, Mark. You'll, uh, be in my thoughts."

At first, the image visible through the window of Jeff's plane was confusing, a misshapen mass like a spot where a god had pressed his cigar against the earth to put it out. Then Jeff realized that he was looking at an island ringed by a fringe of fine sand broken by a few palms and stunted trunks and lapped gently by the waves. The uneven progress of the foam-topped blue toward the shore, as well as the breaks in the waves where a red substance cropped up, then vanished, suggested that coral made access by sea impossible. Jeff was gazing at Nauru, the world's tiniest country, and the only one with no capital. At present, the nation was not only dirt-poor, but it was also at the top of the Financial Action Task Force's list of offenders not in compliance with laws against banks engaged in shady activities—in short, Nauru was a haven for money launderers. Part of the reason for the island's desperation for quick cash was a debt to the corporation to which its newest visitor belonged. Echelon's involvement with Nauru went back three years. Raymond Carr, the regional director of development within what was now Jeff's division, had spent a week on the island, "getting in with" the natives, as he liked to put it.

On the beach next to the airport, a throng of natives greeted Jeff with smiles and songs hearkening back to another epoch. Like the men, the women were shirtless and wore cloths at their loins, while a stray ribbon or bead hung from their straight black hair. Facing the visitor in the foreground was Rene Harris, the president, though probably not for more than a few months. Harris's look was inscrutable. Many doubted that anyone could solve the ills plaguing the republic since the 1970s. Exchanging words with the visitor, Harris gestured at the interior, where the phosphate mines were. Then the two started off toward a jeep resting on a stretch of tarmac that had ringed the island, just inside the circle of sand, ever since Japan's occupation in 1942. The jeep carried the two toward the government's buildings, such as they were, in the district of Yaren. As the jeep set off, Jeff thought he caught a coy look on the face of one of the young women who had dangled their breasts before him. She was in much better shape than most of the Nauruans, whose dependence on processed imports, a.k.a. junk food, had turned them into fat diabetics.

As soon as they sat across from each other in the squat municipal building, the talk turned to Ray Carr's visit three years before. The officer of the world's biggest corporation, in terms of market value, had promised much to this island. The Nauruan president at that time had stressed that he could assure the mining and export of phosphate, on which farmers in Australia, New Zealand, and Europe depended. He knew how much farming everywhere would suffer from the use of a lower-grade phosphate in fertilizers. He needed help expanding Nauru's presence overseas. Carr had stressed that the Nauruans could and should charge ahead with plans abroad. There are only a few things that we need in return, Carr had said. Carr had most definitely wanted the exports to go on. He said in essence: *It's a win-win situation. If you want to buy and develop real estate in Sydney and Melbourne, if you seek investments in Houston, Phoenix, and Honolulu, our financial services division is here to help you realize your dreams.*

"Did he know that the phosphate would be running out in a few years?" Jeff asked.

"Yes. The loan came with a high rate of interest, and our ability to pay it off was totally contingent on the success of our overseas operations."

"Do you really think that Ray Carr grasped the reality of the situation?"

"Why don't we take a stroll together?" Harris proposed.

With three aides in tow, Jeff and the head of state ambled over to Topside and started walking around the outskirts of the mines. Jagged rocks thrust from the denuded interior toward the sky, while the branches of the lonely trees sagged in the ferocious heat. Harris pointed out the mouths of the mines.

"They've been in this nearly depleted state for years," he remarked, "though I can still remember when all this was bush, and my friends and I used to run and hide and kiss girls here."

"You guys didn't go to the drive-in?"

"Mr. Grimes, we were so excited about what the loan might do for us. Then the phosphate ran lower and lower, and we got screwed out of a huge part of the royalties trust. The adviser wasn't scrupulous, he embezzled sixty million dollars, and we're still in courts trying to get part of it back. Even if we do, the legal costs will make it a Pyrrhic victory indeed. The investments in the U.S. didn't work out. We're a fishing and gathering people, we hardly have anyone with a college degree—believe me, Nauruans who are able to study abroad don't resettle here—and we've got no one with any economic sense. It was folly for anyone to think that we could handle big complex investments on our own. Nor was there anyone we could put our trust in."

"So you launched a musical, based on the life of Da Vinci, that closed in London after five weeks."

"We thought it might be one of those moments where a lot of talent comes together spontaneously, and everyone loves it."

"But people walked out before the intermission."

Rene Harris nodded sadly.

The tour went on until the orange dome in the west cast its tint over the tangles of shrub and rock and the rising and falling crests of blue beyond. When the troupe started filing back to the jeep that would take Jeff to one of Nauru's two hotels, he wondered about the woman he had glimpsed on the beach, where she was and to what odd places her mind wandered, and whether she had the privilege of sitting on Ray Carr's ugly potted face. The light waned slowly as the jeep sped away.

The tumult of Flinders Street Station faded from Jeff's mind as he strolled along the bank of the Yarra River on a sweltering day. Businessmen walked by in the heat, a bit loose after sitting at sun-drenched tables in the park and knocking back a few glasses of wine from the red-soil area near Coonewarra in the neighboring province of South Australia. Women pushed strollers through the clear open space in the foreground of the Central Business District. On the grass starting thirty yards from the river, some of the women lying face-down had untied their bikini tops. Jeff sweated heavily and tried not to stare. When walking through Melbourne, it was as if you saw around you a projection of the dream animating the rogues who flocked to the area in the 1850s upon the discovery that gold lay in the depths of the baked soil. Extrapolate from their letters and entries in their diaries, and you could picture something like this megalopolis around you: a place where mostly naked women lolled and smoked while men fortified by wine walked to their offices to negotiate sales and close deals, thinking of the warm soft body with which they would merge after all lights in the office were out. With sweat dampening the light blue dress shirt under his black sports jacket, Jeff turned onto a path that would carry him toward the heart of the CBD, the echoes of frolicking children fading from his ears. To Jeff's mind, the grid of gray and blue steel was like a helmet clamped down over the soft skull of the earth.

Not for the first time that day, Jeff thought of the conference call with Ed Masters and Mark Healy initiated from his hotel the day before.

"Those who abuse their power must pay the price. In the short term, you're going to see receivers appointed to sell the properties developed by Nauru in Melbourne. Then we take further action to recover the debts. The time has come, fellows. Then you'll see a bigger shakeup. I'm going to fold Carr's subdivision and everybody in it. It may have to wait until I'm back, but he might as well start cleaning out that royal suite of his on the seventh floor."

"I don't think you've retained anything I said about caution," wailed Mark.

"You're charging straight into a minefield," Ed put in. "Ray did have a coherent vision, even if he failed to articulate it to you."

"Ray made himself extremely clear to me, Ed."

Jeff walked through the afternoon, past the outskirts of Chinatown, then to the area where the headquarters of Boreal Ltd. sat in a stately gray tower whose elevator rose through a futuristic shaft visible from the street in front. Minutes later, Jeff sat at the desk of Jake Finney, the president of financial planning. Finney was a jovial chap with straight golden hair and the sort of complexion formed by trips to the Outback. He told Jeff of places where the sun mocks the idea of refuge, where the crags and the dust do not care if you are part of a transnational elite. Jake flashed his artificially whitened teeth and leaned forward across his desk.

"Synergy is the *mot du jour*, mate. We're looking to expand our operations, and we need to establish our trustworthiness, to provide you with a solid basis for going forward with a loan. Consider that we're planning to integrate the distribution system for our line of NanoTech G7s and G8s with that of Stuart Blythe's company, the software distributor SpinTech International, over the next two to three quarters. Then SpinTech will be coming out with a computer, pretty much a variant of the G8, with many compatible parts and applications. We believe that synergy among their and our technical and marketing divisions will issue in the highest levels of integrity and recognition, not to say popularity, in this half of the globe," the jovial man finished.

"Allow me to ask if you've read your Keynes," Jeff said.

"Come again, mate?" Jake's brow furrowed.

"I'm sorry, I know you're a community college grad. But let me hazard a prediction. As a result of this synergy, you're likely to corner the market for a while, but then familiarity will breed a swarm of contempt," Jeff continued. "If you'd ever bothered to peruse *The General Theory of Employment, Interest, and Money*—Chapter 22, 'Notes On the Trade Cycle'—you would have a sense of the cycles of growth and synergy that crowd out smaller companies and fuel their dynamism, their innovations that will punch a hole right in your bloated belly."

"That's all a lot of theory, mate—"

"I'm afraid it's far more than that. You should have paid attention to the antitrust cases against Microsoft, which was brazen enough to make Internet access and its own systems dependent on each other. I am not quite old enough to vouch for this, but I heard older execs say that the whole thing is strongly reminiscent of what started happening to IBM in the early 1980s. Not exactly what the world needs more of. Mate."

Jeff sat in a café sipping a rich red wine grown in Coonewarra and sold by Lindeman's to exclusive markets. He liked the way that this wine settled in his system, as his mind roved over the terrain beyond the scarlet-painted partitions and walls of the café. In the slum alleys, in the streets where trucks belched their smoky offal over the streets dark with litter and soot, stood bars and halls where men played pool and chatted about Australian rules football. Beyond the city was the ocean, and on the other side the infinity of desert and rock. Here, in the café, was the rarified air of a place that you might overlook even if you lived near the business district for years. It was a quiet dive where smoke drifted over the booths in which a few businessmen had retired after a grueling day.

The face that appeared before Jeff now was from a time before all of this, or so ran Jeff's confused thoughts as the stranger sat down at his table all of a sudden. On the broad, pitted visage of this dark-skinned fellow was a grin unlike any Jeff had seen in the offices where he had worked. *We have both wandered in the world,* said this grin, *and I come before you now in the light of a shared knowledge.* Yet Jeff had never met someone like this, and was at a loss to name the stranger's race. He could have been an aborigine, but his eyes seemed a tad too narrow, and the stranger could almost have passed for a Malay. The light was dim enough to discourage a guess. Despite the congeniality, as Jeff saw it at first, of the stranger's manner, it was ten seconds before anyone broke the silence.

"You look like you need some *ganja,* mate," the stranger said.

Jeff blinked. "Come again?"

"No, it's a joke. I can tell you've been hard at work, lookin' at spreadsheets and such. You need to unwind some more."

"Did you sit down here for a reason?" Jeff heard himself ask. He was not at all ready for a confrontational mode, and found his own change of tone deeply unpleasant.

"Hey man, loosen up," said the stranger. "Let me get you another drink."

The stranger got up, walked over to the bar in the other part of the café, and returned with a glass which he set down on the table.

"I've seen you in the neighborhood a couple of times," he continued. "You may be angry about somethin', or you thinkin' about a lady with rich hair and a ruby ring in a gold frame. She won't be too impressed by anythin' you spring for, or so you've thought."

A silence.

"Never mind, mate, I'm sorry I bothered you."

Jeff had no idea what to say. Part of him wanted to belt the stranger in the jaw, another part of him felt like leaving, and yet another part of him was transfixed.

"But there's somethin' you could give the lady that I reckon she ain't never seen," continued the stranger with a playful glimmer in his eye. Then he was gone.

Jeff dropped money onto the table and followed the stranger out of the café and up the street in the direction of the Central Business District. He was about to call out, but he could not bring himself to do it, he could only pick up his pace in the expectation that the other man would hear him and turn at any second. But this did not happen even after they crossed Portsmouth Street and continued toward downtown. Without varying his pace, the stranger moved along. Then, in the corner of Jeff's left eye, a figure with a mass of curly black hair stepped from an alley and a bar hit Jeff in the back of the head. He fell face down on the pavement and felt his breath leave him. Another blow landed on his right buttock, and a third, just inches from his spine. But Jeff was quick in his anger. He rose and lurched forward so fast that the next blow met the pavement. In a rage that would have rattled a pro wrestler, he grabbed the attacker's throat and squeezed it as hard as he could, using his left hand to pummel the attacker in one place, then another. He landed a hard blow on the attacker's jaw, then strained forward and tried to bite the man, who started to howl and shriek before shoving Jeff away and taking off up the alley toward a row of tenements. Jeff gave chase, following the man into one of them before he could slam the door. Then Jeff was chasing the dark-skinned man up a flight of rickety stairs, at the top of which the nemesis turned and hurled a chair at Jeff, who lay flat on the stairs as it sailed over him. Then Jeff, growling like a wounded animal, was at the top grappling with the man again, hitting him about the chest and face, clawing at his nose and eyes, then delivering a kick that sent him through a door into the black space beyond. The man got up and slammed the door. Jeff kicked it once, twice, a third time, at which point the door sailed off its hinges and landed with awful force on a child standing on the other side.

On Jeff's fifth day in the penitentiary, he received a phone call from Echelon's corporate headquarters in the United States.

"Jeff, how are you? It's Claire."

Jeff couldn't speak.

"Jeffrey. Going to a house of ill repute and fighting over the price of the whore and critically injuring a kid. I'm shocked," she said, as Jeff imagined how perfect her teeth must look when she smiled ironically all those thousands of miles away.

"We are not going to go ahead with the plans outlined in your report to Mr. Jarratt. We'll find another way to deal with the Nauru problem."

Now Jeff forced the words like a tank crew loading a shell into the tube.

"You dare to tell me that someone's countermanding my authority. Someone grasps the whole picture a lot better than I do!"

"There are many reasons. If you had read your Adam Smith, you would know that it's bad business and bad policy. He argued that a man cannot depend on others' benevolence, but that 'he will be more likely to prevail if he can interest their self-love in his favor. . . . Whoever offers to another a bargain of any kind, proposes to do this.' He believed in cooperation, the accumulation of capital through synergy, which requires examples of successful past collaboration in order to be realized. We need to suggest that we've done it before and it worked out, Jeff. We have to, if we are going to forge the new alliances that will help us protect our interests and show exponential growth from year to year.

"We are trying to merge with the Department of Defense. This will enable us to take new territories, in the Pacific and elsewhere, by force. Banaba. Guam. Taiwan. For a start."

"For a start."

"Adam Smith, Jeff. The God Who's Never Failed."

"Do you care about what Keynes said about synergy? And the Microsoft case—"

"Jeff, Jeff. The real verdict is still out on Bill Gates, and you'll note that even the official settlement doesn't necessarily preclude synergy among their products and services in the future. It is not conclusive."

"But *my* sentence is."

"You shouldn't have frequented such a place."

"I didn't—I—*you screwed me!*"

"That's one pleasure I will never have, hotshot. Good night, or I guess it's good morning for you."

"Claire. *Claire.* I wasn't raised and schooled in order to be sitting here wishing I had a knife to slit my wrists."

"You'll get out someday, and I'm sure there'll be a help-wanted sign down at the 7-Eleven."

"If you look in my office, there's a ring I was going to give you."

"Not the best you could have done for the money, sport," she said before hanging up.

Desolation

The crowds at Mount Rushmore had thinned out considerably when Sean Hamill left the stand where he sold ice cream, climbed into his Honda Accord, and began the trip home through the Black Hills. All around him were silence and a drizzle from the knotty lumps in the heavens. On occasion the trees parted to reveal vistas of white rock and buttes with patches of shrub on plains that seemed peaceful but at times aroused the suspicion that if he were someone else, a military guy, he would take it all in from a different perspective. He would know where the silos lay, and the high-tech bunkers. Right now, Sean wanted nothing more than to score a bag of weed to help him drive all the plump tourists from Middle America out of his mind.

When he got to Keystone, a couple of miles from the monument, he stopped for gas before driving to Randy Lutz's house by the foot of a row of hills like inverted cones of mildew at the outskirts of town. It was so barren here, he always thought. He parked outside the squat white house, got out, and rang the bell and Randy's face appeared, peering from beneath a Mariners cap, three days' stubble under eyes that would betray the chemicals in his body if you knew how to look. Sean followed Randy inside where Derek Coates emerged from the bathroom. When Sean asked for a bag, Randy said that Derek had scored prime weed, which he now went out to his car to fetch as Derek bragged about the properties of this pot, making a further claim:

"We could afford some grade-A stuff this time, man. We killed a kid and took his shit and threw his body in the gulch."

"Ha. You and Randy?"

"No, not Randy."

"Was this before or after you robbed a bank in Deadwood with semiautomatics?"

"After. Next we're gonna cut off Jefferson's nose and sell it on the black market."

"Yeah, then I'm fucked when the tourism goes."

Randy came in with the bag, exchanging it for bills with Sean, then proposing that they hang out on the weekend. Soon Sean was driving through the empty streets toward his father's house, where he lived in the basement. He brooded about what Derek said. Granted, Derek wasn't so bright, but that didn't excuse his unfunny joke about killing a kid and taking all the victim's stuff. Anyway, Sean had a bag and movies to watch. The week before, he'd viewed *North by Northwest* after hearing from Randy that the climax takes place on top of Mount Rushmore. He'd enjoyed the movie but his father couldn't fathom why Cary Grant's character has to run away from the villain Vandamm and his crony at the climax. Vandamm's a middle-aged weakling, his henchman doesn't look that tough, and all they've got between them is a knife, a dinky little kitchen knife from the look of it.

The next morning, Sean climbed out of bed cursing the necessity of dragging himself to work in the tourist trap. Soon, at Mount Rushmore, he was selling ice cream to a chubby man in a red polo shirt, tan trousers, and a pair of loafers. The man began complaining about his cab ride the evening before.

"This driver, he was smoking the whole time and he kept turning his head back and showing this stupid grin when he should have been watching the road. When I told him that, he said 'Fuck it man, I know what I'm doing'—said that in front of my wife and kids. I called the consumer bureau, and it costs five dollars to file a complaint, and you pay again when you follow up on a complaint, so I said forget it."

He inquired about other cab companies in the area, writing down the information Sean gave, before striding off.

Sounds like you got Alan Ostergren, Sean thought. Alan was the guy who, three years before, sold his car and began taking a bus a few miles to Off-Track Betting, where he blew all his money, even the return bus fare. You'd see him trudging all the way home in twenty-degree weather. Now Alan had a cab to drive around in, but the world was not much better off. Sean began thinking he'd rather be just about anyone but Alan, then he thought no, he sure as hell wouldn't like to be Pete Mullen, who'd thrown a chunk of concrete off an overpass and killed a driver. Pete and his victim never saw each other. Now Pete was doing ten to twenty in the penitentiary in Rapid City. Some people thought the sentence harsh because Pete had not set out to kill anyone, while others were incredulous at what they considered a joke—*take a stranger's head off and get out in ten!* Now a tourist, a bit thinner than the man in the red polo shirt, bought four ice cream cones, leaving Sean a dollar before ambling back to his trophy wife and his blond boy and girl. More customers came. By 4:30, the sky grew overcast, the threat of storm audible as the crowd thinned a bit. Within the hour, it was drizzling as Sean took out the "Back in 5 Minutes" sign and strode out under the yellow awning to smoke a Camel. He looked around. Roosevelt seemed troubled. Not in the way Cary Grant perceived in that movie, just kind of brooding.

On the drive back to Keystone, loneliness nagged him like a reopened cut until he pulled into the driveway of Floyd's

Tavern and strode through the swing doors, taking a seat a couple of stools down from a pair of girls he guessed were students at Black Hills State University. It was mid-September, far from crunch time. He wondered how they would react if he told them he sold ice cream to tourists for a living. Two stools down on his other side was a forty-year-old guy with black hair and an impish look. Bob DuBois, the bartender and a huge man, shuffled over to pour Sean a Coors, making talk about the tourists as well as the university where a security guard was a suspect in a coed's rape.

"You're light-years behind if you think that's news," said the man on Sean's left when Bob had moved off to serve a pack of frat boys.

"A woman and her daughter just came home from Disney World, and lo and behold, their house has been burglarized, her teen son's missing, and so's his car. They've been gone just a week, and now their world's totally crazy," the man added.

"Lord," said Sean, more concerned with the fact that in a few years, the kids around him would be working for Boeing or IBM while he served cones for $6.50 an hour, unless—*unless*—he got admitted to the IT training course beginning at the university next spring. He sipped his beer and paid no attention to the man who had the air of a journalist.

At the far end of the bar there was a commotion, until a thin bald man in glasses came over and leaned toward Bob DuBois.

"That guy in the Greek jacket," he said, unable in his anger to identify the fraternity garb correctly, "I want him to leave. He insulted me and I want him to leave *now*."

Bob peered over at the couch where a blond kid laughed and lifted a pint of Stella to his lips, bantering with his friends.

"That kid ain't done nothing."

"I was minding my business and he poked fun at me. If you don't make him leave, I'm never coming back here."

Bob studied the affronted guest, made a calculation, came out from behind the bar, and had words with the kid, who sauntered out of the bar. Instantly the bald man shifted his tone, making light of the weather and the coming elections, leaving good tips for Bob, glancing at Sean as if to ask, *What do you think, my friend?*, but all Sean noticed was that the two girls showed not a flicker of interest in him. Maybe he should have headed right for Randy Lutz's house to score a bag.

On the dreary Saturday that followed, Sean and Randy skirted the edges of Deadwood. Sean drove as his friend stared out at the town where blue-collar folk were cleaning up the mess from the revels the night before, some of them no doubt brooding about the weeks to come when there would be hardly any tourists. As the car emerged from the trees around the town, the desert opened before them, patches of grass dotting the sand extending hundreds of yards on either side to rows of buttes with pink scoring the white of the clefts and folds and the ridges like serrated blades menacing any living thing that approached. Now it was not rainy but between one climate and another. They made their way over the lonely roads toward the spot in the Badlands where they hoped to meet Redskin Mike.

"Damn it'd be easy to die here," was all Randy said in the minutes before they swung off the freeway onto the dirt road, plowing through a wasteland of shrub and grass beginning to give way to weeds.

They got out of the car and rapped on the door of the trailer, which opened to reveal a Lakota Sioux man with a pair of pitted, sagging cheeks and eyes that gave flashes of intelligence. At intervals Mike smiled weakly, a reflex of the mouth muscles. His mouth was the kind that throws dentists into tirades about the filthiness of smoking and what it means to have bad gums. Mike wore a black t-shirt that barely contained his belly and a pair of old jeans. He invited the whites inside, brought them into the tiny kitchen, leaned against a counter with a black satchel on it. Mike wanted to know how much they'd brought him today.

"Two bags, just like we said," Randy answered, pulling the bags from his pockets and setting them on the counter.

"I asked you for more than that."

That reflex: the start of a grin, the slackening of the muscles. Randy and Sean glanced at each other, then Randy scoffed.

"We deal to you, not through you, Mike. We've had this conversation before."

The reflex again.

"I swear it's for me."

"No one does six bags in a week and holds down a job, Mike. Don't play with us. The other Sioux can come to us if they like, but you're not the middleman. And I don't want any more heaps of one-dollar bills."

To Sean it was pretty comical, this two-bit pusher, Randy, laying down the law.

"We deal to you and not through you," he repeated. "Is there something going around that we should know about?"

Mike leaned back against the counter, his belly pushing against his t-shirt and pants, and related that he was hearing more and more about how the knapweed and Canada thistle were spreading so fast you could not traverse parts of the Sioux homeland.

"You know, you little fuckers really could be more polite to me. There's going to be a reckoning here soon. There's talk of suing the Weed and Pest Control Commission. According to sources in the tribe, the weeds were not here by accident. Settlers who think of Little Bighorn like it was yesterday introduced the seed contaminants on purpose, so that now you could sow as much alfalfa as you liked, but you'll never check the weeds."

Again Sean and Randy looked at each other.

"Is there a point to this that I'm missing?" Randy asked.

"Our lives would be just a bit different if no one discovered gold in them damned Black Hills."

"Fuck this. Where's the money?"

"You want to put the heat on me, you loathsome punk?"

Mike had stilled his reflex. He was not being funny.

"What the fuck are you going to do about it?" Randy answered, while Sean felt queasy, this was not what he'd expected when Randy asked nonchalantly what he was doing on Saturday morning.

Mike stared at the kids with contempt emanating from those hurt eyes. Sean looked at the satchel beside Mike.

"Randy," said Sean, extending his palm to the other's chest, "Randy he's a good guy, don't be so fucking aggressive. Back down."

"Shut up."

"Randy. *Please man.*"

The staring continued. Randy was not done needling Mike.

"I said, what the fuck are you gonna do about it, Mike? You people don't have courage anymore when there's hundreds of you assembled, and right now it's just you and two dudes in here."

"Fuck you. You think white people have courage anymore? Think they ever did?"

"I do, Mike. Do you care to contest it?"

"Fuck you. Just fuck you."

Sean's queasiness dipped into nausea and his blood would not sit still. He gauged the distance from where he stood to the door.

"Fuck yourself. Where else are you gonna get it?" said Randy, his voice broken just a bit, gazing over Sean's arm into those black eyes. "Where else? Hmm?"

Mike studied the white punks, some kind of convoluted thought process going on in the stillness of this vast canyon at 10:00 a.m.

Finally Mike reached into the satchel.

"Take your white man's money and get the fuck out of here."

A week later, a woman named Carol Jensen was walking near her property by Sanford Gulch when she noticed something odd lying in the water. On moving closer, it appeared to be in the shape of a man. She called the police. The victim turned out to be Evan Parker, a nineteen-year-old who had lived with his mom and sister in a one-story house in Keystone, had worked at a McDonald's, and by many accounts had been kind of desperate to make friends.

On the following day, Sean Hamill watched a report about the murder on the news. Minutes later, he walked into the police station in Keystone thinking *My friends have made enough assumptions about what's okay with me.* He met with detectives and told them what Derek had confided when he went to score a bag. Through a few inquiries, the cops learned of Derek's acquaintance with Jeremy Rowe, a semi-employed local considered to be even slower witted than Derek, and with George McClure, a factory hand who had arrests for drugs on his record and who went around in a green army jacket with lots of pockets.

On the morning after that meeting, Sean strode through the door of the Best Western Motel in Deadwood, moving quietly into the area closed for renovations, where the chatter of men at work mingled with the music from a radio propped on an alcove by the vending machines. Five guys were busy laying carpet here. Instantly Sean spotted Derek Coates, and shuffled over as inconspicuously as he knew how.

"Hey, man," said Derek.

"Evan Parker, did you know that kid?"

"Yeah man, we knew him."

Derek grinned, his eyes on the carpet.

"Listen," Sean said, moving his face closer, "if they question you, *please* don't say nothin' about dealing grass to me or with me, o.k.?"

Derek studied him, appearing to relish the moment. Then he turned back to the strip of carpet.

"No, don't worry. Unless I change my mind."

Sean's eyes darted around the room, then he turned, pushing his face closer still to Derek's.

"Please, Derek. I've been trying to get into this IT course. If I get a record, I am *so* fucked."

"Oh, well, I promise to be a good character witness at your trial."

"*Please*, man!"

Derek grinned again.

"Don't worry Sean. Now I'm trying to work here, dude."

"You gonna be o.k.? What do they have on you?"

"Not much at all. I'm not worried about traces of hair or anything because my hair was pulled back and we buried the knife, all the shit that had blood on it."

Sean did not quite look satisfied, but he reiterated his request in whispers before sliding out of the hotel as stealthily as ever.

Panting, sweating, cursing under his breath, he climbed into the Honda Accord, took off toward the freeway, and drove a mile to a rest stop where he parked and maneuvered his body through the crowds in their t-shirts and beige shorts. He fought his way through the parking lot toward the restrooms. Sean entered the men's room, found an empty stall, staggered inside, and locked the door before unbuttoning his shirt and reaching down to inspect the recording device, which appeared not to have slid around much. *Why were those people looking at me like I'm crazy?* Minutes later he was back on the freeway, swerving past the boathouses ringing the shore of Pactola Lake, continuing on past the outskirts of Lead until he was back in Keystone, the police station a beacon amid the Kwik Shops, parking lots, and bars.

The detectives pushed Derek Coates into the spare clean room, sat him down, and pressed the record button under the table.

"If this goes to trial and you're convicted, you'll get the needle."

"It wasn't fair to have someone talk to me wearing a wire. I got Miranda rights."

"Derek, it's in your best interest to fess up. Where'd you meet Evan Parker that night?"

"At his house. I came over and we smoked some joints and played PS2 for a couple of hours just like any night."

"Who brought the weed?"

"I did, of course."

"Had you sold it to him before this occasion?"

"Once or twice."

"You don't remember how many times?"

"I honestly don't."

"So you played PS2 and then you knocked him out?"

"No, I got up to go take a piss, and on the way back I snuck into his mom's room and felt around in the drawers until I found the pistol."

"What did you do with it?"

"Slipped it into the back of my pants, like on those cop shows, it was stuck in the crack of my ass."

"Then you rejoined Evan in the living room."

"Uh-huh."

"What was he doing?"

"He was killin' monsters on PS2. I said hey, let's go to my house."

"He agreed."

"Dude saw no reason not to."

"Describe the trip to your house. Someone saw you in the filling station on Thorn."

"We got in the Blazer and went down Cedar and turned onto Thorn to get gas—then we got back on Cedar and drove two miles to my house. As soon as we were there, I pulled the gun on Evan and made him hit the floor."

"What did he say?"

"I think he was even more confused than scared at that point. He kept sayin', 'I'm your friend, I'm your friend," and then we—I—kicked him in the head so hard he passed out."

"How long was he out?"

"Maybe twenty minutes, and when he came to he was tied up in a chair. He was still sayin', 'I'm your friend' and askin' why this was happening."

Derek's interlocutor was silent, then another detective broke in:

"You don't appreciate the nastiness, the evil of this whole business, luring him to your place on the pretext of being friends and then doing this cowardly thing to him?"

"That's how it was done."

"That's how it was done," the second detective repeated.

Derek nodded.

The questions continued, drawing an account of how Evan was forced back into his own Blazer and taken six miles away to Sanford Gulch, where the kicking, stabbing, and stoning began as he cried and begged, his attacker chortling and giggling.

"What else did he say?"

"After about two and a half hours, he stopped screaming, and he said, 'Just let me die. Please just let me die!'"

When Derek was back in his cell, the detectives agreed on the unlikelihood of his having acted alone, given Derek's slip of the tongue and the inconvenience of going to a gas station on Thorn when there was another one, closer, on Cedar, as anyone who lived in that area knew. Another party had made a sudden unilateral decision to turn onto Thorn.

Sean Hamill was sitting in his basement smoking a cigarette when the phone rang and he picked it up and received the information that Derek Coates had hanged himself in his cell.

He drove around for a while and then parked in the mud outside Gallagher's Pub, the only Irish-themed joint in Keystone, surprisingly enough for a place tourists liked so much, he had always thought. It's always Irish this, Irish that for the swarms of people who could not tell Flann O'Brien from Eamon De Valera. Sean had avoided his place since an evening in March when he'd stumbled outside to find that someone had keyed his car, back and forth, back and forth on the passenger's side. *God, you have to be cowardly to do a thing like that.* Tonight he felt brave. He walked inside and bought a Stella, taking a seat amid the chatter and the ascending smoke of the bar, near the left end of the counter where all the stickers and slogans were. Here were signs demanding justice for the McAllister family, signs with anti-British mantras and exclamation points, and another sign: SNIPER AT WORK. Certain people were likely to be here on just about any evening, in fact here was one of them: Jeremy Rowe, putting away glasses of Guinness, talking with a girl sporting a tattoo on the back of her neck, hard to make out in this light, and here also was Melissa Fuson, smoking American Spirits.

"How's things?" asked Sean, raising his glass.

Sean and Melissa chatted until George McClure, a gaunt but muscular dude with a pitted face, came in and sat down beside Melissa, who kissed his cheek tenderly. George wore his trademark army jacket, and worn dungarees.

"I've got some great shit," Sean told George. "Don't know where you're shopping but it ain't nothing, man."

"Is that so?" George replied. "I think we should catch up one of these days, maybe head out on the lake on a weekend."

Sean nodded. The half-wit named Jeremy Rowe made a few insulting remarks until Sean remembered the aphorism about discretion and valor, not word for word but the general sense of it, and ducked out of Gallagher's Pub.

In Sean's dream that night, a ceremony was underway on the pavilion below the visages of the four presidents, the governor beaming before his entourage and the reporters in the clear air of the middle of September. Sean felt grateful to be in attendance as a park employee. It came time for the governor to mount the stage and stride behind the podium, where he began naming people who deserved notice for their service to South Dakota. They began to file past the podium, accepting their certificates, moving down away from the stage. They were legion, these men in their thirties and forties in blue shirts who executed their duty behind clean desks, getting things done with efficiency, solving crimes, drawing up contracts to erect dams, reservoirs, and bridges across the breadth of the Badlands, the distances they refused to let cow them. Still they came, receiving certificates and the politician's praise. As they filed off across the pavilion, the governor left the stage, taking a seat with his wife at one of the tables, with one more address in order until the banquet began. Before Sean and the others started eating, a new speaker, a man of about thirty-eight in a dark suit, opened up:

"Our ancestors came to these parts, they were here in the midst of a wilderness such as they had never seen. They faced hostile tribes, brutal winters, terrain that can wreck you, dangerous predators. To survive here they adopted a code—"

Sean wasn't really listening, nor, he suspected, were the others at his table, transfixed as they'd been by the governor's voice. Now the governor turned to Sean.

"What's a young fellow doing here on a day like this?"

It was not a question requiring an answer. The politician gestured at the reaches all around the valley where bison roamed, thistle contended with the arable acres.

"You could be swimming in Pactola Lake, climbing the Black Hills, following one of the trails not far from here," the governor added.

On the stage the speaker droned on: "They adopted a code to live by, as exemplified by Lieutenant Colonel Custer. You would be strong. You would not run away just because you were outnumbered, nor would you take advantage of a situation where there really was no contest. . . ."

"So many things in the bright day to occupy a young man," the governor continued.

Now the governor's wife turned to a guy two seats down from Sean, striking up a conversation. She asked about the prospects for farming in the uppermost parts of Lawrence County, how things were going, and the guy, a Lakota Sioux, said things were fine, he and his brothers got up early every day to pick and pile crops into their flat bed, driving to Keystone Saturday and Sunday.

"And the Black Hills today are a national treasure," said the man on the stage, "where you'll find not only some of the most productive gold mines on the planet but the publishing industry's greatest resource, our forests. . . ."

At length, the diners stood up, shook hands, and dispersed quietly. Sean did not talk with anyone before he strode away from the pavilion, the chatter behind him dissolving into the crisp air. He was walking on one of the side roads in the direction of Keystone, but now he strode off the road out onto the plains where the buttes loomed in the distance. All around him were gravel like the essence of mountains that giants had destroyed in a rage. At length Sean passed a pair of cowboys on steeds, with beige caps, boots with spurs, but they paid him no attention except for a moment when the younger of the two turned his head slightly, the rim of his hat hiding his features, offering what sounded like a few words of caution.

Sean plodded on into the barrenness until he spied a figure a hundred yards ahead on the gravel.

"Hey!" Sean yelled.

The stranger ignored him.

"Hey there!"

He called a few more times. Still the stranger didn't turn around.

"Hey, hold on!"

All around Sean and the stranger, shadows grew as a breeze swept through the canyon, the gravel and the trunks and the buttes like white coals in the distance dimming as he felt the need to meet this man, shake his hand, say *I can aspire to be like you*. He was in full pursuit of the man in the shades of 5:30. Sean quickened his pace, realizing now that it was someone younger than he'd thought, clad not in one of the dress shirts on display before but in a polo-style shirt and black trousers, the upper parts of his body kind of indistinct. Sean ran through the dusk calling out until he stood just behind the man who turned, reluctantly it seemed, something about his ear quite odd indeed, it hung by a thread from the side of the boy's head. Sean saw him face to face and realized that never before had he seen a person who was mutilated while he was alive.

Sean Hamill and George McClure pushed the motorboat free of its moorings, wading in the fringes of Pactola Lake until the moment came to leap in. Between them in the boat lay a metal box containing bait beside a cooler and a coffee maker. George guided the boat toward the center of the lake as Sean gazed around in wonder, taking in the trees along the circumference of the water, the mountains to the north, the edges of a house barely visible among trunks at the bank furthest from the vessel, admiring the reaches of undisturbed blue in the quiet of 8:00 a.m. George seemed to have an idea of the promising spots in the lake, so Sean said nothing, eying the rods beside the box at his feet.

The vessel sped in the direction of the mountains to the north, in the stillness of this perfect morning, until they reached the center of the lake. George killed the motor and reached into a bag, withdrawing a pair of bagels as Sean made coffee and poured a cup for himself.

"Here Sean. Chow down, man."

"Thanks."

Sean munched on his bagel though he wasn't hungry. He could not spy a single ranger, tourist, or jogger on the fringes of the lake. He almost began to tell George about the contents of a letter concerning his application to the IT course at the university, but aborted the sentence. How might George react to the news that Sean's life was about to improve?

"Damn if I've seen a bigger lake," George said.

"No shit."

"The West is so much more than people ever take in. And I'm talkin' people who live here, not fuckin' tourists."

"Yeah."

"Sean, my man, we can sell grass to the Sioux every week for the next two years before they've got their own supply network. They get so used to doing things a certain way, you'll never persuade them otherwise if their ass depended on it."

"Never persuade them, I agree on that much."

"I've got good suppliers, bitch."

"Do you?"

"The best."

"How are you paying them?"

"Let me deal with it. They're not guys you want to piss off, if you know what I mean."

"O.k.," Sean assented, then added: "Are they the ones you bought from after Evan died?"

"Maybe so."

Now came a breeze, caressing Sean's black hair like a mother's fingers, as he reclined in the aft of the boat.

"He didn't die for nothing then, I guess you'll agree."

"Jeremy and I couldn't agree more."

"Jeremy's not so bright."

"I never said the bitch was bright."

"Jeremy drove the car?"

George nodded, his attention straying.

"Did he ever handle the knife?"

At this question, George looked up and peered at Sean.

And in that moment, the queasiness verging on nausea came back.

"Huh?"

"Never mind. Got any more bagels?"

"No. Why'd you ask about the knife?"

"Nothing."

"Why'd you ask about the knife?"

"That's some grade-A cream cheese—"

"Answer the question."

"Oh, I was, like, you know, trying to visualize what happened. I was curious—"

"No you weren't."

"I was, like—"

George reached into his army jacket and withdrew a .45 pistol.

"*Open your shirt, bitch!*"

"All right, be cool man."

He obeyed. As soon as George saw the recorder, he leaned forward and ripped it free of Sean's chest and flung it on the floor of the boat. Sean tossed his steaming coffee into George's face, seized the tackle box with both hands, and jumped, and then he was sinking, plummeting thanks to the box's weight, as one bullet, then another, shot past him. Sean waited until the boat was a blur way overhead, let go of the box and swam toward the shore where he thought he had spied a trail just moments into the trip. A bullet sped past inches from his leg as he fought to hold in his breath until the shore came into relief before him, sensing that George could not see him and was firing wildly. He came to the muddy bank, scrambling up into the line of trees, gasping, wheezing, as George talked into a cell phone, not appearing to see Sean. He fled into the woods, thinking now of that Hitchcock film he had watched. As far as most people were concerned, *You're a regular Cary Grant* was a compliment, but he felt distaste as he thought of Grant's character. *Roger Thornhill, you're not the first New Yorker to come to the Badlands and have your courage put to the test. Not only do you show cowardice, but you do it literally in the face of a man who set a different example. And now look at me, look at me, I'm a coward!*

He fought his way through the weed and shrub and found himself in a field of buffalograss, thin with stolons leaning forward. How easily George's guys could trap him here. Now a row of trees beckoned to him, buffalograss segueing into a mix of thorny shrub and wheatgrass growing from the clay-like substance that had gotten on his shoes and pants. The blue and green of the grass here pulled at his eyes. Sean reached the tree line hugging one of the elms as sweat ran into his eyes, his body squirming in the damp of his soiled clothes. He fought through the bushes, realizing again how far Canada thistle had encroached in these parts, the prickles cutting him as rays coming through the canopy above mottled the blackness of the leaves. He wheezed and cried. He made himself shut up. Now he thought he made out a clearing ahead. In moments Sean stood at the opening of a field scored by a road, a scar of tarmac through the white, a pickup parked by the side of the road half a mile away. Nobody moved. Sean was not nearly close enough to make out anyone in the vehicle which sat there like a cat full of confidence, ready to pounce.

Abruptly, the pickup pulled onto the road in his direction, and just as suddenly he vanished into the elms. A hundred yards from the road, he panted as he tried to shrink behind a trunk, just like a child, wanting the might, the immensity of the elm to protect him. Detecting no movement between himself and the road, he stole in a northerly direction. In half an hour he was ready to emerge again from the cover of the trees, spying a clearing with a house in the distance that reminded him of a dwelling a couple of miles from where the Hamill family lived before his mom's death. He and his friend Matt Lane had spied that rickety house with rotting boards in the barrenness of the fields beyond the limits of Spearfish, in days when neither of them had the vocabulary to convey what people do in this world, and Matt said, *Don't ever go there, Sean, no don't go there, a bad man lives there*. For some reason, the house he was looking at now had that aspect.

As he started toward the house, he saw a man with a rifle slung on his shoulder coming up the road toward him. He had overalls and a hunting cap on, and conceivably he was just a hunter, but he walked right toward Sean. Sean bolted toward the hills to the west, kicking off his shoes so there could be no *squish squish* as he ascended the nearest slope. Soon he was about thirty feet above ground level and he stole behind a boulder, his heart like one of those hammers used by road crews. He realized now that *Sean Hamill had shit himself*. He was a pathetic excuse for a man, watching, sweating, scanning the ground below where the man with the rifle strolled through the whispering air, to the north and back again. Then he was out of sight. After thirty minutes, Sean descended, trudged across the field, and pounded at the door of the house.

It was a pretty dead night at Gallagher's Pub when Sean Hamill burst in and went right past the tables piled high with glasses of Guinness and Stella and the kids from the university tossing darts at the wall until he stood face to face with Jeremy Rowe. Looking like a cowboy in a scarlet shirt wide open at the collar and with his curly blond hair pulled back in the manner of a mid-career Matthew McConaughey, two days' stubble on his plain features, Jeremy looked up at him inquiringly. For a moment, Sean stood there, taking in the features of this not very bright man sitting in the tumult of the bar with his glass of beer. Then Sean said:

"I'm here upon a matter of personal honor. I have no physical evidence to prove it, but I happen to know that you drove the car that took Evan Parker to the gulch the night he died."

Jeremy grinned, shifting his eyes with a look saying *You believe this guy?*

"Fuck off."

"No, I'm not going to fuck off, Jeremy."

"Well why don't you go to the police?"

"I'm not going to the police. Get up."

Jeremy repeated the shifting movements, but his manner was changing.

"Why don't you fuck off before you get hurt?"

"I don't mind getting hurt. And I'd like you to get up right now."

All eyes in the pub were on them now—the kids from Black Hills State University, the pair of middle-aged alcoholics, the woman seated at the far end of the bar, and the bartender.

"Fuck it."

Jeremy Rowe stood up and they strode out into the parking lot.

The first blow to Jeremy's nose made him shriek as his eyes filled with water, too distracted to check the punches that followed on his chest and jaw. Sean kicked him so hard he feared he'd fucked up his own foot, then when Jeremy keeled forward he stomped on his head, almost as he imagined Derek Coates had kicked Evan Parker. Sean kicked Jeremy again before crouching over his back and getting his right arm into a chicken wing and pushing it with all his might up toward Jeremy's neck. The half-wit screamed. The people from the bar looked on like a silent tribunal. Now Sean demanded: "Tell them what you did."

"I drove the car that took Evan Parker to the gulch."

"Louder."

"*I drove the car that took Evan Parker to the gulch!*"

Sean stood up in the drizzle, feeling the breeze and the scattering drops on his face. He thought of what he had been, stumbling out of the hills down into the field where he'd spied the stranger's house, panting, terrified, the evidence of that terror all over the seat of his trousers, yes he had really shit him-self, and he thought of the man in that house, the flannel shirt and overalls and thick hair like bundled hay and the cold hard face that had seen so many seasons in the Badlands, looking at Sean with pity, saying to the excuse for a man who'd come strag-gling to his door: "Well now, why should I help you?"

Speed Demons

It was before the age of e-mail and the internet. Computers were not as universal a fact of life as they are today, but my father knew which way the wind was blowing. He demanded that I leave our palace in Palm Springs and head off to a computer camp at a site in Riverside County twice a week. *You'll never be a success if you don't stay ahead of the curve, Richie,* was his banal line. *You'll end up like those losers who come around asking to clean the pool. They are without character. I don't care what your friends are doing this summer, I've given you marching orders, now get on with it.* As it happened, one of my friends was under the same stern sentence from his father, and it was a good thing for me, since I wouldn't get my driver's license for another year. Matt Ross not only had a license and an '82 Audi, but he was also socially acceptable in the eyes of my investment banker dad and his trophy wife.

So twice a week, we set out from Palm Springs into the desert in Matt's car. For a couple of hours every Tuesday and Friday, we sat in a big room bisected by three long tables with computers on either side, while a balding, overweight man in small round spectacles explained the basics of WordPerfect. Matt branched out, became friendly with a few of the other kids in the class, but I didn't do so well. The teacher, Mr. Eggert, humiliated me by correcting me in front of the class, but I soldiered on. God forbid that I should turn out like one of those "losers" who went around to rich people's houses, asking to clean the pool for chump change.

About midway between Palm Springs and the computer camp, there was a diner and truck stop that we quickly became curious about on our way back and forth along the freeway. One evening on the way home, Matt proposed to stop there. I told Matt that surely the truckers would be hostile to a pair of brats from Palm Springs. Matt Ross and Richard White, sitting down among burly guys with tattoos on their biceps and amphetamines in their veins. He shrugged, his look said *Fucked if I care* as he pulled off the road into the lot in front of the elongated silver exterior of the diner. As it turned out, the five or six truckers in the place paid us no mind, and our waitress, a girl named Sandy in a pink apron, was disarmingly warm.

"Her smile could give a corpse a hard-on," Matt said, studying her swishing buttocks as she moved down the aisle with the coffee pot from which she'd just filled our cups.

I asked Matt what he thought of Mr. Eggert. Matt thought the guy was explaining things lucidly. If I didn't know better, I'd have said that my friend was starting to enjoy the class a bit. I wanted him to feel as unhappy as I did. When I got home, my father would start up again. Somebody got rejected by a college he had thought of as a safety school, so-and-so just got fired because he was not keeping pace with the IBM revolution in California, on and on. How unbearable to think that I might submit to this torture, computer camp, and still end up like those children of my father's acquaintances. But there were worse ways to end up. Matt and I began talking about a woman who had been spotted hitchhiking in the area before going missing for several days now.

At this point, I noticed a face at the booth in front of ours. It belonged to a guy a couple of years older than Matt, wearing a gray tank top and a pair of soiled jeans. He had stubby dirty blond hair and hadn't shaved in a few days. He was eating intently, not looking at us. I couldn't help thinking of my father's warnings, noxious though I found them to be in spirit. Matt and I had hot fudge sundaes and a few cups of coffee before he got up to use the restroom.

The punk in the adjoining booth made eye contact with me.

"Starin' at the waitress's ass. I should have you both tossed outta here," he said. His voice was starchy, like sandpaper on a rough surface. I kept up a poker face, trailing my spoon through runny puddles of ice cream. He laughed.

"You guys from the computer camp?" he asked.

I acted as if I hadn't heard, wished Matt would get back from the men's room.

"Come on, you can talk to me. I'm Dean," the punk said, with levity in his tone. Still I studied the fascinating patterns in my bowl. Still Matt did not come back. The diner seemed so small and remote, like a station on the moon. In my peripheral vision, I could see Dean watching me. Then I heard him say, "Fuck you, man," before he dropped some bills on the table, slipped on a leather jacket, and walked out of the diner. Only now did Matt reappear in front of me.

"There must have been some fascinating graffiti in there," I said with a nod toward the men's room.

"Let's cut out," he said.

But I'd see Dean again.

The computer class fell on Tuesdays and Fridays, so it was only two evenings a week that I got back to Palm Springs too late to dine with my parents. On the other five evenings, we sat in the garden with a range of ragged mountains in the background, talking mostly of trivia as my mother drank glass after glass of red wine and my father smoked a few of the Marlboros that would eventually do him in. My father preferred Scotch with his cigarettes, but he had cut back on the stuff lately, as if *that* were the long-term danger. Sometimes he talked about things going down in Tinseltown, where my father held shares in the major studios. Lately his talk focused on a screenwriter who had gone off the deep end, cutting his wife into little pieces after receiving word that one of the studios had declined an option on his most ambitious screenplay to date, a project he had been shopping around for years. My father saw a kind of symmetry between the crime and one of the scenes in the screenplay, so maybe the murder had achieved the drama associated with a personal breakthrough after all, in my father's perverse view. Of course he was careful to qualify this point with expressions of shock at so horrid a crime, empathy for the victim's family.

"How can you just sit back and analyze the screenplay so dispassionately, after what's happened?" my mother asked.

"If there were any journalists worth their salt out there, they would have picked up on this," my father replied, taking another drag on his Marlboro.

"So, Richie, what's your sense of Mr. Eggert?" my mother said.

I groped for banalities to toss in her direction. In reality, I had little sense of Mr. Eggert or of anything he'd imparted.

Without warning, one of Matt's grandparents died and he had to go off to the East Coast for a while, so when it came to getting to and from Eggert's class, I had to fend for myself. I buckled to my adventurous streak, hitching rides either way, assuring my parents with the fiction that I had another friend making the jaunt. I continued to stop at the diner. On the first

Tuesday I ate there alone, I pretended not to notice the leering, grinning young men seated a few booths away in either direction. Here I could eat whatever I pleased, without the company of a pair of middle-aging blowhards. I put away a cheeseburger with extra fries, three cokes, and a hot fudge sundae, and I was wondering if Sandy, whom I tipped more than adequately, just might let me order a beer. Then in my peripheral vision, I detected a couple of guys in a booth ten yards down staring at me. I tried to ignore it, but it went right on. There are places where you can't act like that, I wanted to scream. In the South, in the Upper Midwest. They would politely ask you to step outside. I looked up, right at them. It was Dean and another guy, with stringy brown hair like a guitarist in a metal band.

"Does your mommy know you're out this late?" Dean asked.

They both laughed. I weighed the consequences of chucking something at them. But then Dean's tone changed, suddenly and completely.

"Look man, I'm not trying to be a jerk. You just struck me as a guy who doesn't make friends too easily. I know the type when I see it 'cause I've been there, believe me. My dad's a mechanic. How do you think I felt when they sent me to a private school in Riverside when I was little—"

I wanted to interrupt, to interject, to clarify, but he brooked no interruption.

"Look, we don't spend all our time drag-racing our cars on lots behind supermarkets. We have girlfriends and we have lives. We're wondering if you'd like to step out of your privileged shell for just a moment. Have a beer with the Speed Demons. What do you say, man?"

In his eyes, there was something very close to sincerity. Maybe I'd misjudged Dean, maybe here was someone I could conceivably become friends with. I thought I'd rather find out

than go through my life wondering about an unexplored possibility. And that was how I agreed to meet up with Dean Hayes
and Steve Trelawny on Friday night, at a campsite a mile up the
road from the diner. I made this decision even though there was
something menacing about Dean and something sad in Steve's
eyes, something that never went away on any of the occasions
I saw him.

When I got to the camp grounds on Friday night, having
hitched a ride to the diner, eaten, and walked a mile and a half up
the freeway, a fire blazed in a garbage can. Around it, a dozen or
so black leather jackets were on display. It got cool in the Valley
at night. I knew I'd look ridiculous in a leather jacket, but I might
have weighed that against the awkwardness of standing there,
arms clasped, shivering, while the Speed Demons laughed and
guzzled Coors. I moved toward the flaming barrel. Before I got
there, Dean and Steve approached me, handed me a Coors. I had
no idea how to tell them that beer still tasted kind of nasty to me,
that I was more than a bit uncertain about what might happen to
my body if I went beyond two beers. We might see the beer again.

The two Speed Demons and I talked for a while, and they
confirmed my suspicion that they liked to talk about all the ugly
stuff that went on in the world. School shootings, spouses mur-
dering one another, highways collapsing onto cars, all this held
a perverse fascination for them, making me wonder whether
there was anything more to them than morbid nihilism. But
some of the talk was just about their crappy jobs. Steve said that
Dean, who liked to complain about his dad, had nothing on
Steve. Trelawny senior was a paralyzed vet in a wheelchair, and
it might have made things simpler if the government made out
his checks directly to the liquor store.

"Poor bastard never stops bitchin' about his dad," Dean
confided to me when Steve went off to find more beers.

"Uh, look Dean, I don't know if—"

Dean was not listening. He pointed out some of the other guys lounging around, drinking, smoking, mock-shoving one another. There was "Red" Connor, a huge guy whose parents just might have conceived him atop a motorcycle; Eddie Gauchi, a kid with an unruly mop of greasy black hair; Boz Burnham, a sullen guy with a dead baby earring and patches on the elbows of his jacket; Mike Haroz, who, it was whispered, had a Syrian dad and a blond American mom. They came here, just about every Friday and Saturday night, I gathered. A couple of them had criminal records, but I could have told you that without Dean sharing the information. I wanted to get to know them, to be able to say to Matt and my other rich acquaintances that I knew them. Now Steve returned with more beers, handed me one. I made a show of downing it in long, consecutive gulps. Dean and Steve watched with amusement, handed me another, let me repeat the stunt. As I did so, I had a third spectator, it might have been Eddie. I checked my inner exhibitionist, slowed down, listened as my new friends speculated about the hitchhiker who'd vanished in the area. Someone said he thought he knew who was responsible. At this intelligence, the others nodded. I already had a buzz, I was not thinking straight enough to challenge them for pulling my leg, for surely that was what they were doing. My overriding sensation was a giddy one I had come to know well enough.

Still I was not in the others' league. I could not have told you how many beers Dean had put away at this point. I kept hearing his laugh, a keening, shrill sound coming out of a long narrow pipe, rather as I imagined an eel might sound if it could laugh. Everything I said was funny to him. Just the fact that I was standing here saying it amid all these tough young men tinged every word, every syllable. I began to listen to a voice, small but insistent, telling me to chill out, to wind it down for the evening before I did something really stupid. In it I could hear my father, I could hear his rich buddies.

They had no place here.

Steve brought over two more six-packs of Coors, and I reached for a can. Before I knew what was happening, my feet were off the ground, but I wasn't falling—my body arched diagonally, one Speed Demon clutching my ankles while another had my armpits, and a third, it might have been Dean, began to pour the beer down my throat. I started to cry out, but only regurgitated a portion of the beer, which kept coming and coming like a waterfall. A new can replaced the first. I went along, swallowing as fast as I could, as a chant went up around us: *"Oouh! Oouh! Oouh! Oouh! Oouh!"* If waterboarding were a common term then, it would surely have occurred to me. Still the fluids came as if the space inside the can was infinite. I swallowed, gasped, tried to speak, swallowed again, and again.

"Ddd-Dean! MMMMPH! MRRRRRRRRRRRPH!"

Now the contents of a third can were entering me. And now a fourth. My eyes watered and began to rotate in Dean's direction, I tried to spit the beer out again, resumed swallowing madly, began to fold my right hand into a fist—

And then the Speed Demons, cackling, laughing, whooping, dropped me on my back in the dust.

I rolled over onto my belly, propped myself up on my palms as more of the bitter liquid left me, spattering the dirt. Most people who drink beer have only vague memories of a long-ago time, ancient history really, when the stuff tasted nasty. Not this boy. I began to pick myself up, thinking that I must not misconstrue the spirit in which the Speed Demons had done this thing. It *was* kind of funny. Finally I managed to stand up straight, wipe my mouth with a soiled hand. Dean was chortling. Now a shape moved up on the other side of the flaming barrel, spoke in a low voice:

"Where'd you find this asshole?"

I strained my eyes, made out a figure silhouetted against the vast expanse of desert. Red Connor. He had a mohawk and the physique of a pro wrestler, not one of the ones you're supposed to like, but one of the dirty fighters. He glared at me. Neither Dean nor Steve said anything. Red took a step toward me, another step. He looked like someone right out of the Mad Max trilogy, but I don't think anyone was going to mistake me for Mel Gibson.

"Who invited him?" Red demanded.

Dean and Steve weren't owning up to anything. I felt liquid slipping from my stomach down to my intestines, felt my scrotum tighten. Now I realized how long it had been since I had seen the tail lights of a car receding into the night in any direction. Red Connor had made calculations. He took yet another step toward me. Desperately, I looked to Dean and Steve, wondered what I might say in the lingo of my Palm Springs mom: "Dean, you're being rather a poor host." But Dean and Steve wore poker faces. Red bent down—what was he doing? I looked around. Most of the Speed Demons seemed to be savoring the moment.

Red Connor picked up a chain, raised it so it was about level with his mohawk. Angry red eyes leveled with mine. It is hard to write this: I pissed my pants. He relished the chance to get even with this pansy who had treated the Speed Demons, the whole scene, as an amusement I could later brag about to my friends in the comforts of our rich man's playground. He was going to hurt me in ways I hadn't dreamt you could get hurt. He was coming. Yes, he was almost upon me.

Now came a voice ten feet away.

"Fuck off, Red."

It was Boz Burnham. One of the Speed Demons I hadn't deigned to speak to all night. Boz didn't even look that tough: a thin guy in a faded leather jacket, with medium-length brown hair curving around ruddy cheeks. For a moment, as Boz and Red locked eyes, I thought that I should run, bolt to the freeway, take my chances. Then I thought no, if there is anything in me worth defending, I can't flee now. Red stared icily at Boz, but did not take another step forward. He looked at me, looked back to Boz. Finally he dropped the chain, walked off toward the cluster of Speed Demons furthest from the road, spat into the dirt, opened yet another Coors.

"Come on. Let me give you a ride home, kid," said Boz.

I gratefully accepted. We climbed into his '73 Chevy and set out into the California night. Boz drove with the effortless grace of someone who's been doing it every day since age 15. Not once did either of us look back. I assumed that Boz knew how to get to Palm Springs, so I did not say anything most of the way, not until he did something unexpected. Boz pulled off the freeway onto a side road, drove southeast past the vast ominous form of a hill toward an area where I thought nobody at all lived. I turned to the young man in the driver's seat. He was watching the curving dirt road. Then he pulled off it, onto the rough shoulder, and put the car in park.

"What is it?"

Boz sat there, his eyes scanning the hills. I looked where I thought he was looking, and I thought I detected something, faint but unmistakable, like a flashlight being turned on and off again. I repeated my question.

"Nothin', kid. Be quiet, o.k.?"

I obeyed him. For a few minutes more we sat there. We didn't see the light again. When Boz appeared satisfied, he started the car, drove for about ten minutes, and stopped in front of a trailer with a dirt yard strewn with plastic chairs, a grill, and sacks of charcoal. Boz got out, walked up to the trailer and through the front door, then I saw a light come on in one of the rooms. Moments later he reappeared, got back in the car, and then he did not say another word until he had taken me all the way to the limits of Palm Springs. He asked if I could get home from here. I nodded. When I started to thank him, he said, "Never mind, kid. Take care now," and then the Chevy was gone. I never found out what was going on out there that night.

The following Tuesday, after class, I was sitting in the diner, staring at the cheeseburger I hadn't touched. There were Dean and Steve, barely suppressing giggles.

"Hey, man. I heard you were a little green over the weekend," said Dean.

"Like, puking up rivers," added Steve with a smirk.

I tried to ignore them. They weren't my friends, they never had been. If it hadn't been for Boz . . .

"Listen, man, we're just riding you. So was Red. He wasn't gonna do nothin' to you, at least not with all of us there," Dean said.

I went on staring at my big, high-calorie meal.

"Don't you get it, man? He just wanted to, like, gauge what your attitude was toward us," Steve said.

"Come on. You want a good time, ditch that pre-professional shit and come out with us on Friday night. We're goin' over to the Freak House," Dean added.

Ah, the Freak House. The decaying place on a side road off the freeway, with weathered green shutters on the grimy windows. People seen leaving there reputedly included members of bike gangs and the Mexican mafia. There would be naked women there, I gathered, under the supervision of the proprietor, a mysterious retired director named Dave Nolan. I shook my head, but part of me thought it might be pretty fucking awesome to enter that place. Strangely, Steve did not appear to share Dean's enthusiasm. Perhaps he knew something about the Freak House that neither Dean nor I even suspected.

The next time I dined with my parents, my mother wanted to talk about Mr. Eggert.

"Does he seem strange to you?"

"No, not more than other teachers I've had."

She'd heard a rumor that the middle-aging computer instructor had inappropriately touched a female student a couple of years ago in L.A. His defenders said he just wanted to look at a pendant hanging from her neck, he had not meant for his fingers to brush anything they shouldn't have.

"Are you sure you feel comfortable with him as your teacher?"

I said yes and it didn't really matter anyway, since I'd never go anywhere I shouldn't.

"Why did you get in so late on Friday night?" my father wanted to know.

"Mr. Eggert did a demo of a WordPerfect 2.0 for those of us willing to stay a bit later," I said, knowing my father wouldn't try to verify this information.

With the majestic mountains rising behind the garden of his palace, my father leaned back in his deck chair, took a long sip of Scotch, and lit another Marlboro. I guess it was kind of ironic that he so enjoyed a brand whose icon was a cowboy, a working-class dude.

"Don't worry about his teacher, Linda."

"I know I shouldn't trust rumors."

"But I mean even if they're true. Just because people are sad and lonely it doesn't mean the world has no use for them," the investment banker said from the heights of magnanimity.

She nodded sagely, drank some more merlot. I suppose my father felt the need to put his earlier comments about pool cleaners into context. Now he turned to me and said:

"I ran into Matt Ross's dad on the golf course. He said that Matt came back from the East Coast and you didn't want to ride with him anymore. Which was fine with Matt because you didn't ever seem to take the course seriously."

"Well, I don't think Matt can read my mind—"

"You are not to hitchhike again. If Matt won't take you, go with Alan McGinnis."

"He's a jerk—"

"Is this the kind of class where they give marks?" my father interrupted me, blowing smoke through his nostrils.

"Uh, no. It's not even pass/fail."

"But they do give you exercises?"

"Yes."

"Well, you tell Mr. Eggert I want you to receive a grade. He can track your performance, don't you even try to tell me otherwise. And if that grade is less than a B, I'll ground you for the rest of the summer."

"Dad—"

"Richie, don't argue with me, or I'll just go ahead and ground you right now," my father finished.

Don't ask me how I refrained from seizing my fork and thrusting it in that face, somehow both self-satisfied and insecure, as he sat there smoking and drinking in the garden of our palace in one of the wealthiest places on earth.

On Friday evening, I hitched a ride from the computer camp to the diner. Sandy smiled at me as if she would have been happy to go to a back room and do everything with me. But even at my tender age, I was beginning to wonder if this manner of hers might be just a ruse to extract ever more generous tips.

I ate my cheeseburger and fries with relish, weighed asking her for a beer, then decided I was kidding myself with so trifling a request. I did not see Speed Demons anywhere in the diner, but that was as it should be—I knew where they were tonight.

I wasn't going to linger here, in a place whose novelty had quite worn off. Leaving yet another excessive tip on my table, I got up, strode out through the front door, and out of the parking lot to the freeway. I scanned the length of it. The air was clear and sweet like in a Midwestern town when they're burning leaves. It was the manzanita shrubs in the hills, coming into bloom. The sky was getting dark and there were hardly any cars passing by. I waited, and waited. A couple of cars came along, one of them slowed a bit as it neared the diner, but it did not stop. I lingered for what seemed like hours. It was getting cool once again. I thought maybe I should go back into the diner, call my dad, and beg him to pick me up. He would probably be so furious at me for hitchhiking, in defiance of his orders, that he would ground me for the rest of the summer right on the spot. I shivered, cursed, rubbed my hands together. Yet another car passed without slowing.

But at last a car did slow down, its headlights in the darkness looking almost like the eyes of an empathetic robot. I dared to hope that it was Boz, that he'd spirit me right off to Palm Springs, no questions asked, but I saw that it was not a '73 Chevy. The blue Ford eased to the shoulder 20 yards ahead of me. I ran up to it, looked through the open passenger's side window at the driver.

It was Steve Trelawny.

"Get in, hump," he said with a grin.

I quickly obeyed.

"Where's Dean tonight?"

"He's going to do what he's going to do," was all Steve said.

He looked more than ever like a guitarist in a metal band as he drove us out into the desert, and the scent on his breath was not mouthwash. But his driving was not erratic. He seemed fully in control, in fact. Though I had spoken to Steve only in Dean's presence in the past, and hardly at all even then, I had picked up on something about him, the sort of emotion a man might have when he has left a dog all alone in a house somewhere and knows the dog is starving, but tells himself insistently that it's not his problem. As he steered the Ford slightly to the southeast, I thought I knew where we were going. His next remark stunned me.

"How far would you go to protect a weaker person?"

I couldn't speak. I spluttered. I wanted to formulate an answer, but first I had to probe his meaning—

"Forget it. You've got your whole life ahead of you, Richie."

This time, I had a ready answer.

"That's the sort of thing my dad tells me. I've got a future to build, I need to train for it, and all."

"Yeah, I know, it's exactly the kind of shit dads say. But it's true, man, you're lucky."

I considered this. The engine of the Ford was moaning, the desert pitch dark. The vague shapes of the terrain around us here were oddly menacing.

"I won't take that to mean that I should never bust loose and enjoy myself."

Steve laughed.

"Well, who in his right mind would?"

I studied the curving road as the sleek hood of the car swallowed yard after yard. Beyond the headlights' glare, the hills loomed all around us.

"I'd like to ask you something, Richie."

I didn't think he was waiting for my consent, but I said, "Sure."

"What's the sickest discovery you've ever heard of?"

I honestly had no idea what to say. He went on:

"I don't mean a big event, like the Holocaust, or Hiroshima. I mean, like, small-scale and personal, a discovery, a scene that a guy walked in on."

"Ah . . . I don't know, Steve. I really don't know. Finding Sharon Tate's body with her dead child inside. Does that count?"

He considered my answer, but I don't think it impressed him very much.

"Well, what about you, Steve?"

He stared at the road. I knew he had something in mind, but perhaps words were not up to the job.

Then he said: "In Australia, you know how they have these bush fires? Fires that move like cyclones, heat that can turn you to ash? This one case I heard about . . . after a fire destroyed a whole town, they went in and found big piles surrounding little piles. Adults tried to shield kids, not even necessarily their own kids, until the fires turned them all to ash. That's just totally inexplicable to almost anybody you know."

I couldn't speak. I wanted to ask him if this was what Speed Demons talked about when they weren't drag-racing or getting wasted off their asses, but thought better of it. I searched Steve's eyes for some clue as to why the image made such an impression on him. Of course, in the hills not far from us, there were dwellings not so unlike the scene of what he'd just described.

"You know, Steve, I'm the first to admit that some rich people really are assholes. But I just wish you'd look beyond—"

"No, Richie. You're totally missing the point, man."

It was pitch dark and we were all alone on this stretch of road. I did not know what to say, so I just sat there listening to the aging motor. A couple of minutes later, I heard myself ask Steve if this was the way to the Freak House.

Instead of answering me, Steve said: "There's just so much out there in the world you're too young to make sense of. I'm not, like, a fountain of knowledge and wisdom myself, but I see, what's the word, I see continuity here. I'm on my back road, you're on yours. You may get off someday. I may never."

Now when I began to open my mouth again, the Speed Demon said, "Don't—save your breath, man. Just think about it, o.k.?"

We continued on into the night. I imagined what sort of time the other guys must be having, right now. Outside the land was dark and quiet. As the minutes turned into a half hour, I heard myself say, "Steve, where the fuck are we now?"

He pulled over, stopped the car.

"Palm Springs. I took a shortcut."

I started to thank him, only to get cut off again.

"No. Save your breath. Go home and have a good sleep, Richie."

I got out. He drove off.

Over the next few days, the crowds would descend—the police, the forensics people, the morticians, and of course the reporters—as the news spread of a gruesome find at Dave Nolan's place, a.k.a. the Freak House. Dean Hayes's body was in such a state that they had to identify him using his teeth. There were others, a man and two women, whose identification was pending. The gore had a splendor to it, said someone in a white uniform as he passed in front of a camera outside. Though he did not elaborate, though a news anchor quickly took his place before the camera, I can't help thinking that everyone who watched picked up on the connotations of *splendor*. Perhaps there was a splendor, a glory, a majesty, like the brilliant fulfill-ment of someone's fondest dream. I could have been there, but I still had my life before me.

I might get off my back road, Steve Trelawny might never. I wonder if nobler words were ever spoken.

The Burning of Los Angeles

The multimillionaire bankrolling my feature film, Reid Hamilton, sent his aide Jimmy Cavanagh to visit the set one afternoon.

Of course we didn't need any intrusion. But for Jimmy, here was an unheralded honor. For an afternoon, he was in charge of assessing the potential of a director and his cast. I'm sure pride welled within Jimmy's $300 Gucci dress shirt as the limo wended its way east on Santa Monica, then headed south to a region on the fringes of Pico Rivera, an area where neither Reid nor Jimmy would normally set foot. Here was a vast weed-ridden field among clusters of dirty, rotting, white clapboard buildings and roads frequented by those craving coke or smack. In the distance to the east was the back of a supermarket. Far off to the west were the shapes of a few buildings including a crumbling church and a shuttered pre-school. When Jimmy stepped out of the limo, he saw that my people were in the middle of filming a scene for which we might have used a stunt double if it were in our budget. Jimmy got to witness a chase. A beige Ford plows up the field and a man tries to run up alongside it on its right and climb into the passenger's seat through the space where the window used to be.

Jimmy scanned the edges of the field. Besides myself, there were a few women he'd never seen before. I and a pair of assistants stood getting ready for the action.

"Chase sequence—take one!"

The car began rolling eastward across the vast field. The assistant directors murmured, exhorted, prayed. I bellowed through my loudspeaker. As the car gained speed, Jimmy saw a stuntman who looked a bit like a younger, blond Kurt Russell charge up on the car's right, at first feigning desperation in his efforts to keep pace with the vehicle, then betraying the real thing. The car swerved one way, then the other, but the pursuer seemed to anticipate what it was going to do. The stuntman, Steve Rawls, put both his hands on the sill of the shot-out window, started to leap, then lost balance, jerking, spilling forward onto his stomach as the car zoomed out of reach.

I yelled, "Cut, cut!" and got into a tense exchange with my two assistants about the staging of the chase. One of them seemed to think we needed a pro, not this guy Steve, while the other believed that we should have Steve walk up to the car and climb in, then speed up the whole thing in post-production. No, I replied. Then all they'll see is a man walking fast, not bending his legs.

We tried again, with mixed results. Steve kept pace with the car more effectively, but when he tried to hoist himself high enough to slip into the passenger's side, he hung there on the flats of his hands for a couple of surreal seconds, seemed to deliberate, decided it wasn't happening, then let go, banging his thigh hard against the side of the car, landing hard on his ass. I wondered what we were thinking when we hired this guy. On the third try, he actually managed to swing his legs over the top of the door and slide part of the way in but grew so flushed with his success that he rode there, his torso sticking out, as if he were a passenger who wanted to flip off another driver. It was all a waste of film. I began to hate Jane for hiring this incredibly dumb stuntman, Steve Rawls. I thought he'd never be more than a poor imitation of a pro.

When the cast took a break, Jimmy approached me. I thanked him lavishly for coming. I introduced him to publicist Jane Jeffrey, who had thick glasses and hair that was striking but was probably not its natural color. Then Jimmy met Steve's girl-friend Rachel Getz, who had clipped blond hair and an unaffected smile and looked utterly unpretentious in her jeans and denim jacket. Next he met cashier and amateur actress Alice Kern, a dumpy woman in early middle age. Finally he met Max Rose, a comedian who dabbled in film and resembled a young Beat.

Jimmy had questions for Jane and Max, but he hardly got a chance to speak with either, for they'd launched into animated talk.

"We need to jump right from this sequence to the bar scene," Max said.

"No. We're already way over budget for this part of the shoot."

"Actually, we're not over budget."

"You know fucking well what I mean, Max. When we finish the chase sequence, we'll be way over budget—"

"If we end it now and cut to the bar and the meeting with the cops, we're fine."

Max wanted dialogue, he wanted brainy, Woody Allen humor, he wanted allusion, metaphor, symbolism, he wanted a subtext about cops being as selfish as any cartel, but he was not persuading Jane, our publicist and media advisor. Rather than allow this quarrel to go on in front of Jimmy, I ushered them to the sidelines, away from the cameras, before beginning preparations for the next take. This time Steve did more or less what he was supposed to do. Rachel started cheering, but Jane quickly shut her up. The cameras were still rolling.

But Max was not done arguing.

"He shouldn't hit the driver, he should start arguing with the driver."

"Oh, sure. They could get into a debate over whether free will exists. Then one of them whips out a cell phone and calls a professor."

"Something like that, yes. He calls a professor and they talk about Epictetus and the role of free will at critical moments."

For all his intellectual talk, Max looked like he wanted to strangle Jane. She'd intimated before that Max might be replaceable.

"So, Max, you want to dilute all the action to the point where no one can sit through the film."

"Jane. Look at some of the action movies that have come out in the last few years, and that you want us to imitate."

"What about them?"

"Some of those films would actually work much better if they hadn't filmed them in such a hyperkinetic style—"

"I'm sorry, Max, but *The Expendables* made more in the first week of its release than you've made in your life," Jane said.

"That's quite beside the point—"

"Max, you should know that you are here out of kindness, not because of anything irreplaceable you bring to the picture," Jane said.

"But—"

"Don't argue with me."

Never before had Max held a job where he endangered his prospects by being smart and sophisticated.

"Jane, I really think—"

"Please, Max, not now!" I said.

"You can see we're trying to work, Max!" said an assistant director.

Now Jane did not look at the comedian. She stood gazing out at the set, where Rachel stood facing Steve, exchanging inaudible words. On Jane's face was an expression not unlike a smirk.

"I think the consensus is that you should shut up," someone called in Max's direction.

"Oh, fuck you all! Idiots!"

The profanity escalated. I felt something bizarre began to happen. I heaved and pouted and sighed as if at the onset of a heart attack, began to walk away from the set, toward the cluster of buildings off to the west, then stopped.

"Al, are you okay?" one of the crew called.

At first I could not answer. Then I turned around again, my black hair mussed, not with the appearance of an English-speaking USC graduate, but rather the look of a French surrealist who'd walked right off the set of *The Passion of Joan of Arc* during a critical moment in the filming.

"Al? Everything okay?" the assistant director called.

I quoted Artaud. "Perhaps now someone will distract me with a false suggestion."

I probably looked as if I might slit both my wrists, were someone kind enough to hand me a dagger. At this point, Jimmy, who was standing fifteen feet off toward the east side of the field, retreated to the limo, slid inside, and reached for a phone to call his boss.

Riding in a limo was a new experience for all of us who accompanied Reid Hamilton to the museum, with the exception of Max. Friends had hired the comedian to perform at their lavish weddings on Catalina Island or at a resort town along the coast between L.A. and San Diego, so he had had a taste of the luxuries Reid enjoyed daily. For me, Steve, Rachel, and Alice, the ride through Los Feliz down to Santa Monica Boulevard was either a harbinger of what would come when we made it big, or a dream with no purpose other than to taunt us. Soon the limo swung into the parking lot on Santa Monica where it dispensed Reid along with me and the cast. Somewhere among the crowds milling inside the new annex was Jane Jeffrey, who no doubt already had a drink in hand and was chatting up the rich collectors. Jane was in with Reid these days, to put it mildly. He was eager to discuss new ventures with her and had even lent her a key to his house in Riverside County. But it was Max who acted like Reid's cultural advisor, lending him books, from contemporary works such as Michael Tolkin's *The Player* to tomes like *Moby-Dick*.

Once inside the annex, we split up and began to wander among the men in $3,500 Gino Valentino suits, the women in elegant $1,000 MNM Couture gowns, the photographers and flacks, the tables with bottles of champagne and gleaming glasses, and the paintings representing dozens of schools and styles lining the walls. Rachel was glad she'd dissuaded Steve from wearing his windbreaker or his denim jacket. I spotted Jane, a glass of wine in hand, the grin of someone in on a joke spread across her face, but then shuffling bodies blocked my view. I tried to fight my way over to the wine. Max wandered among the crowds until he got list amid a tableau of canvases by a cut-rate Klimt who confused frenzy with technical élan. I thought that Alice wanted to follow Max, who was so bright and had so many clever things to say, but she decided he didn't want her tagging along like a fat kid in a schoolyard. There were dozens of single men here, of course. Surely Alice could see what an oddball Max was.

Rachel, who weaved through the crowds with two glasses of champagne looking for Steve, had not been in a crowd half this size since the funeral of the wealthiest man back home in Brady, Texas, years ago. She hoped and believed Steve could suppress his oafish qualities.

When Rachel tried to make her way toward the center of the room, a tide of well-dressed bodies rebuffed her, nearly making her spill the drinks. So Rachel headed toward the rear of the annex, perhaps figuring she could cut around the mass of people and spy Steve somewhere, his hands in his back pockets, gaping at one of the canvases.

Now I managed to get my hands around one of the glasses of white wine on a table lining the north wall. I wandered back toward the center of the room, hoping I might bump into Jane, but the crowds were as dense as on a pavilion outside the Oscars ceremony. I stood sipping the wine, finding it sweet and pungent for such an official function, when I noticed Andy Warhol staring at me. I reeled, meditating soup cans. Okay, maybe it wasn't Warhol, but the man's black blazer, shades, and graying hair that not long ago must have been platinum blond, inevitably drew comparisons. I wanted to stop and make his acquaintance, to say something about the derivative quality of a number of the canvases I had spied, but I pressed on through the crowds. The silence of that stranger in dark shades had something of the eloquence of a cat that knows a person has done something rotten.

Soon I reached a point near the center of the room, where I wished I had Reid Hamilton with me to lend prestige. Here a number of people had scurried away from and stood in a circle around a situation I felt powerless to defuse. I just stood there feeling queasy.

"How *dare* you insult me?" a young woman said to a thin man in a blue dress shirt, a brown blazer, and a pair of chinos.

The man moved in closer to the woman, trying to slide his arm around her waist and whisper to her, but she pushed his arm away. She was one of the young people hired to carry around trays of drinks and hors d'oeuvres, but that her tray lay face down on the floor amid chipped and broken glasses and puddles of champagne. Even as people gasped and pointed, the thin man moved in again to whisper to the girl. Reluctantly, as if it took heroic efforts not to grab a shard off the floor and stab him in the eye, the woman allowed him to escort her over to the wall, where he continued to whisper to her while fishing something out of the breast pocket of his blue Abercrombie shirt. The woman's sobs began to subside. Clutching the small of her back with his right arm, the man moved a cluster of bills toward the girl with his left hand. She saw the bills, brightened ever so faintly, reached for them. Suddenly the man jerked his hand away, as if she were a child whom he must teach a lesson about waiting her turn. She began to sob again. He moved the bills closer, jerked them away again, then taunted her a third time. Finally he gave her the bills while whispering in her left ear. She nodded, went to pick up the tray and crushed glasses. When a couple of security guards, young men with bony heads, dressed in blazers and chinos, moved up to the thin man, Reid Hamilton stepped through the crowds and had words with them. The guards walked away.

At this point, I noticed Jane Jeffrey standing next to me.

"Al Duchamp, my favorite director!"

"Hello, my favorite PR shill."

"Don't criticize Dave Ware."

"Excuse me?"

"That man over there who caused the scene. He's a friend of Reid's, and he's a happening guy."

"This isn't the first time I've seen something like this. The other night at Reid's—"

"Yes, I know, he offered the maid a lot of bills, except the bills were wrapped around his penis, and she started to take them, but then—"

"Jane! Could you come here?" called one of the collectors, who was trying to arrange a photo-op with a number of up-and-coming artists. She smiled, excused herself, and glided off.

I later heard from Rachel the following. As Rachel moved through the annex, she saw a fat bald man in a black blazer turn to follow her progress as intently as if she were naked. She tried to ignore him. Still, in her peripheral vision, she caught that guy feeling her up with his eyes, probing, storing away visual data that he could upload at a time and place of his choosing, until Rachel moved past a cluster of exquisitely dressed Angelinos holding glasses of white wine, filling the air with their chatter about newly chic neighborhoods and the gentrification in Echo Park. Rachel pressed toward the back of the room, then when she had closed about three-fourths of the distance, cut across toward the other side. She bumped right into someone, spun around to apologize, and suddenly she was face to face with Alice Kern.

"Oh, Alice, I'm so sorry."

"No worries, sweet buns."

"Do you need a drink?" Rachel asked, though she'd meant to give one of the glasses she held to Steve.

"Uh, yes, I guess I do."

Something about Alice had seemed peculiar to Rachel, all the way from Los Feliz down to the museum, but only now could Rachel define it. Alice had slapped some kind of oil on her body, primarily on her breasts. The substance was peppermint oil, and as much as you might feel disinclined to turn your head toward Alice's breasts, it was so hard not to react when you encountered that scent. Nor could anyone fail to notice the air of sadness or disappointment about Alice.

"Alice, I hope you've had a chance to get out there and mingle and meet a few people," Rachel said.

"'Been doing it my whole life," Alice said with a forced smile.

"Have you seen Steve?"

The overweight cashier shook her head.

"Uh . . . is everything okay, Alice?" Rachel asked, studying the rugged, ruddy features of the cashier-turned-actress.

"Yes . . . but could you please just stay here for a minute and talk to me?"

"Sure."

Alice began to talk about the film shoot, in such a way that Rachel knew that was the furthest thing from her mind. Then Alice started sobbing a little, pressing close against Rachel, whispering to her, pouring it all out.

"Oh no, nothing's okay. I'm thinking about Max. Max Rose. The comedian who keeps arguing with Jane about our film. I approached him earlier tonight."

Rachel must've thought, *Uh-oh.*

"'I cannot help but admire the seductive qualities of the abstract paintings,' I said when I sidled up to him."

Rachel winced at Alice's poor imitation of discernment. Alice continued.

"I know that Max is, like, really unstable, but he looks so sexy with his hair slicked back and his white jacket and black pants tight around his waist. So I said to him, You know, Max, I can only admire the *provocative, unadorned* beauty of the landscape paintings and the barrio etchings. I was trying to sound smart, Rachel! But Max shifted his eyes as if pleading for someone to rescue him. You know how his nostrils seem to recede as if beginning to inhale, then drop back as if they didn't at all like what greeted them? Max must have known that I meant *unadorned* as a synonym for *naked.*"

Rachel let out a groan.

"And I told him that my favorite painting, the one I would swoon for, is *Black Dahlia Suspect.*"

Alice's eyes registered what her brain through a sort of cognitive dissonance refused to acknowledge.

"I'd dropped all the right words, with perfect timing, but Max couldn't get far enough away from me."

"It's okay, Alice," Rachel assured the woman who was older yet so much more emotionally needy.

As for Max, he milled about, bumping into people and apologizing and receiving his share of apologies. Soon he found himself in an area of the annex devoted to framed pictures of a few of the new wave of buildings downtown, the Department of Transportation headquarters with arches like the hull of a parked spacecraft, the Art Center College of Design with its leaning blue and beige walls like an enormous elongated radar attuned to every pit and crevice of the hills and the desert, the Armenian School in East Hollywood that seemed poised to walk away on its twenty-foot pillars like a tripod from the mind of H.G. Wells. Here were pictures of a handful of Neutra buildings: the Lovell Heath House with its tasteful arrangement of white rectangles, the spacious Miller and Kaufmann Houses in Palm Springs, the elegant Tremaine House in Montecito. Then there was a canvas showing the exterior and interiors of the Jai House in the Santa Monica Mountains, where you can stand in one rectangle of framed glass surmounting all the others, where the distances in the brilliant day around you beckon and call to the recesses of your memory and imagination.

Max weaved or spun or slid through the crowds until he came shoulder to shoulder with a couple of the wealthiest collectors in the city, viewing the very painting Alice had mentioned. Contrary to what he had expected, *Black Dahlia Suspect* was an abstract painting. Max knew a little about the murder case, he remembered the line from *Sunset Boulevard* in which William Holden's friend jokingly calls him a suspect, but nothing could have prepared Max for the tall canvas with a round dark face whose features, represented by lines and circles, hung in proximity without quite meeting. The black circle appeared against a blazing yellow background, as if falling into a star. Max studied the painting, decided he had had enough, then turned to make his way back to the entrance. But now he ran smack into Steve and Rachel, who huddled together, sharing the glass of wine that Rachel had spirited from the far side of the annex.

"Max, have you seen the painting by Tod Hackett?" Steve asked.

Tod Hackett. *Tod Hackett.* That was the name of a character in a novel, not a contemporary artist. Even someone as unlettered as Steve ought to know that.

"I'm afraid I missed it."

"That one's not my favorite. I like *Black Dahlia Suspect*, but Steve here doesn't get it," Rachel put in.

"Look at the buildings in these photos! I thought people were so proud of the historical stuff in the place where they live. Not all this newfangled junk," said Steve.

"I see that *innovation* and *opportunity* and related terms are unassimilated concepts for you," Max said.

Steve grinned. Max sensed there was something Steve wanted to share but could not do so with Rachel hanging onto him.

"Should we fight our way over to the wine?" Max asked.

Steve shook his head.

"Are you sure?"

"I'm fine. Good luck, partner."

Max must have known it would be remiss, even rude, if he did not circle back to Reid or me to say thanks for bringing him to the event. But before he made much progress toward the former half of the annex, enough bodies spilled away from the canvas by "Tod Hackett" for Max to get a look. He trained his eyes. *No way,* was Max's first reaction, *oh no way did someone conceive of this and paint it and actually persuade the museum to display it here in front of all these silk suits!*

He looked away. Looked at it again.

Out of the question. No way.

But it was there.

The work, entitled *The Burning of Los Angeles*, was a meticulous realization of the painting mentioned briefly at a couple of points in Nathanael West's famous novel, the one Tod has been contemplating since moving from an elite school on the East Coast to L.A. Against the backdrop of a city in flames, West's characters, Tod Hackett, Harry and Faye Greener, Claude Estee, Homer Simpson, and Abe Kusich are running from what in another age might have gone by the term *la foule*, a mob of seething, leering, drooling faces. Scarcely any viewer who has read the novel can expect them to make it. When looking at this canvas, you could not help wondering how, when, and where life would imitate art.

Though it had been months since I had fixed up my place in the hills in anticipation of guests, I fulfilled my duties fairly well, at least to Jane Jeffrey. She stood in the living room where I had run a couple of tables together, admiring my collection of books on independent *auteurs* and film theory, and my neat desk and cabinets, pushed into a corner of the room. I refused to let her help with anything. When she pressed the point, I asked her to be ready to answer the phone should someone get lost in the hills again. No one did. First Max Rose showed up at the door, holding a bottle of merlot in a plastic bag, then Alice Kern, then Steve Rawls and Rachel Getz. Jane said she wanted the cast to get past the arguing and develop their bond through a joyful party.

Everyone sat down. I made the rounds with the bottle of malbec, filling each glass at the two tables, brought out the meatloaf and mashed potatoes, then moved to the head of the table. Before sitting, I proposed a toast to the film.

With impeccable timing, Jane spoke up.

"It's a *wonderful* opportunity for all of us."

"That seems premature," Max said.

"Come on, Max, there must be any number of films you admire that were stuck in development hell far longer than this one has been," Jane replied.

"Yes, I suppose so."

Suddenly Rachel spoke up, volunteering information she must not have known was unneeded:

"You do know that Jane here is a *New York Times* bestselling author?" she inquired, looking earnestly at Max's eyes.

Max said nothing. Alice laughed.

"Jane is, without question, a publicist and liaison of the first rank," I said.

"We're all sitting here together in this room now thanks to her," Alice reminded everyone.

Max nodded, sipped his wine, let the burden of conversation rest on others.

"To return to my point: Show me a film that millions of people around the world have seen and admired, and I'll show you one that people said would never get made, and never get noticed if it did," Jane added, with a knowing, playful gleam discernible behind her glasses.

"Absolutely," Alice concurred.

"You all know Tarantino used to be a clerk in a video store, with a few ideas kicking around and not much else to his name," Rachel added.

"I can see you've read *People* magazine," Max said.

Whether he was earnest, or was teasing Rachel a little, I couldn't guess.

The meatloaf made the rounds again. Max barely touched his food, but Steve and Alice were stuffing their faces. Not until he had put away a second helping, and started on a third, did Steve finally speak up.

"So tell me, Max. Suppose for a minute that you had a little more creative leeway here."

I wanted to kick Steve under the table, but he wasn't sitting anywhere near. Jane pleaded with her eyes. But Steve wasn't looking at her.

"Okay."

"In what direction would you take it? What would it be like creatively? I guess what I really want to know is, What directors and films would you want to emanate?"

"*Emanate?*"

"He means 'emulate,'" Rachel said.

Max sipped his merlot, considered the question, took another sip. Then he said:

"I really don't think it's a sin to include a strong social message. This film can't be *Bowling for Columbine*, but it doesn't have to be totally brainless either."

Steve scoffed at this answer, not under his breath, but out loud. Max made eye contact with him.

"Is something funny?"

Steve paused, as if remembering his manners. Maybe someone *had* kicked him under the table.

"I'm sorry, Max. You talk about *Bowling for Columbine* like it *is* something to emulate. I happen to believe that Mr. Moore's film seriously misrepresents the social reality, is all," Steve said.

"What do you mean?"

Steve spoke in a calm, measured voice.

"I know that nobody in this room would ever expect me to say this, but I find him rather crude."

For a moment, we stared at our plates.

Max said: "How so, Steve?"

"Moore argues that the fear of crime feeds a craze for guns. The media exaggerate crime to make us ignore other issues. We—"

"Yes, I'm familiar with the argument," Max said.

"Do you remember the scene in the documentary where they're walking around South Central and they stop at the corner of Florence and Normandie?"

"Yes."

"And they say, 'Look, we're here, and nothing's happening to us. It's all a lot of hysteria and myth that says a pair of whites would get assaulted here.'"

"Yes, I recall that scene."

"Oh, you do?"

"Get to the point, please."

"Well, to my mind they didn't prove a damn thing. Yes, you can go there, in broad daylight, accompanied by a camera crew, and you might not be assaulted. That doesn't mean that what people say about the area being so dangerous is wrong."

"It doesn't?"

"I wonder if Michael Moore would go there by himself, late at night."

"I never knew you had such a considered opinion about this, Steve," Max said, a look of utter contempt.

"Well I do."

"Or about *anything*, for that matter."

"Then there are those short comedy videos of yours, Max," Steve went on.

I thought, *How in the hell did we get into this?*

"Yes? What about them?"

Max looked at Steve expectantly.

"That one you made about fighting the bigots—"

I stared at my hands. Jane continued to plead in vain with her eyes.

"Yes?" Max asked.

"Frankly, I don't think you understand the social reality, either. Minorities get shot and stabbed to death every day in this city, and not one in a thousand of these murders involves the Klan—"

"Steve!" I spoke up now. Rachel looked ready to beg Steve to cut it out.

"Steve, can we please talk about *our* project?" Jane said.

But Steve went on:

"The crimes that happen are gang-related, or drug-related, or two people start arguing at a party and one of them pulls a gun and shoots the other."

"*Steve, would you shut up!*" I cried.

"So why, unless you are totally cut off from reality, would you make a video calling for an end to the bigots, and not for an end to the Crips, or the Bloods, or one of these other violent gangs?" Steve said.

Max's face was red. Alice stared. Rachel's hand rested on Steve's right arm, but she was silent.

"I didn't come here to argue with you, you—you—bumpkin!" Max hissed.

"Steve, get out of my house!"

Without another word, Steve rose and left. As he did so, Rachel leaned and whispered something to him. I gathered that she wanted him to stay, or at least not to go far, but I felt so relieved to be rid of that amateur whose art would never rise above poor imitation. I could not fathom how he had ever gotten an invitation.

I eased back into my chair, panting, my face the color of ripe radish. Jane put her face in her hands. Alice looked on the verge of tears. Rachel touched Alice's shoulder gently. For a while, no one spoke.

"Uh, Max, it was Jane's idea to invite—"

"Oh, *please*. You could at least face up to it!"

I looked at my hands again.

Now it was Rachel who spoke up.

"Ah, everyone. I think there's some wine left. And I know for a fact that Alice here brought some Boston creme pie for all of us."

Rachel reached down into Alice's handbag, felt around, brought out the cardboard box. Jane leapt up, served the pie on paper plates, and before long a bit of geniality crept back. But as the others feasted on pie, swilled coffee, or drank up the remainder of the wine, Max kept turning his gaze to Jane with a curious look she had never seen before. Clearly he was making Rachel and Alice nervous again.

"I thought it was a nice idea, inviting us out here," Jane said.

"Oh, a very nice idea."

"I think we've had more than our share of setbacks. I think if it's at all possible, Steve should continue to work on the film," Jane replied.

"I don't necessarily disagree."

"You don't?"

Max spoke up.

"Here's the thing, Jane. Steve raised a matter that frankly I haven't been able to stop thinking about since you came on board. It's about the creative direction of the film."

Jane froze.

Max continued:

"You know what? I want to back up here for just a minute and say a few things. Then maybe you'll have an idea of where I'm coming from here. What do you say, Jane?"

Jane leaned back in her chair.

"Just for the record, I happen to think that Renee Zellweger is a fine actress."

"Er . . . I've never said otherwise, Max."

"Don't tell me you haven't ever made fun of her. I've visited that blog of yours. Once was quite enough, thank you."

"If no one makes fun of you, you're not a celebrity."

"That's funny, Jane. I thought you were going to say you were just joking. As in, you know, 'I said this cruel and hurtful thing but I'm not responsible for it because I was joking.'"

"What's so wrong with ridiculing pretensions? You do it yourself."

"I like to read, rather than watch TV, and I don't consider myself a 'pretentious fuck.' I would think that kind of language is better reserved for a more serious order of offense than being intelligent and liking books."

"It's all in a humorous spirit, Max."

"'It's all in a humorous spirit, Max,'" he mimicked. In his eyes was an unsettling glow like the fire at a marauders' encampment outside a lightly defended colonial citadel.

He continued:

"Well, let me tell you something, Jane. You are loud, crude, vulgar, obnoxious, rude, offensive, and nasty. You are never funny. Your sense of humor is a shade different from mine. For example: you seem to think that it's uproariously funny when you say 'fuck' or suggest that a prospective employee would have to pull something out of her rear."

Jane couldn't speak. Max leered at her.

"It's not funny just because I didn't expect you to say it! Do you understand that, you stupid, debased bitch?"

Jane's eyes darted to either side of Max, as if she wanted someone to save her. She needed the equivalent of a rape whistle right now.

"You know what else? I've actually taken a look at the books that have your name on them. You're not the author. You're not even the co-author except by a generous definition of the term. A couple of authors were too lazy to finish the book, so they got you to do ten minutes of online 'research' in return for a check and a credit as 'co-author,'" Max said.

Jane was ready to call me or somebody to come and rescue her. If she had a rape whistle on her, she'd blow it, loud and shrill, bringing out all the neighbors in a four-block radius. Yet Max went on:

"These two guys who wrote one of the dating manuals got you to contribute a few paragraphs—on how to get out of a bad date and stuff like that. The book reached maybe number eighteen on the bestseller lists for a week or two. Just based on that, your title, in every single byline, every single credit, everywhere your name appears from now till you die, is '*New York Times* bestselling author'!"

"But Max, the book was on the bestseller list!" Jane cried.

"Jane! Oh, Jane. What book is not a bestseller, if you look at the data a certain way?"

"Max . . . please just calm down for a minute."

"You come on to men because you're in need of an instant husband, or maybe an instant dad. Well once again, I understand concepts like love and commitment a little differently," Max said, spittle flying from his mouth.

"Okay Max—okay. I don't think both of us will continue our association with this project."

He pretended to reel.

"Jane, why don't you go home and burn your stupid fucking script?"

"And what else should I burn?"

"All of the books you claim to have authored."

"Are you obsessed with burning things, Max?"

"It's better than total inertia. Nathanael West understood that just as well as Walter Pater."

I said, "Max. That's not at all what Pater—"

Max reached behind his back with his left hand, pulled up the flap of his shirt, and with his right hand withdrew a big Sig Sauer pistol from the band of his pants. He waved the gleaming silver barrel at Jane, Alice, Rachel, and me. Alice cried out. Rachel burst into sobs. Jane looked at me, her mouth a dark oval, and back at the gun. My interest in the development was almost detached. I had had no idea how much he loathed us.

"Okay, now we're going to be democratic about this. None of you deserve to live, but I have to admit I'm slightly curious."

We were listening.

"Better that the city should burn than saunter on without any passion or gamble. I do believe all of that. But on a micro level, I'm curious as to what choices you'll make."

He looked at Rachel.

"Which of you should I kill?"

She sobbed.

"Come on. Tell me or you all die," Max said.

Though her sobbing did not ease, she got the words out.

"Shoot me."

Max grinned. "I'll take it into consideration."

He pointed the weapon at Alice. She too was crying.

"Well, I hate to say this, Max, but Rachel has offered herself. It's her choice."

Max laughed. "The vote's leaning one way already."

He pointed the gun at Jane. She deliberated, but dared not tempt him.

"That man there. Al Duchamp. The B-movie director who thinks he's fucking Artaud! He's failed to offer any kind of guidance and vision. That's why the shoot is such a mess. He's brought things to this point, Max!"

Max gave me an eager probing look. Maybe he did not dismiss what Jane said. Now Jane was shrieking.

"*Shoot him, Max! Take his head off!*"

"No, Max, shoot me," Rachel said in her gentle voice.

"SHUT UP! SHOOT HIM IN THE FACE, MAX!"

"I thought we were so very democratic around here," I said.

"COME ON, SHOOT HIM! HE WANTS A THEATER OF CRUELTY, LET HIM HAVE IT!" Jane screamed.

"Please, Max," said Rachel.

"KILL HIM!"

"And how do you vote, Al?" Max said.

"I say, put the pistol in your mouth."

He grinned and aligned the barrel with my forehead.

The door flew open so hard its knob entered the plaster wall. Steve rushed in. Before Max could turn his right arm around toward the front of the bungalow, the stuntman got his hands onto two points on the arm. We heard the crunch of bone breaking, nearly simultaneous with Max's scream and the thud of the pistol hitting the floor. I thanked every deity whose name I knew that the bungalow was so fucking small. Steve kicked Max's prone body repeatedly in the head and face, until his shoe was invisible beneath blood and garb. Then, straightening out and catching his breath, the stuntman looked over at me inquiringly.

The Enemies of Order

When Reid Hamilton first set foot in the occult bookshop, at the base of beige-red cliffs partly covered by bush and shrub, books on the shelves and dark things in jars and bottles piqued his curiosity. The books had strange titles but the allure really came from authors' names: Aleister Crowley, Helena Blavatsky, Israel Regardie, Rudolph Steiner, Colin Wilson. Reid was unready to spend his money on these obscure books, much less on graveyard dirt packed into a jar, but he empathized with a small business that locals had tried to close down. He wondered what beliefs could be more outré than the thoughts and impulses that drove people to kill strangers over a look on the streets of this city.

Reid resolved to give up his amateur interest in the occult and be a serious patron of the arts. Close to noon on a blazing Thursday, his limo pulled into the parking lot of the hippest modern art museum in Southern California. Reid and his aide, Jimmy Cavanagh, got out and walked through the concrete pavilion to the lobby, where Gerald Baxter, a director of fundraising and investor relations, came out to shake their hands. Gerald ushered them into the cool and sterile hall, where a redhead sat at a piano, playing a lovely rendition of "It's Crazy But It's True." Reid found himself wanting to stop, to listen, to study this girl, whom he was already beginning to imagine in other contexts. But he and Jimmy followed Gerald to the section devoted to California art, where Elaine Bauman joined them. After spending years cultivating galleries in Tribeca, Elaine was now the owner of one near MacArthur Park. Although past fifty, she was the life of the parties at her gallery, bumping and grinding with young guests.

Elaine led the men on a tour of the contemporary pavilion, where they took in an array of canvases by artists whose work sold fast at galleries. These canvases featured cityscapes or coastlines glowing with an eerie incandescence from countless lights in the style of artists like Peter Alexander or Carlos Almaraz, or semi-surreal imitations of Hockney's coastal watercolors, or blue within blue or blue on green. The artists on display here preferred bright colors to the ghostly evocations of Goya and Daumier alluded to in Nathanael West's 1939 novel, *The Day of the Locust.*

Reid thought: *I was wrong. I'm wasting my time. The maker and master of all existence doesn't lie here, but out in the desert among the crags and crevices and rocks.*

Jimmy could not fathom why a lady from New York was leading a tour of this part of the museum. Elaine clarified the matter by outlining plans similar to those she had helped execute for the expansion of two of New York's top museums. She was here to explain the aesthetic and logistical aspects of the venture, and Gerald to discuss costs with Reid. Gerald held up an *L.A. Times* article trumpeting the growth and potential of the art scene, with blurbs from dealers and exhibitors about how the scene on this coast would eclipse the more famous one. But Reid's mind was wandering. That girl, that redhead, her eyes, her lips! Reid caved to the urge to turn matters over to Jimmy and go back to the steel ring enclosing the fountain and the piano. He introduced himself to the redhead, whose name was Christine. He'd planned to visit a film set today, but never mind.

Two nights later Reid stared into Christine's clear brown eyes. They sat in the dim back room of a wine bar on Franklin, the kind of tony place where the bartender tells you, the moment you sit down, that you just missed Clooney or DiCaprio or someone. You are likely to spot kids who perform at the Upright Citizens Brigade or other venues in the area, or a writer for late-night comedy chilling out with a martini. Though Christine had dated guys who lived in Los Feliz, no one had ever taken her here before. Reid had done so under a pretense that he found Christine gifted and they had opportunities to discuss, but Christine was no naïf. She returned his gaze guardedly. When Reid asked if she had a boyfriend, she tried to laugh off the question, but knew she wore her tensions on her sleeve.

"Please don't ask me invasive personal questions."

He wanted to know all about her, what her parents did, the name of her first dog, where she'd lived and gone to school. Christine had grown up mostly in Placentia, she told him. Her parents were nobody special. What avocations did she have besides piano playing, Reid asked.

Now came the explosion.

"Why all these questions you barely give me time to answer? Am I a fucking playmate? 'My dislikes: standing in line, selfishness, dirty fingernails, people who think money is everything.' You're insulting me, Reid!"

Heads turned in the dim light. Reid begged her with his eyes to calm down.

"Christine, I apologize. I didn't mean to bombard you."

A waiter in a white blazer with a rose in his breast pocket stealthily made the rounds. When one of the patrons held forth about something, the man listened, with astonishing forbearance, and went off to correct what was wrong.

Reid realized how far he'd strayed.

"I have a lucrative opportunity to tell you about—one that does involve some evening hours."

"All you have to do is describe it and I'll tell you if I'm interested or not. How's that?" Christine answered, knowing that Reid Hamilton wasn't used to anyone speaking to him as she had this afternoon, relishing the chance to do so.

He outlined the gig he had in mind. Christine would play the piano at his house in the Hollywood Hills three or four days a week. She said she would ponder it. Christine wanted to know what brought Reid down to the museum that day. When he told her that the museum might open a new annex and wanted Reid on board as a sponsor, she brightened.

"Oh, I don't know. It'll be nice if they go ahead with it. But their usual approach is to form a committee to draft a proposal to consider a plan to explore a possibility—"

"It's news to me, I only work there," Christine said, laughing.

"If you come to work for me, your life will change. You may have the chance to meet and interact with a few of my business associates. I'm sure you'll love them."

"Really? What are they like?"

"Oh, colorful, funny, passionate."

"Those sound awfully like euphemisms to me."

"What are you, some kind of socialist?"

"I'm not a socialist, but I'm not an Ayn Rand follower either."

Around them in the wine bar, people were settling into the sort of easy familiarity well beyond the province of a first or second date. He envied them. Christine said:

"Look, I know this is a little direct—"

She paused. His eyes neither encouraged nor discouraged her.

"—but when a man like you occasionally does something nice for the city, I have to wonder why you're limiting the scope of your philanthropy."

"That's an excellent question. Do you remember the riots, Christine? No, you were a small kid nowhere near the eye of the storm."

She wanted to clarify, to correct, but he pre-empted her again.

"Well, I happened to own a lot of property that burned down in those three days, Christine. I had buildings and stores on Sunset and on Santa Monica from La Brea to Vermont Avenue. I think you can guess why I've been a little sore at the city since then."

Christine nodded. The waiter appeared at their table, pouring some more Prosecco with exquisite poise.

"The cops didn't protect what was yours."

"Not only that, but they arrested one of the store owners who shot a rioter. They didn't quite have all their priorities straight, to my mind."

It wasn't every day that millionaire investors justified themselves to kids who waited tables and could barely make rent.

"You know, 'the city' isn't responsible for what happened to your property. Not everyone who lives here should have to pay for the mistake of one police official."

"That's one way to look at it."

"Do you really know or care anything about art, or is your involvement in this thing a p.r. stunt, like when a tobacco company sets up a minority scholarship fund?"

Reid almost blew his Prosecco on Christine's lovely white blouse. He leaned forward until their noses were inches apart above the candle on the tastefully designed table, and said without a trace of uncertainty:

"Honey, was Picasso Spanish?"

Three days later came awful news. Reid languished in a deck chair by the pool of his house at the eastern end of the valley, admiring the sleek contours of the building crafted by a disciple of the great Richard Neutra, reflecting on his failed marriage to a ravishing woman named Sarah. He looked out over the valley, at the mountains and cacti and ocotillo plants with their crazily twisting stalks. Dust plumed up behind a car just barely visible on the horizon. He almost hoped it might be a drifter who'd break in, kill him, and torch the house for good measure. But recognizing the limo, Reid braced for Jimmy's nasal voice. Soon Jimmy got out of the vehicle and strolled up the stone path, through the long rooms, and out to the pool to face his boss.

Everything came out now. They were going to nail him to the wall over Dave Ware, the short, insecure man who had weaseled his way into Reid's good graces by offering to steer the top investors of two of the largest pension funds in the country to Reid's hedge fund. Dave had begun to engage in such "placement" quietly yet with glee at what he could pull off and the leverage it gave him. Then a kid at one of the pensions read an email on Dave's screen when Dave was busy and began talking to the SEC and the D.A.'s office.

Reid's eyes, normally alive with a restless longing, were inscrutable behind his dark shades and Jimmy stood there watching, two men near the base of majestic mountains in the silence of an infinite valley.

"Thank you. You can go, Jimmy."

Reid thought all the way back to when he was a skinny kid spending at year at one of the tough high schools in the valley, before he was able to transfer to an elite academy. He sat in diners in Polo shirts and glasses sipping ice cream sodas, as the mechanics' and truck drivers' sons, unshaven guys in leather jackets who liked to drag-race their souped-up hot rods on dis-used back roads, came in and sat down and grinned at him. He thought of computer camp, where he always had a table to himself at lunch. He thought back to when he had earned his MBA. That was way back during the Reagan era, morning in America, morning for a generation of money managers bent on fostering pools of private capital.

Reid had this classmate, Victor Tsui, who was living proof that being smart and being an intellectual are not even distant relatives. He had no interest at all in books unless they had practical utility. He spoke English, his third language, fluently enough, but his writing was unselfconsciously riddled with errors. At first Reid had no idea why he felt a tinge of unease around Victor. Later he decided it was because on some level, he clung to a notion that people living in an adopted home-land should be polite around those whose ancestors were here for generations. Abrasive and immature, Victor was eager to discuss classes, professors, theories. or tools of financial analysis, but often made fun of Reid's lack of a girlfriend. For his part, Victor always seemed to have a smiling Asian girl clinging to him. They saw each other nearly on a daily basis over the years at classes, talks, and parties around and off the campus. On occasion, Victor asked Reid to edit a misspelled resume or a letter.

Victor used spoofing and mark-to-marketing and other illegal tricks of the trade to parlay his funds into a fortune, learned about commercial real estate, became a landlord with six rental properties to his name. He brought Reid along with him once when the time came to serve notice to a delinquent tenant in Van Nuys. It was a young stoner named Andrew with long blond hair and a pin on his black trench coat: "Normal People Make Good Pets." Though Victor had no evidence, he'd long suspected Andrew of selling pot to kids from a high school up the street.

Andrew wanted to know whom Victor would put in his place when he left. The pouches under Andrew's eyes were either from not having slept in days, or clinical depression.

"Andrew! You're not listening to me. At this point, I don't give a flying fuck who replaces you as long as it's someone who is working, responsible, reliable."

"I'm going to have the money—"

"And when's that going to be, Andrew?"

"I don't know exactly, the student loan check is going to come—"

"You're not a student, Andrew. You're a fucking parasite."

"But the check—"

"Andrew. I want three hundred and fifty dollars, or I go to the sheriff."

So it went with those who ran afoul of Victor. The guy was hell-bent on being rich by age thirty. After graduation, Reid and Victor stayed in touch over the years, getting together for a beer or to watch CNN Financial Network. Reid recalled a day in February 1997 when he and Victor were getting wasted together in a bar on Santa Monica. News helicopters had caught something incredible. They swilled beer, gazed up at the screen where a man clad from his neck to his ankles in body armor made from threads of woven aramid shuffled down a back street in North Hollywood, weary after firing thousands of rounds and getting hit multiple times, squeezed off a few more bullets at the police, dropped his Beretta when a round grazed his hand, then stooped to pick up the gun. It was briefly unclear what the bandit was doing. Then the man on the screen slid the barrel of the gun under his chin and paused. Reid and Victor saw a wisp of smoke marking a bullet's exit from the back of the man's head before he folded and fell in a heap as yet another round from the cops across the street cut through his spine.

"Now there's someone who *really* wanted to make it rich by thirty," Victor said.

"Hah! That's a High Incident Bandit, Victor. And he's got himself a new ventilation system. Watch, the camera's still rolling," Reid said. With fascination, they joined millions of others in following several more minutes of footage, taken from a news copter, showing the second bandit as he tried to navigate his way out of the maze of streets around the bank, only to engage in a shootout with a trio of cops. The second bandit, the big guy, Matasereanu, kneeled behind a getaway car beside a pickup whose owner had fled with the keys when Matasereanu drove up. He fired his AR-15 wildly at the cops using their squad car for cover, until one of the lawmen shot beneath the vehicles and shredded the bandit's feet. Victor wondered aloud why the bandit hadn't stepped out in front of the pickup and fired at the windshield of the approaching squad car. At the time, neither Reid nor Victor could have known anything at all about that second robber, who was born in Romania in 1966 and bled to death on the sunny streets of North Hollywood that day in February 1997. Matasereanu's parents were a bit like Victor's, having fled life under a regime of a dictator whose grip held millions of people in a static state.

Reid would have liked to stay friends with Victor over the years, but it wasn't easy. Victor fired employees, hurt people, broke off relationships like tossing out empty cartons. "Reid, do you consider yourself a loser?" Victor asked on one occasion. It was a rather general question, but no doubt alluded to the maddeningly slow, incremental growth of Reid's hedge fund, to the fact that Reid lived in fear of investor lawsuits and owed most of his wealth to an inheritance.

Suppose Reid made an effort to get to know Victor as a man, to grasp what informed Victor's success? But the closest he ever came to such knowledge was in dreams. In one dream, Reid was strolling late at night on a suburban street lined with palms trees, somewhere in Van Nuys, or it might have been Inglewood, trying to find Victor's house. He came to a house that didn't have "high-end real estate" written all over it, in fact it was a rather plain two-story white house, yet he sensed that this was it.

Reid walked right up and opened the door. Inside was a dark room illuminated by burning lamps where a fat bare-chested Asian man sat facing the entrance. He didn't look much like Buddha but his height and muscle mass made him a giant and he would have been frightening if not for a bit of flab around the cheeks, like baby fat. Around him in the dark, small skinny men with beads of sweat dripping down their faces scurried and pleaded and catered to his wishes. Reid stepped inside. The big man looked at him and laughed and said Reid should know it was unprofessional not to wear a watch, and from the depths of the room, the dark corners, there came jeers and laughter from all the supplicants and attendants, as if *that* could explain the arc of Reid Hamilton's career.

Reid thought it a blessed thing that he hadn't spoken to Victor in months. He thought of someone else with whom he'd broken off contact. Sarah Hamilton, *née* Collingwood, used to come home from cocktail parties at $10 million homes in Palm Springs to find him slumped in the long room at the house's center, legs crossed, with a mixed drink. In this room, nothing was simply what it was. The extrapolations implied by a book, a nightstand, a typewriter, a trowel from outside propped in the corner, Reid's discarded shoes lying on the pristine floor, were maddeningly insistent. But when Reid sat here, he was like a man paralyzed from the neck down. His body's sagging, wasting appearance comported oddly with his resolutely mannered, polite demeanor. Sarah came through the front door, saw him, cried, "Reid, would you go sit out by the pool so I don't have to look at you?"

His head rotated toward her, his eyes made a vain plea.

"I wish you wouldn't say that, it's very hurtful."

"Go, Reid, get out. *So I don't have to look at you!*"

The memories seared. He got up, strode out of the empty courtyard into the house, went to the kitchen, reached for the forbidden stuff he had stocked up on since the divorce. Bourbon in hand, he went to the living room and for a moment had the bracing sensation of being twenty-one and unattached once again. He felt he must call someone. He could call Christine, explain that all other things being equal, he was a genuine philanthropist, except she knew that was crap. *Oh Christine, oh undeflowered youth of my middle-aged fantasy.*

Out there somewhere in the vastness of L.A., out there in the night, was a young man whom Christine probably had in mind when she mouthed the words to accompany her piano playing at the museum: *"It's crazy but it's true / I only want to be with you."*

Reid downed the bourbon, set the glass on the nightstand at the room's eastern end, and walked over to a side room, where he racked his memory for the combination that would open a trunk. Inside it was a loaded Browning Hi-Power pistol with a smooth oak grip. Though he struggled, he could not recall the combination. 21-34-something. Well, he guessed he was going to be around just a bit longer. He slammed the lock against the hull of the trunk, listening to the sharp sound reverberate in the vastness of the house. He shuffled off to find more bourbon, drank a fourth glass, a fifth, a sixth. Again he tried and failed to recall the combo that would free the gun.

Reid's director friend, Al Duchamp, did not want to come over. Jimmy had already broken the news that no more financial support for Al's projects was in the pipe. What was Reid to him now? Reid thought the bond between them transcended such factors but realized that was not a type of reasoning Victor Tsui would ever use. Reid slammed the receiver, buried his face in his hands, then sauntered off toward the room with the trunk once again. Maybe he could rip that lock off with his teeth. *21-34-?* He thought of how the Browning would feel in his hands, against his temple. But there was more bourbon, and if he didn't drink it—no, fuck that, what he really wanted was to caress the smooth oak barrel of that pistol, smell it, feel it, taste it, suck on it. *21-34-come on, for fuck's sake!*

Two nights later he was back at his other house, in the Hollywood Hills. Christine's head edged closer to Reid's and her legs shifted slightly on the plush couch across from the plasma screen where a reporter was talking to a camera outside City Hall. The middle third of the window spanning the western edge of the room was open and a breeze came, tepid then stronger, an invitation to come outside and explore the steep slopes and the unsuspected depths of the dense bush. Reid felt a special type of fear and decided he needed to conquer it right now, in order to bolster his confidence in the presence of the young lady he'd heard playing the piano in the museum not so long ago.

He got up and went to the window and looked out, at dark within dark, at branches spreading like the fingers of a lunatic in a pose of supplication, at vines that crept and slid and coiled and turned back on themselves in defiance of any external concept of order or utility, and he listened. The wind grew fainter, as if ceding the floor to another voice, one that must come any moment now. He stood there until he thought Christine must be starting to wonder, then went back to the couch and put his arm around her. She welcomed this.

Now he knew his sense about the wind had been right. The news program presented a couple of law firm partners weighing in on the scandal embroiling Reid's hedge fund, and then the camera alighted on Scott Dwyer, the most aggressive U.S. Attorney for the District of Southern California in living memory. Dwyer looked at the camera with such intensity you might have thought he could see Reid Hamilton here in this living room of a house in the Hollywood Hills and the sight fueled a Biblical fury.

"You think your twelve-hundred-an-hour lawyers can get you out of this, Reid Hamilton, and then you can go on bilking retirees out of their savings. That might have been true in the nineteen-nineties. Look around, mister. We have zero tolerance for this kind of malfeasance and you will answer to the people of California."

Christine turned her face to his, with a look of concern tempered by curiosity, as the news program shifted to the trial of the two UCLA athletes who'd beaten parolee Jermaine Wilson nearly to death after Wilson's attempted carjacking.

He liked chatting with the clerk in the occult bookshop, who was knowledgeable about every single thing in the place. Coming here wasn't like visiting the Barnes & Noble over in Glendale where a young clerk had thought James Joyce was the title of a book by Stephen Hero.

Today a strange feeling eclipsed his curiosity about the books with all the intriguing names. It wasn't the graveyard dirt in a transparent jar or the photos of rituals involving hooded gurus and naked women or the sign with a pointed message. ("If you are bigoted racially, ethnically, sexually, or religiously, FUCK OFF!") No, it was another item, hanging from a rack at the rear of the store, easy enough to miss. The orb was four inches in diameter and its smooth ochre surface glinted intelligently in the light from the red-shaded bulb above. When the young clerk saw him gazing at it, in the grip of a strange unclassifiable power, she slid up alongside him.

"Not the kind of thing you usually pay money for," she said.

"Why are you selling it?"

"It's got to be out in the world serving some kind of purpose. If we kept it indefinitely we'd get in a bit of trouble with certain parties."

He chuckled.

"Certain parties. Gosh, I'm not even really sure what I'm looking for."

"Why'd you come in?"

"I couldn't stay outside. Have you seen what those hills look like in this glare? We have to make a stand in a hostile and terrifying world. But my immediate response was to step in here."

"Yeah, I know. And I saw a baby with two heads in a stroller over on Hollywood Boulevard. They say go home and lock your door when you see stuff like this. But you came in here."

"Never mind. Tell me about this item, please."

"It's a portal of sorts. They found it among the personal effects of one of the High Incident Bandits."

He thought back to that violent day in February 1997.

"You think I'm stupid."

"I know your kind well enough. Okay, it's a piece of junk some wino came in here and pawned."

He laughed. "So what happens if you touch it?"

"You have to deliver a certain invocation. If you do it right, you'll achieve unity with a person who did the same at some point in the past."

"I'd like it—what's your name?"

"Samantha."

"Do you happen to know anyone who seeks the kind of unity I have in mind?"

"Possibly."

She explained the invocation to him quietly and patiently, and then talked about herself for a bit. As he walked out of the shop, into the glare, it struck him that a place good respectable folk had tried to close down was the only refuge he could have hoped to find.

He'd learned a lot about the shop's young employee.

At this time of life, Samantha did not indulge in her own dreams of stardom, but one of the perks of working on a film set was that they let her enter and sit in a trailer during breaks. The trailer sat at the edge of a canyon that lit up brilliantly every evening, countless bulbs illuminating the shacks, apartments, trailers, bungalows, and lofts where the complex experience of transplants from all over America had inspired innumerable dreams. There Samantha sat on a vinyl excuse for a couch, a cigarette or a joint in hand, cursing the director who made her get up at 6:00 a.m. every day and come to the set and hang around for hours and then leave because somebody in the props department fucked up and they couldn't shoot the scene. The shoot was killing her. She wouldn't give up the shoot for anything on this earth.

Boyd walked through the door of the trailer and sat down across from Samantha and an assistant director. Boyd had a fury in his eyes. He stared at Samantha, asked questions about her hours and pay, something in those eyes registering that everything was all out of proportion, that they were using Samantha, the starry-eyed girl with black hair and an olive complexion, in a manner that would have sent nineteenth-century robber barons into throes of self-disgust.

"You're kidding yourself with this stuff," Boyd said with a look around the room and, by implication, at the subculture outside. If Boyd thought he was right, he said what he thought. Now he got up to go, leaving Samantha wide-eyed and speechless. Samantha turned to the AD with a pleading look. *He's so young and hotheaded, please forget this happened.* The AD, who couldn't afford to be choosy about her friends, took it all in stride.

To the extent that it is possible to have memories of somebody at second hand, Samantha found herself having them about Boyd. His name probably wasn't Boyd. That was reputedly one of a number of *noms de guerre* used by this angry youth who had passed in and out of her life, noticing her to a lesser degree than she did him. Perhaps memories is the wrong word, maybe they were only imaginings, extrapolations such as you might engage in about a stranger based on bits of overheard talk. Call them what you will but some images are hard to banish. Here is Boyd, gazing through the window of a white Sedan as he passes through the hills of North Hollywood, between rows of nice but not fancy one- and two-level white stucco homes and narrow sidewalks set apart from the street by gently sloping tufts of grass so uniform in height and thickness it is like Astroturf.

How often she'd heard him say, *You're kidding yourself with all this. This isn't a real gig. This is nothing.*

This is nothing.

Here is Boyd, turning left onto a wider street where the palms are not quite so far apart, where the houses begin to have an atmosphere of contrived ornateness like dyed gingerbread on a 50th anniversary cake. He drives further north on a road that can seemingly carry him right off the end of the earth if he pursues it far enough.

You're kidding yourself. Just forget it. Either get real about what you're doing or get real about you and me.

Here is Boyd, wending through the tree-lined streets until he comes to a dead end that meets in an upside-down T with the street he is on, pulling in behind a parked Porsche, killing the engine, sitting there in the dusk where he can hear a cat mewling to be let inside four blocks away. At the corner where the dead end meets the street stands a mansion with walls the color of congealed buttermilk and a balcony half the size of a tennis court looking out over the dead end, the stately houses beyond. Nothing moves in the dimming air. Boyd rolls down his window and breathes in the scent of the acacia leaves drifting on the faintest of breezes during this hour when the Mexicans who mowed the lawn have packed up and left but the rich kids aren't yet ready to climb into their Ferraris and Porsches and Lamborghinis and head to the bars and clubs and theaters down on Santa Monica and Wilshire, and it is as still as anywhere on earth.

You're kidding yourself. Get real about your life, or get real about us.

Amid the monotony of sprinklers, the green pulls hard at his eyes.

Now the door joining the balcony to the second floor of the mansion opens. Out strolls a woman in a white dress whose neckline curves in a demi-oval just above her breasts and a pair of brown leather high-heeled slippers. There follows a man maybe five years her senior, in a dark suit over a dress shirt the color of margarine and a pair of loafers. He may be a partner at a law firm or the co-head of a brokerage house. As they move in the dusk, sitting at the table in the center of the balcony and setting down their wine glasses and taking in the sights and sounds of this hour, Boyd thinks he hears the woman say something about the texture of the wine, about how this is the place to enjoy it, remarks that bring a chuckle from the man, who says in a faux-wino tone, "Thish' is the life, honey," making the woman titter. Not a sound comes from the surrounding yards. Boyd doesn't think anyone will notice him sitting there by the curb, but knows he'll look more than a little curious if someone does. D.A. Scott Dwyer has come down hard on Boyd in the past for a real-estate scam.

Fine, then, go on with your acting gig. Maybe in a couple of years, you just might be able to afford a trip to Tijuana.

Fuck you, Boyd, just fuck you. Get fucking lost before I call security.

The grand double doors facing the curb open. Two teens come outside in the deepening blue. Boyd twists the strip of metal in the ignition.

The verdict in the athletes' trial came down at 1:12 p.m. on a sunny Thursday. The riots began immediately. For once, drivers throughout the city felt grateful for the lack of movement on the roads, not wanting to enter or even pass by certain areas. As they sat in their motionless metal frames, they took in the distant edge of expanding catastrophe, plumes of smoke rising into the cobalt blue, flames consuming buildings coated with gas, sirens like the shrill cries of paralyzed sentinels, news helicopters hovering over the flashpoints, low but not too low. Cries, screams, bursts of terrified chatter came from all around.

The streets outside City Hall were near the epicenter of the riots, but Scott Dwyer, in his desperation to get home to his family, did not weigh different routes and modes of transport. He ordered the driver of his limo to cut right through the streets toward Holmby Hills. The driver raised concerns. Dwyer threatened to have him fired. The limo advanced several blocks into a montage of sights. Babies screamed in strollers racing up the pavement. A woman sat on the curb, her face in her hands, weeping. People fled every which way and cops ran from rather than toward the danger amid cries, curses, flames, explosions, and the noxious, ascending smoke.

The limo advanced through the streets past terrified citizens with torn clothes and blackened skin. A rioter took careful aim and let loose with a brick which made a big crack in the windshield. Dwyer ordered the driver to floor it.

Then, just as the limo began to accelerate, an apparition up ahead on the right caught Dwyer's attention. A sociopath, a High Incident Bandit in full body armor and a ski mask, stepped forward brandishing an illegally modified Bushmaster XM-15 assault rifle and stood there for a moment, as if relishing the sight of the limo and its helpless occupants. Then the bandit let loose a burst of armor-piercing rounds. The windshield and chassis might as well not have been there.

Dwyer barely had time to scream.

F. Scott Fitzgerald told us that there are no second acts in American lives, but now, in the second act, Reid Hamilton spends hours upon hours sitting on a deck chair between his house and swimming pool, out in the vastness of Riverside County. This is a period of reflection unmarred by too much anxiety. Prosecuting Reid will be tougher now. The new D.A. has a different approach from his predecessor's, and Donald Trump has really shaken up the SEC and changed its focus.

Shortly after the riots, he found himself thinking about Christine. He'd thought that she would never speak to him again, partly for legal reasons. But after the riots, after his ordeal passed, she felt just enough sympathy for them to be on speaking terms once again. Soon Reid brought Christine out to the house in Riverside County and poured drinks for them out by the pool in the crisp air.

Now, in the second act, Reid sits out here every day. He thinks often about the ending of *Moby-Dick*, which he has just recently finished, and also about the inscription left inside the book by a comedian, now dead by suicide, who gave it to him. *It just might be easier for a sperm whale to pass through the eye of the needle than for you to get to heaven, mister. Enjoy.* When he starts to feel too down, he gives Christine a call and arranges to take her out to a play or a live jazz show at one of the venues springing up rapidly in smart modern buildings around the city, almost as if the riots had not happened. They are having fun, and Reid, at least, is beginning to see potential. But now, in the second act, an instinct is developing in his breast, as he contemplates the time remaining to him on this earth. Reid Hamilton is in many respects a callous, selfish man, but not an unreflective one. Hollywood has been the perennial source of hope for L.A., of faith in its potential to be far, far more than a mail-order town. He finds himself thinking about the final words of *Moby-Dick*. He begins to feel that if you could grant him one wish, it might be to support a project that would out-pace even *Ben Hur* or *Sunset Boulevard*, a film that might be a topic of discussion when people stand here and look out at the desert, at the ocotillo branches like the fingers of a man bent in prayer, at the blue oaks lining the base of the bare majestic mountains, three hundred years from now.

Corrupt Spring

I.

Neil and Heather stood near the edge of the red carpet, blinking at the flashes around the room. At the entrance there came a rise in the chatter, such as might have greeted Louis XIV's appearance in a hall at Versailles. Then up the carpet came the celebrity, a smooth-skinned young woman shrouded in the majestic white of a dress trailing just above her ankles. F. Scott Fitzgerald could hardly have described the obsequiousness here as everyone fought to catch the attention, to inhale the perfume of the guest of honor.

Heather had grabbed her husband's hand as a gesture of support but he sensed now she that wanted to let go of the clammy, slippery thing. It was getting hard to overlook the distance between them, though their marriage wasn't a case of opposites attracting. Neil was a screenwriter and sometime playwright, and Heather had literary ambitions of her own.

The actress's lips were like a red flare on a February afternoon. As she strode up the carpet without deigning to return the gazes of the paparazzi and fans, Neil wondered whether he was alone in thinking, *I've worshiped this star, when she was twenty-five, twenty-six. This is her moment, but five years down the road, I wonder, I can't help but wonder.* Next came a director, a pair of assistant directors, a screenwriter, and a producer named Martin Boyle to whom Neil had pitched a number of projects in Martin's palatial office. Martin grinned, shook hands on either side of the aisle, paused for photos. Neil called out the producer's name, extending a hand. Martin Boyle strolled by as if he hadn't noticed.

Sitting in a restaurant in Bel Air later that evening, Neil racked his brain for anything it wouldn't be awkward to discuss. Other people's kids, jobs, promotions, *no*. Well, what? As if it weren't bad enough that people kept commenting on the age difference between Neil, forty-three, and Heather, twenty-nine, Martin had to humiliate Neil. They picked at their food.

"Richard Neutra knew Freud," Neil said.

"Did he? He must've been pretty young."

They hoped to take up residence soon in a new property, a recently discovered Neutra house in Riverside County. They both craved time to write, and Heather wanted to indulge her amateur interest in photography.

"We'll be in a totally natural setting, Heather."

"There are wolves and coyotes out there."

"As if I've never dealt with those!"

The weak attempt at humor drew a faint smile from Heather. Neil ordered a bottle of red wine and tried to change the topic, since he really knew little about the architect Neutra or Freud for that matter. When the wine came, Heather drank less than her husband. He couldn't lose the sense that people at other tables were listening. Well, fuck them. Neil thought of himself as an auteur in the grandest Hollywood sense, with ideas worthy of Billy Wilder. He'd taught himself to analyze the psychic tensions that compelled viewers to follow *Sunset Boulevard* and *The Lost Weekend*.

When the bottle was empty, they walked away from all the curious eyes and headed home in Neil's aging car through the dark silent streets. In this area of two-million-dollar homes, you little expected that a thug might blow your brains all over the dash for the change in your pocket, but gruesome crimes had taken place lately. It could happen, a stranger might roll on a bicycle from the shadows up to your window and pump rounds into your soft white skull.

At the traffic light, Neil held his breath, attentive to the dark areas in his peripheral vision, as Heather smoked a Pall Mall, leaning her hand out the window. On either side the Mandarins had retired in the security of their ultra-sophisticated alarm systems. After mocking Neil for what felt like an hour, the light changed.

Not quite twenty minutes later, they were back at their bungalow on Laurel Canyon Drive, navigating a path to the bedroom through the boxes of notebooks, photo albums, works on screenwriting and acting, tomes on film theory from Verso or Yale University Press.

A letter awaited them. He opened it. The company that owned the rural property had turned down Neil's application, citing his meager income and bad credit.

The prospect of temporary escape no longer beckoned. Lying in bed in the dark tight space, listening to the heave of Heather's chest, Neil felt himself squirm like a rat sucked down a drainpipe.

II.

Chuck Lyons's house would have been easy to find even if it didn't stand alone near the foot of a mountain in Riverside

County. It practically screamed *Look at me, admire me.* Much like the Neutra house where Neil and Heather couldn't become tenants, this one consisted of a series of sleek raised rectangles, each segment of the house overlying another, making you feel you couldn't quite leave the center of it unless you walked out to the garden by the pool. The place was elegant and stately, on par with the Mosk House or the Kauffmann House. Beyond the pool lay a vista of dark mountains, a dry river bed, dense cacti, ocotillo plants with stalks twisting and curving toward the sky.

A few dozen guests stood in the garden, drinks in hand, as Neil drove his aging Saturn into the lot out in front and parked between a Ferrari and a Porsche before trying to compose himself in the rear-view mirror, feeling naked. Neil wore a pair of soil-colored chinos and a white button-down taffeta shirt beneath a tan blazer. He climbed out and walked up a gravel path to the high double doors.

People might wonder why Neil should leave the cocoon of L.A. to pay a visit to Chuck Lyons. The fact was that Chuck was a name in a town swarming with locusts. Chuck sat on the board of directors of a studio to which Neil had pitched his biggest project to date, not that that was saying much. Neil had only a few credits as advisor or co-screenwriter on a bunch of short films made during his USC days. One of these was about a man, closely resembling Antonin Artaud, who goes off to live among the Tarahumara of Mexico, studying the tribe's way of life, trying peyote, upturning all his assumptions, exploring galaxies. Neil craved fame and knew that something differentiated him from all the poseurs who dignify themselves as screenwriters.

On this evening, Neil was in search of a studio to adapt his story of activists and anarchists during the heyday of the mighty steel industry of Fontana, California. Among the strapping young men in the cast, there'd be radical intrigues, closeted dalliances with the most powerful officials in the state, insights into the future of America's industries in a world increasingly shaped by Asian capital. When Neil pitched the idea to Chuck and a few fellow execs over lunch at a café on Santa Monica, they were, if not in love with the project, at least visibly interested. This fortified him.

Upon striding through the double doors of Chuck's house, Neil found himself gazing into the face of a thin man with short black hair, a stubbly face, and glasses like a young Allen Ginsberg's. Some people aren't born to wear black sports jackets and ties, and this guest's looked like a Halloween costume. He looked surprised at the appearance of such a nobody. Neil thought he knew him from somewhere.

"Neil Payton," he said, sucking in his gut, trying to look important.

"Oh yeah—you just pulled up in the rusty Saturn with the pizza box on the back seat," replied the guest in a nasal drawl. The stranger grinned at the silence that ensued.

"Max Rose," he said, extending a hand. Now everything fell into place. Max was a stand-up comic who performed at The Laugh Factory on Sunset and less-known venues in Hollywood, Burbank, Sherman Oaks, Glendale, Tarzana, and Pasadena. Though a lot of Max's humor was raunchy, even vile, Neil had once heard a monologue where Max speculated before a hushed room about what Nathanael West might have done for the world of letters if that writer hadn't run a red light on the way home from Mexico and had lived just one more year.

"I take it Chuck saw you perform and had someone invite you out here," Neil said.

"The man thinks I'm a pitiful excuse for a comedian. But he has what they call a big heart. Anyway, let me give you a tip. Nobody here ever calls him Chuck!" Max replied.

"Sorry. I'm adjusting."

"Let's get you a drink."

Neil followed Max through a living room with a beige marble floor and plush black chairs facing each other at the opposite end from the fireplace and the dais surmounted by a bronze baby angel blowing through a horn. A few guests were in here, including a fortyish man in a dark blazer, clutching a mixed drink and holding forth about the picture industry to a pair of women in their twenties.

There was also a rancher who reminded Neil of Earle Shoop, the sullen cowboy in West's novel *The Day of the Locust* who competes with Tod Hackett for the attentions of the ravishing actress, Faye Greener. Over six feet tall, the man wore a long-sleeved yellow shirt of coarse fiber over a thick leather belt, a pair of worn corduroy trousers, and a pair of black rancher's boots. He swilled beer from a plastic cup while shifting unselfconsciously on his rawhide heels and talking with a woman in a scarlet keyhole wrap-top blouse and gray shift dress.

Neil followed Max through another big room, and then they were outside under constellations not even faintly obscured by smog. Each star in that vastness glittered like all the ardor of a desperate life. They stood between guests milling on the edges of the pool marking the northern edge of the property, and a bar where a guy in a white suit with a rose in his breast pocket poured Daiquiris, Woodpeckers, Jack-and-diets. Over here were Ralph Lauren Black Label suits to make you feel naked, Halston Heritage dresses you'd have to have fucked the retailer just to lay eyes upon, and over there were Brioni and Kiton suits that sold for $10,000 and up.

Max slid to the bar to order a whiskey-and-soda for himself and a Corona Light for Neil, who looked around for someone he could thank for the courtesy of inviting him here after that lunch the week before. In truth, inviting Neil had been a spontaneous act, made when Chuck was tipsy after four glasses of 1978 Montrachet.

Max handed Neil the beer and began to ask a bullshit question about the climate for indie filmmakers, but then another guest dashed right up.

"Oh, Max! Max Rose!"

Here was a tall woman with a fairly magnificent head of flowing copper hair and a pair of Kensie Hipster glasses that magnified the wonder in her deep brown eyes. She wore a deep blue dress and a pair of maroon high heels. The woman had an air of something Neil couldn't quite name, a peculiarly self-referential quality. Neil felt as if they weren't three people mingling at a party, but the subject of a photo op for a celebrity magazine. It was like running into Annie Leibovitz.

"Jane Jeffrey, *New York Times* bestselling author," she announced, extending a hand which Max shook, not without reluctance.

"Er, hi. You obviously know who I am. This is Neil Payton, a rising screenwriter," Max replied.

But she took no notice of Neil.

"I've seen a few of your shows, Max. Hilarious. Hysterical. I think I could be of help," Jane said, pressing a business card into Max's hand.

Neil could tell that a *frisson* crept down Max's spine and it wasn't disagreeable at all. This lady just might help open doors for Max Rose, making him a comic presence to be reckoned with on the Strip and beyond.

Neil stopped listening to his new acquaintances, gazing past them, out at the vastness of the valley. At the base of the mountain were blue oak trees that had started growing before California existed as a state, when the advent of Hollywood and its dominance of world cinema were about as plausible as anything else one might have predicted. From this distance and in the near-dark, the bark of the trees looked pale, sickly, though the trees thrived in the arid air of the valley. To the west was desert where men broke away from their parties, got lost, grew dehydrated, moaned, cried, scrawled words to relatives with blood-dipped fingers on their pants or their bare arms.

Neil turned now and saw the man he'd come here hoping to meet. Chuck stood down by the western end of the swimming pool, sipping a martini, rocking gently back and forth in his dark polished shoes when a member of the throng of executives standing between Neil and the window of one of the gilded bathrooms made a joke. *A cowboy, an operator, a successful Hollywood man, all we need now is a dead horse in the pool,* he thought.

Chuck deserved his reputation for being tricky and erratic. Here was a new breed of super-capitalist who took pride in his social awareness. The only criticism that stuck, because he sensed the truth of it more and more, like a cancer, was that he lived in too small of a world, that he'd refused to let the unwashed multitudes from the streets of L.A. walk into his pampered existence and share his wine.

"There's your man, if you'd like to meet him," said Max.

"Nice to meet both of you. Now if you'll pardon me," Neil said, shuffling off toward the far end of the pool.

Now Chuck finally noticed Neil. In his jet-black Valentino wool suit, Chuck actually looked something close to casual.

"Neil Payton. Grand to see you," the multimillionaire said, taking a sip of Chateau Mouton-Rothschild which swirled in his glass like the blood of a ruby.

Chuck grinned and took Neil aside, easing his arm gently around the curve of Neil's left shoulder, on the very edge of the pool shimmering in the moonlight. With the lightest of nudges, he could have tipped his nervous guest into this pool. Instead he pressed his face up close to Neil's stubbly cheek and began to confide.

"Look here, buddy boy. I know talent when I see it. I'm not just being kind when I say that I've always believed in you. But we watched both of your short films down at the studio the other day. We talked about your proposal. Here's the scoop: We think you're a talented guy, but we're not sure you've got the instincts of a good commercial screenwriter. So the short answer is no."

With a sigh, Neil studied the dancing reflections on the water. Back at the bungalow on Laurel, there were a congealing mess of leftover egg rolls and fried rice, and recycling bags full of bottles he'd been too lazy to take out.

"Now I said the short answer. The future's hard to predict. Tell me: do you have more business acumen than other screen-writers out there?"

Neil quickly nodded.

"Think you can prove it?"

"I don't think you even need me to answer that, Ch— Mr. Lyons."

"Swell. Now listen to me. I need something done. The guy who does it can't be someone who's got an in with me. Should the question come up, it needs to be someone who, to all appearances, resents me and would never want to help me. Someone I turned down rather nastily. You'll be getting a rather pointed letter from us in a day or two."

Neil nodded again. Chuck went on.

"You resent Marty Boyle? Welcome to the club, buddy boy. A lot of my associates don't like the way he's lured the A- and B-list talent from our projects before we had a chance to make a proper offer. He's a shark."

Neil's eyes widened in sheer disbelief that he was hearing this.

"And, since we're on the topic, there are a few other predators I think we'd be better off without. Not all of them in showbiz, mind you. We need something done."

Neil nodded.

"I assure you, Neil, they're all thieves, looters, backstabbers, scum. Not one of them deserves to live. Have you read the Hebrew Bible, Neil?"

"Not recently."

"Well, different parts of it differ on certain points. Jonah and Nahum don't agree at all about the fate of Nineveh. The wicked elites did or did not redeem themselves, depending on whom you believe. But if you believe Nahum, it took a whole constellation of forces to clean up Nineveh and dispose of its corrupt elites."

Neil nodded again.

"You thought I was another subliterate trust-funder, didn't you?" Chuck said.

"I don't know what I thought."

"Never mind. Your life has purpose now. The cowboy can tell you more."

"You mean that dude who looks like Earle Shoop in *The Day of the Locust*?"

"Exactly."

Before letting go, the host tightened his grip, tilting Neil ever so slightly further toward the pool, and in a completely different tone, whispered:

"Don't you dare show up at my house looking like this again."

Then he smiled and clapped Neil gently on the shoulder before resuming his genial manner.

While he was talking to Chuck, Neil later learned, Max wandered inside the house in search of a bathroom. The one near the door opening on the courtyard had a line, and he couldn't wait, so he sauntered through a maze of halls at the rear of the house. Sarah had hired a crew to paint these halls a bright yellow, and had adorned them with the works of a roughly equal mix of Weimer and California artists.

Finally, Max found a bathroom at the back of the house with a window looking out on a small porch, and, beyond that, the infinite desert. As soon as he stepped into the john, he heard the voices of a couple of people outside on the porch, engaged in low, conspiratorial talk. The cowboy was talking to a young woman.

"Want to buy a Glock?"

"I'll consider it."

Max finished up in the bathroom as quietly as he could, then made his way back to the courtyard by the pool. As soon as Neil saw Max again, he approached him and asked where the cowboy was. Max gave him directions.

"You gonna do a service for the man?" the cowboy asked.

Neil nodded.

The cowboy shared the name and location of an operative who lived in South Central. He handed Neil a couple hundred dollars.

Then Max led Neil back to where Jane Jeffrey stood with a glass of sauvignon blanc and a broad smile spread across her smooth, creamy features. He re-introduced Neil to Jane, who noticed Neil now, listened with compassion, and then invited Neil to a corner of the garden where they could talk further. From nearby the pool came gay laughter, and from far beyond, out at the base of the mountain, a faint, immensely leisured rustling in the blue oaks.

III.

Max consented to let Neil drive but gave directions rather brusquely as they headed south on Normandie, away from the respectable parts of town. The comedian lolled toward the passenger's side window, taking in the squat houses and the palm trees as they moved down into South Central. It was a bracingly cool evening. As they passed corner after corner, the vastness of the town's layout hit Neil once again and he felt acutely the distance between the New Age coffee shops of West Hollywood and the bars and bistros with signs for "Cold Beer" down here.

A couple of blocks above Slauson, when they had to pause as a big Latino family shuffled across the street going east, Max rotated his head and eyed Neil reproachfully, as if daring him to let something slip. Neil wanted to tell Max that he loved Latinos, the women especially, but he knew that just doing so would concede the relevance of whatever vile charge Max might have felt like making. The light changed.

When they were right about to hit Slauson, Max gestured for Neil to make a left and go east. They pursued Slauson for only a couple of blocks before he indicated the dingy concrete façade of a place with bars in the windows and a neon Budweiser sign in one window. In the lot on the other side were half a dozen aging cars and a grimy purple pickup. One of the cars had mismatched paint all over its lower parts suggesting it had been in many bang-ups. Neil swung right into the lot and parked beside the pickup. They got out and strode into the place.

Here was a cookie-cutter type of bar, with a counter running down the west wall and a dozen circular tables filling the
interior, but it was dingier, scruffier, than any place you'd find
in the supposed borderlands up around Pico. A black girl with
a cone of frizzy hair and a tan dress falling just below her skinny
knees carried a tray between the tables and the counter. A few
heads turned as they made their way into the dimmer recesses,
but that didn't concern Max. He hurried past them in his urge
to get to the rear, where a calm but guarded face regarded the
pair of whites. On the table before that face were a half-empty
glass of beer and two fidgety hands.

As they approached, Neil waited for this stranger's look to
change, to register the presence of someone with whom he'd
shared a laugh and a drink, but the face went on watching stolidly.

"Malik. Thanks for agreeing to meet at short notice,"
said Max, extending a hand toward the fellow, who shook it
mechanically, out of obligation. Words like "Drinking again?"
must have sounded odd even from a comedian who delighted
in rubbing salt into wounds and then staring at all the faces out
there in the seats before him, writhing under garish lights.

"Malik, this is Neil," said the comedian.

Now as Neil shook Malik's hand, he really got hit with the
odor on his breath. He seemed miserable and resigned in the
manner of someone who's blown his last cent at the racetrack.
At last Malik spoke.

"Who's this chump?"

Max and Neil laughed uneasily.

"He's a screenwriter. Maybe he and I'll make a series of
films and do something without precedent in the history of
cinema."

Malik's fingers raked the fabric just above his knees as his
bleary eyes fixed on Max.

"Well, hello, my friend. Nice of you to venture out of your cocoon, down into the world below Pico for once."

"Actually, it's not quite the first time—"

"What d'you chumps want?"

The interlopers looked at each other anxiously.

"I'm just runnin' with you, man. Why don't you boys relax, hang out a while?"

As they settled into the wobbly seats, the girl with the frizzy hair came over to take orders for a round of drinks. Behind them were whispers, curses, but Neil didn't mind because this place was becoming real in a way as unexpected as it was thrilling.

"I thought I'd bring the screenwriter here in person, and ask whether you might be interested in a role in a movie," Max said.

The bleary eyes rotated from Max's face to Neil's and back.

"Lord. Well just what sort of movie is it? And how many X's does it come with?" he breathed as a feeble grin spread across his tired features.

Max laughed.

"No, no, Malik, what do you take me for?"

"I won't answer that."

"I dare you to."

"Ever notice how upset people get when you generalize about people below Pico, but it never works the other way?" Neil said.

"Look, man. I don't know what I was thinking. Maybe both you fellas better leave. Fast, like you just remembered you gotta be someplace. You don't know the talk I hear in this place sometimes," Malik said.

"Really, I think this could be the break you've been waiting for, forever," Max replied.

Malik took a good long swig.

"I haven't seen someone this wasted for quite a while," Max added.

"I doubt that."

"We could leave now."

"I have to say I ain't got much respect for a pair of guys that feel entitled to brag about roughin' it just 'cause they insert and extricate themselves from any situation as they please. But this one here, mister screenwriter, I do feel a certain sympathy for, because I have this sense of him, and it's a strong sense, that he's a deeply lonely person. Now we all have rough spots but there's somethin' kind of sadistic about a fella's life dragging on this way for years and years. If his life isn't going to achieve high art, then maybe it's better to achieve the thrill of seein' stuff burn. You get me?"

"Look Malik, I know we barged in here at this maybe not the best moment for you so let me just say—"

"Tell me what you chumps're here for."

"Come on, Max, this was a terrible idea," Neil said.

"No. No, fellas. Stay here and finish your beers."

Neil took a furtive look around.

"Here's a list of names and addresses," Neil said, holding out a slip of paper. Beside each entry was a dollar amount. $20,000, $25,000, $30,000.

Malik studied the list.

"Here's an advance," Neil added, sliding a thick roll of bills under the table.

"I see all you middle-class folks gettin' swept along in tidal waves of blood that come roarin' from South Central up to Hollywood, to Los Feliz, and all the way out to Altadena. If you don't respect each other how's others ever gonna respect you?"

"I love the part about torrents of blood—very cinematic. Kind of makes April '92 look like a playground scuffle, doesn't it now?" Neil said.

Max spoke up.

"We're glad to have you on our side, Malik. Come on, Neil, you're designated driver."

As they left, they heard Malik slam his bottle down and say with a loud laugh:

"I sho' hope you suckers got a spare in the trunk!"

IV.

As Neil drove home through a drizzle, names on the list he'd handed to Malik flitted through his mind. Scott Boyer, Dave Atkinson, Nate McCormick, Angela Drakos. A corrupt prosecutor, a hedge funder who used reporting tricks and ponzi schemes to screw retirees out of their savings, an inside trader at a securities exchange, a talent scout who extorted sexual favors for her friends from desperate young men and then tossed them aside like tissue.

Waiting for a light to change a few blocks from the bungalow on Laurel Canyon Drive, Neil thought that he'd rejected complacency in the face of evil. He tried to recall a line from the Book of Proverbs. It was about how a righteous man who falls down before the wicked is a tainted fountain, a corrupt spring, something like that. Neil hadn't bowed or kneeled or fallen down. Maybe the line would have been easier to recall if Neil hadn't just downed ten whiskies at a place on Wilshire. The booze was all the more potent for the fact that he hadn't eaten.

He pulled into the drive at the bungalow, went inside, and confronted a young woman with a savage look on her face. Then he noticed the open envelope and letter on the table.

"Congratulations, Neil. You got a letter from Lyons Associates, and I opened it by mistake. It seems the brilliant idea you said would put you on the map isn't such a hit. They're not greenlighting it."

Neil blinked.

"You read my mail?"

"I opened it by mistake."

Neil parsed her sentences in his mind. Opening the letter, even if it was an honest mistake, did not explain reading it, or at least reading past the salutation at the top.

"You read my mail."

"Neil. I could smell the liquor on your breath a mile away. Would you just get out of here right now so I don't have to look at you?"

She shifted a bit, defensively, as if she half expected her husband to become violent, but he quietly pivoted and walked back out the door.

Sitting behind the wheel again in the driveway, he pulled out his phone and dialed Max's number but got no answer. He imagined the comedian, in the company of sexy appreciative fans in a café somewhere, glancing down at his phone and seeing Neil's number and going right on talking and laughing. Maybe Neil had exposed himself as the worst kind of amateur by calling Max.

He drove to the restaurant in Bel Air and walked in self-consciously with no reservation. Nevertheless they found a seat for him by the big window overlooking the garden. The light in here was too bright. A young waiter stood by the table with a polite smile as Neil gazed at the menu and struggled to say the name of the pasta he wanted, mangling it several times. Finally he made himself understood.

"And the pinot noir."

"Certainly, sir."

The waiter came back with the glass of wine. No sooner had Neil emptied it than he signaled for the kid to bring him another. Neil finished it quickly and then noticed Martin Boyle sitting across from a gorgeous blonde on the far side of the room. He got up and made his way over without falling down.

"Hiya Marty," Neil said.

Boyle kept talking to the blonde as if hadn't heard.

"Marty!" Neil said, his legs weak and wobbly.

Still Boyle went on talking, as if Neil were just as invisible as that evening he'd humiliated Neil in front of Heather. But the blonde eyed the interloper nervously.

"Hey Marty! You fucking well see me standing here!" Neil screamed loud enough for everyone in the restaurant to hear.

The blonde turned her head toward Neil, then looked around the room anxiously. Thinking he'd fall down any second, Neil eyed one of the knives on the table.

"MARTY!"

Finally Boyle turned and made eye contact, with a look of infinite contempt, but didn't say a word.

"Marty. You don't have to ignore me, even if you think my ideas are garbage. But then you really don't have much of an opinion at all, do you, you spoiled mandarin? I don't think you've ever paid attention to my pitches. I have so much more to show you and I can't wait till we're alone. There's this one story about a man, he lives in a city for many years and then he goes out and gets lost in the desert—"

A strong hand seized Neil's elbow. He cried out in indignation, but the real outrage was that Martin still wouldn't say anything.

"You'll have to leave, sir," said Neil's waiter, his kind demeanor gone.

"Say something, Marty!" Neil cried.

Two more servers came over. Neil seized the tablecloth and gave it such a quick hard tug that only one of the glasses, the blonde's, toppled as it shot out. Surely Boyle must register some complaint now, with his Montrachet all over the table and on his lap. But Boyle looked on stoically.

"No, Let go of me. I just want him to say something," Neil cried as they hauled him off.

He managed to find his keys and to drive through the dark streets without hitting anything. But his fear of a random assault grew inexorably as he turned one corner, then another, on the way back to Laurel. All the while he tried but failed to banish the image of Boyle's stolid, silent face.

If only Boyle knew what he knew. Neil thought himself clever. Only an idiot would make such a scene around someone whose murder he'd helped orchestrate, and everyone knew Neil was a highly intelligent loser. Here was the perfect defense.

He drove around, eying the dark areas outside the penumbras of light nervously, until he felt reasonably certain Heather had gone to bed. When he pulled into the driveway, he was still too drunk to think in a linear way about Heather and her possible reaction when he flopped down on the bed beside her. He walked into the bungalow.

Once again he thought of Max. He wondered at what point exactly that bastard was right now out there amid all the glittering lights on the boulevards under the dark hills. He found his phone, fumbled with it, dropped it, and knew he'd never find it in his present state.

A bit of her upper back and hair were visible in the moonlight coming through the window as Neil slid into the bed. As he drifted off, he thought again of the comedian. Max's disdain for him wasn't the social snobbery of Martin Boyle, no, it was a different animal.

He had a vision of the comedian up on a stage, standing in a penumbra of light in an otherwise pitch-dark space, grinning, joking, using Neil's name often. Now, in his wasted semi-conscious state, Neil thought he finally got it. The joke that Max put to brilliant use before his audience out there somewhere in the night was that a local guy, a screenwriter manqué, an incomparable idiot named Neil Payton, had actually thought he and Max had entered into a plan to work together to put out a contract on someone's life, or the lives of several people, on behalf of a rich man. Max stood on the stage in the dark room, laughing so hard he nearly cried, pushing others into spasms of hilarity with his account of this preposterous fool. Neil actually thought this was how you did it, this was how you arranged a hit, you went with your pal down to South Central and walked around in full view of others until you met the other party, and you barely tried to avoid letting others hear you discuss the plan.

Hilarious indeed.

Neil drifted off with the vision of the acerbic, chortling comedian on the stage filling his mind.

When he woke up in an empty bed, his first thought was that he'd never see Heather again and his life was over and he might as well take his time with things. But when he came out of the shower twenty minutes later, a familiar voice called to him from the living room.

"Neil. Horrible news this morning."

Groggy, hungover, he pulled on his bathrobe and went into the living room. Sitting on the plastic chair, her back to him, Heather gestured at the TV.

"They haven't even solved the Ronni Chasen murder and now another rich mandarin in Beverly Hills has died in the grisliest way. A hedge funder, David something."

Neil nodded and went into the kitchen to make coffee.

"Only the good die young, right?"

"How original."

He was beginning to love his wife again, but he could barely think coherently and he still badly wanted to know what Martin Boyle might have said if those idiots hadn't kicked him out.

About the Author

Michael Washburn is a Brooklyn-based writer and journalist. His short stories have appeared in numerous journals and magazines including *Green Hills Literary Lantern, Rosebud, Adelaide Literary Magazine, Weird Fiction Review, New Orphic Review, Stand, Still Point Arts Quarterly, Lakeview Journal, Black Fox Literary Magazine, Bryant Literary Journal, Meat for Tea, Marathon Literary Review, Prick of the Spindle,* and other publications. Michael is the author of an acclaimed cover story in the *Philadelphia City Paper,* entitled "Home and Abroad." He is the author of a previous short fiction collection, *Scenes from the Catastrophe* (2016).

Made in the USA
Columbia, SC
26 September 2021

45671731R00143